To Dance with a Devil

Girls Who Dare, Book 6

By Emma V. Leech

Published by Emma V. Leech.

Copyright (c) Emma V. Leech 2019

Cover Art: Victoria Cooper

ASIN No.: B07YFV2NXW

ISBN NO.: 978-1674793436

All rights reserved. Without limiting the rights under copyright reserved above, no part of this publication may be reproduced, stored in or introduced into a retrieval system, or transmitted, in any form, or by any means (electronic, mechanical, photocopying, recording, or otherwise) without the prior written permission of both the copyright owner and the above publisher of this book. This is a work of fiction. Names, characters, places, brands, media, and incidents are either the product of the author's imagination or are used fictitiously. The author acknowledges the trademarked status and trademark owners of various products referenced in this work of fiction, which have been used without permission. The publication/use of these trademarks is not authorized, associated with, or sponsored by the trademark owners. The ebook version and print version are licensed for your personal enjoyment only.

The ebook version may not be re-sold or given away to other people. If you would like to share the ebook with another person, please purchase an additional copy for each person you share it with. No identification with actual persons (living or deceased), places, buildings, and products is inferred.

Table of Contents

Members of the Peculiar Ladies' Book Club

Prunella Adolphus, Duchess of Bedwin – first peculiar lady and secretly Miss Terry, author of *The Dark History of a Damned Duke.*

Mrs Alice Hunt (née Dowding)–Not as shy as she once was. Recently married to Matilda's brother, the notorious Nathanial Hunt, owner of *Hunter's*, the exclusive gambling club.

Lady Aashini Cavendish (Lucia de Feria) – a beauty. A foreigner. Recently happily, and scandalously, married to Silas Anson, Viscount Cavendish.

Mrs Kitty Baxter (née Connolly) – quiet and watchful, until she isn't. Recently eloped to marry childhood sweetheart, Mr Luke Baxter.

Lady Harriet St Clair (née Stanhope) Countess of St Clair – serious, studious, intelligent. Prim. Wearer of spectacles. Finally married to the Earl of St Clair.

Bonnie Campbell – too outspoken and forever in a scrape.

Ruth Stone – heiress and daughter of a wealthy merchant.

Minerva Butler - Prue's cousin. Not so vain or vacuous as she appears. Dreams of love.

Jemima Fernside – pretty and penniless.

Lady Helena Adolphus – vivacious, managing, unexpected.

Matilda Hunt – blonde and lovely and ruined in a scandal that was none of her making.

Chapter 1

I feel like I'm running pell-mell towards a cliff's edge, and though I know there's a sheer drop to face, I can't seem to stop myself. I never considered myself a stupid girl, but surely this is madness. Yet the alternative is to give in and do as I'm told and marry a man I don't want and live in a place I have no wish to be.

The cliff's edge it is then.

—Excerpt of an entry from Miss Bonnie Campbell to her diary.

10ᵗʰ September 1814, Holbrooke House, Sussex.

Bonnie contemplated the inside of her eyelids, shining red as the sun warmed her face. Sleep tugged at her mind. She was drowsy from the lazy afternoon and the delicious picnic she'd eaten with her friends. It would be easy to drift off, to forget all the worries that had crowded her thoughts of late, like spectators to another's misfortune, gathering to gawk and gossip and thank the heavens it wasn't them run down by the mail coach, or fallen on their face in the dirt.

Bonnie was used to spectators, used to people casting her disapproving glances and tutting and whispering. It was jealousy, she told herself; they were jealous that she had the guts to do the things they wanted to do but hadn't the nerve. What did she care if they thought her a hoyden?

She opened her eyes, dazzled by the midday sun, and blinked up at a sky of azure blue, as blue as Jerome Cadogan's eyes. Lord, but she was a cliché: a foolish little nobody, in love with a devilishly handsome man far beyond her reach. He was a wicked charmer with a roguish laugh and twinkling blue eyes, and he was no more of a mind to put a ring on her finger than to become the next Archbishop of Canterbury. She might be a ward of the Earl of Morven, but her family was not illustrious. They were respectable enough, but Jerome Cadogan, brother of the Earl of St Clair, could do a great deal better.

Her only hope had been to get him to fall as madly in love with her as she had with him. Bonnie let out a soft huff of laughter as she considered just how well that plan had worked. Jerome loved her all right, just like he loved the rest of his motley band of friends. He thought her a *jolly good sort* and *merry as a grig,* and treated her just as he might one of his boisterous roaring boys, not as a gently bred young lady. Not that Bonnie *was* frail and gently bred. There was nothing the least bit fragile about her. Her figure was voluptuous, verging on plump, she thought herself nigh unshockable, and she had a knack for saying the first thing that came into her head... usually loudly enough to be heard several streets away.

No, she knew well enough by now the type of lady Jerome fancied, and it wasn't her. Not even nearly. He had a reputation for falling in love at the drop of a hat, and always with women who were far from suitable, much to his older brother's despair. Apart from their unsuitability, these women had other things in common. They were blonde and blue-eyed, daintily pretty and in obvious need of rescue. Bonnie might be the epitome of unsuitability, but there the comparison ended. She had dark hair, vaguely green eyes, a robust figure and was more than capable of knocking a man out cold with a well-aimed blow to the nose if the need arose. She sighed, aware of her own idiocy and, worse, aware that her friends all knew of her infatuation and pitied her for it.

They'd done their best to warn her off, to tell her that Jerome just didn't see her that way—would never see her that way—and it wasn't that she didn't believe them. She did. She knew they were right. Even Jerome, bless his soul, had warned her that he wasn't the marrying kind when he'd caught her eyeing him with something more than friendly affection and the penny had finally dropped. He'd been sweet about it, too, making sure she knew how much he valued her friendship and assuring her it was his loss, for he'd make the most appalling husband if ever he was forced to take a wife. He'd caught at an imaginary rope and pretended to hang himself with it at that point, and Bonnie had laughed at his antics even though her heart was breaking. Ah well, better to have loved and lost... *pfft*. What drivel! If she could fall out of love with Jerome Cadogan as easily as she'd tumbled into it, she'd do so in a heartbeat, but her heart beat for him alone, and she didn't know how to make it stop.

Why couldn't she have just pleased everyone and fallen for Gordon bloody Anderson? She shuddered at the thought. The glowering, bad-tempered fellow and his glowering, unwelcoming castle had nothing to recommend them. He wouldn't know fun if it fell on its head with a label attached pronouncing FUN in capital letters. Well, she was damned if she'd marry a man who thought her frivolous because she wanted the society of others and longed to dance and enjoy life. She didn't care what plans Anderson had for her dowry or what Morven had promised her father before he'd died. That had been his promise, not hers. She'd not let them lock her up in some ghastly castle in the Highlands, away from all her friends and with no other occupation than to give her husband as many brats as she could manage, before the activity killed her just as it had killed her mother. No, thank you.

The trouble was that she couldn't avoid it indefinitely. She was living on borrowed time. Anderson would come for her soon and, as she lived on Morven's money, there was no escaping her fate. She could and *would* put it off for as long as possible, however. Perhaps if she behaved badly enough, Anderson would refuse to marry her. He only wanted her for her dowry in any case, and if she was damaged goods....

Perhaps that would be enough to make him refuse her?

The idea persisted, though she knew it was dangerous. Yet it meant she could have what she wanted, for a brief time at least. She could give herself to the man she loved and be honest with Anderson about what she'd done. Either it would change her fate, or it wouldn't. Perhaps Morven would disown her, but she didn't think so. No doubt he'd pack her off to somewhere she'd cause him no further embarrassment, but that had to be better than mouldering in some godforsaken castle in the back end of nowhere.

Well, it would likely come to naught anyway, she thought, huffing out a gloomy sigh. Jerome simply didn't see her in that light, so he'd probably not want to ruin her, even if she handed herself to him on a platter… though it had to be worth a try.

Bonnie stared at the lake in front of her as she considered the idea, her gaze falling upon St Clair and Harriet. They'd finally sorted themselves out and were very clearly in love. Lucky Harriet, she thought, unable to hold back another despondent sigh.

Matilda, who was sitting beside her, glanced over at the sound.

"Lucky things," Bonnie said, smiling wistfully as Matilda nodded her agreement.

"Indeed."

"We're not all so lucky, are we?"

"No," Matilda said, and there was a bleak note in that one word that Bonnie heard and recognised. "But you are young and pretty, Bonnie. There's time yet."

Bonnie shook her head. "No," she said, wishing her voice hadn't quavered. There was no point in bleating about it. "No, there's not. I told you, I'm already living on borrowed time."

Matilda reached out and took her hand and Bonnie squeezed it in return, grateful for her unerring support and understanding. Matilda understood, because her time was running out too.

"You'll not be alone, Bonnie. Not forgotten or abandoned, whatever happens. We won't allow that. Your friends will always be there for you. I'll come to Scotland and stay with you, I promise. No matter how far into the wilderness they try to bury you."

Bonnie made a choked sound as emotions crashed about inside her, and then laughed. Matilda followed, blinking back tears.

"Lud, how maudlin we've become," Matilda said, shaking her head. "This won't do at all."

Bonnie nodded. She couldn't agree more. You were a long time dead, and the living could join you in the blink of an eye, as she well knew.

"Aye, there's time enough for tears and wailing," Bonnie said, scrambling to her feet, determination swelling in her heart. "I won't waste a moment of what's left to me."

Taking a deep breath, Bonnie snatched up her drinking cup and headed for the lake.

***

Jerome sighed, content and stretched in the sun like a lazy cat. He considered himself a simple fellow with simple tastes, and it took little to please him. A sunny day, convivial company, and good food, and he wouldn't have swapped places with a duke or a king. He certainly didn't envy his brother the responsibilities of the earldom. No, no, the life of a younger son was by far preferable. No accounts ledgers and tenants bleating about this problem and that roof and the price of barley, no expectations to marry well and provide an heir and a spare, though it seemed Jasper had that in hand, the sly devil. Harry Stanhope, who would have thought it?

Why hadn't he seen it earlier, he wondered? It was as clear as the besotted grin on his brother's face. The two of them adored each other. They'd been at each other's throats for years and all the time… well, it just went to show, no one knew for sure what went on in another fellow's head. Probably for the best, too, he thought, suppressing a smile as he turned his own thoughts to a comely new barmaid he'd spotted down at The Swan in the village. She was blonde and pretty, slender as a reed but with curves in all the right places, and she'd given him a smile that might have stopped short of *come hither*, but only just.

He'd just settled himself down to indulge in an agreeable daydream of how to get an invitation to come hither, when a shock of icy water hit him in the face, and he jolted up with a yelp. For a moment he just sat, dripping, too stunned to react further, and then he saw her.

"Why you little brat!" he thundered, as his outraged glare fell upon the culprit.

Who else?

"I'm going to throw you in the lake, Bonnie Campbell," he warned, pushing to his feet as she hitched up her skirts and gave a shriek.

Jasper cursed and set off in pursuit. Bonnie glanced over her shoulder to see him belting after her and crowed with laughter. She turned and stuck out her tongue at him.

"You've got to catch me first, clod pole," she taunted, before running off into the trees.

Despite his annoyance, Jerome laughed and charged after her into the cool shade of the woods. Bonnie squealed as he lunged for her and twisted out of his grasp before running on again. She was faster than she looked, though her face was flushed now, her eyes sparkling with devilry.

"Wretch!" he yelled, before snagging his toe on a root and falling heavily to his knees. "Curse it," he muttered, hauling himself up to discover Bonnie had vanished.

He could still hear her, so he ran on, following the sound of crunching leaves and snapping twigs. After what felt like a lifetime, he paused, gasping, to lean against a tree. Good Lord, but his lifestyle was taking a toll on his stamina. He had to make an effort to exercise more often, before he ran to fat like his friend Cholly. Forcing himself onwards, Jerome broke from the tree line where it gave out onto the edge of the lake.

There was a small inlet here, out of sight and secluded, which was just as well as he took in the sight in front of him and froze with shock.

"Bonnie Campbell, you'll be the death of me yet," he murmured as his gaze held on the woman before him, standing on a large rock that jutted out into deeper water and wearing nothing but her shift.

She turned to grin at him.

"Bonnie, no!" he called, but too late. With quite remarkable grace, considering what a hoyden she was, she dived in.

Jerome ran to the lake's edge, his heart in his mouth as he stared down into the dark water. It was deep here, so deep neither he nor Jasper had ever swum to the bottom. Not so much as a ripple disturbed the surface and panic gripped him.

No. Oh, no, no, no.

He stripped off and dived in, swimming down and down until his lungs were bursting and he was forced back to the surface, coughing and spluttering. About to take a breath and dive once more, he almost screamed as a hand gripped his shoulders and dunked him under.

It was only for a second, but when he came up, he found Bonnie shrieking with laughter and he had to fight the urge to throttle her.

"Plague take you!" he shouted, wiping water from his eyes. "That's not funny, you diabolical creature. I thought you'd drowned, curse you."

"In this little puddle?" she said, pulling a face and obviously unimpressed. "I hardly think so. I've been swimming in lochs since I was a bairn, far deeper and darker and colder than this. This is like taking a bath."

"Perhaps I'll drown you myself, then," he muttered, and swam after her.

She gasped and tried to evade him, but she was too slow this time and he grabbed her about the waist.

"Let go," she protested, wriggling in his grasp, but Jerome was too incensed to do as she bade him. Though she had likened the temperature to bath water it was icy and, in normal circumstances, enough to cool any man's ardour. Having a generous armful of barely clad female in his arms, however, was all the encouragement Jerome's body required to sit up and take note of the situation.

Behave, he told himself sternly. Bonnie was out of bounds. He knew it. If he hadn't known it, his brother had hit him over the head with the fact so repeatedly that there was really no escaping it. Jasper had warned him his last amorous adventure was the final straw and the last one he'd bail Jerome out of. To be fair, it *had* cost a pretty penny and *hadn't* been his finest hour, and Jerome had been trying to behave himself since. Besides, Bonnie wasn't his type at all. Yet when she turned in his arms, the fine fabric of her shift doing absolutely nothing to make a barrier between her nearly naked form and his own, his cock didn't seem to be of a mind to make a distinction.

Though the water was too bloody cold, her breasts were warm and plump. They pushed against his chest, and the hard little nubs of her nipples against his skin made his blood heat despite the frigid lake. She gasped with surprise as his erection pressed into the softness of her belly and Jerome held his breath, waiting for her to shriek in horror and slap him. Except this was Bonnie—bold, wicked Bonnie—and he ought to have known better. She wrapped her legs about his waist, and pleasure jolted through him as his cock nestled between her thighs, and her mouth pressed against his. The sensation was so intense and so unexpected, that he forgot to swim, and they plunged under the water again.

They came up a moment later, coughing and splashing. Jerome threw back his head and roared with laughter at the insanity of it and Bonnie watched him with delight ablaze in her eyes. He saw the devil in her then, recognised it as it called out to the devil in him, a terrible siren song which would lure them both into deep water and destroy them on the rocks if they weren't careful. It was why they ought to stay far, far away from each other, and why it was so hard to keep her at bay. They were alike, two wicked peas in a pod, and all too ready to go to hell together.

With regret, Jerome turned away from her and swam back to the shore, stumbling across the rock to the grass and sitting down in a heap, gasping for air and willing his arousal to perdition. He looked up then and knew that would never happen as Bonnie emerged from the water. Her long dark hair clung to her body, thick coils dripping about her shoulders and framing the mouth-watering abundance of her breasts. Jerome's tastes had never run to excess—a tidy handful was quite enough for any man in his opinion—yet he wondered now if he'd not been a bit hasty as he took in Bonnie's lush curves. His breath hitched at her all-but-transparent shift, which left nothing to the imagination. Her nipples were clearly defined, as was the dark triangle of her sex.

Heat exploded under his skin and his body throbbed, all the hotter and more insistently for knowing she'd welcome his advances. She'd made that plain enough. Yet she was an innocent, a young lady, not a willing petticoat or a Cyprian. There were rules. His father had imparted that much to him before he'd died, and Jasper had taken up where he'd left off. This particular rule had been drummed into Jerome from the moment he'd first been caught casting a look of longing at a pretty girl. If one did not expect to offer marriage, one had no business in dallying with virgins.

As Bonnie knelt beside him, however, her pale green eyes darker than he'd ever seen them, this was almost impossible to remember. She pressed her lips to his again, and he groaned, pushing her down onto the grass and filling his hands with her. She arched beneath his touch and sighed with pleasure as he gave one full breast a gentle squeeze and then took her nipple in his mouth. The wanton little cry she made jolted through him and the longing for more was so fierce it hurt.

Oh God, he was doomed.

He licked and teased and grazed her with his teeth, desire a wild thing in his blood now, thrashing inside him and demanding release, and then he looked up. For just a moment he was caught in her gaze, in the emotion he saw there… the love. Jerome felt his pulse thudding unevenly and was trapped by the soft look in her eyes, and then panic won out and he pushed away from her. He got to his feet and strode away, his heart crashing about in his chest.

"Jerry," she said, her disappointment all too clear. She should get used to that, he supposed. He'd always be a disappointment to her if she looked at him like he'd hung the moon.

"No," he said, trying to keep the word as soft and gentle as he could make it, even though frustration and desire were simmering beneath his skin as if he was boiling in a cauldron, the witch's brew that Bonnie seemed to stir in his blood fighting to control him. "We can't, Bonnie. No."

"We could," she persisted, and he wanted to curse her for putting temptation in his way. "I wouldn't—"

"No!" He almost shouted the word, his fists clenched against the desire to fling himself to the ground beside her and take everything she offered him. He took a breath and said it again, softer, his regret audible. "No."

"No," she repeated, and he hated the sound of it, the way it sounded so defeated, as though she'd known it would be the answer.

Of course she'd known, he raged to himself. He'd told her so, hadn't he? He'd told her there was no future for her with him. He had no intention of marrying, not for a long, long, time at any rate. Why on earth would he tie himself down with a wife and children when his life was so agreeable? He need only stay out of trouble and Jasper wouldn't nag him to settle down.

Jerome dried himself off as best he could, discarding his wet drawers for now. He'd have to retrieve them another time before they scandalised some visitor or other, or his mother, heaven forbid. When he turned around, Bonnie was dressed too. He caught her eye and let out a breath, smiling at her. If he wasn't so dashed fond of her this wouldn't be so hard, but he was. He did love her, but not in the way she wanted him to. He'd been too much the wide-eyed innocent in his youth, giving his heart away at the drop of a hat and making a blasted fool of himself. Never again, he'd sworn to his brother and himself, and he'd meant it.

"We're friends, Bonnie," he said, his voice soft. "Don't spoil it."

She nodded and flashed him a grin which didn't reach her eyes. That unpleasant ache took up residence in his chest again.

"Come along, you nuisance of a female," he said, holding out a hand to her. "We'd best smuggle you into the house, *again*," he added, tutting at her. "You look like a half-drowned cat."

"Such a way with words you have, Jerome," she said, pressing her free hand to her heart and pretending to swoon. "I'll faint if you keep saying such romantic things."

He snorted and tugged her hand into the crook of his arm. "If you faint, I'll leave you here and you can find your own way home. I'm famished and I've not energy enough to haul your lifeless corpse all the way to the house, I can tell you."

This time Bonnie slapped the back of her hand to her head. "Oh, my," she said, as her knees buckled, and she slid elegantly to the floor.

A moment later, she peered up through her fingers at him and grinned. Laughing and shaking his head, he reached down and grasped her hands.

"Addlepate," he said with too much affection in his voice but unable to stop it.

"I know," she said with a sigh, before hauling herself to her feet with rather less elegance than she'd fallen.

Relieved that she'd recovered her good humour, Jerome grasped hold of her hand and escorted her back to the house.

Chapter 2

Dear Alice,

*I'm so sorry you're missing out on all the fun.
We've all been so lucky to be asked to stay on
for the earl and Harriet's wedding. You'd think
Lady St Clair would have had enough of us by
now — me, anyway — but she's always so
gracious. I wish I had an ounce of her
sophistication. I'm sure she thinks me an
unruly hoyden and will be glad to see the back
of me.*

**—Excerpt of a letter to Mrs Alice Hunt from
Miss Bonnie Campbell.**

**18th September 1814. Harriet and Jasper's engagement ball.
Holbrooke House, Sussex.**

Bonnie laughed, delighted as Harriet's brother Henry spun her
around. He looked a little unnerved by her unabashed enthusiasm,
as well he might. Well-behaved young ladies did not laugh their
heads off and bounce about the floor like Bonnie did. Well-
behaved young ladies gave shy smiles and glided about as if they
were floating just above the parquet on little fluffy clouds made of
innocence, rainbows, and pink ribbons, or something equally
nauseating.

If such a thing had existed, Bonnie would have stomped her
little cloud into the dirt and gladly a long time ago. She didn't want
to simper and be a good girl and do as she was told. She'd had

done once, a long time ago, so long ago that she could only just remember it, only just remember the cold stone beneath her bony knees as she prayed to a God who'd refused to listen to her pleas, her promises to be a good girl. Being good hadn't gotten her what she'd wanted then, and it never would, so she was done trying. She'd get what she wanted through her own efforts or she'd fail, but it would be her doing and no one else's, certainly not some capricious deity who'd ignored a desperate child.

She didn't dare look at Jerome, too certain he'd be glowering at her. He'd promised to help her with her dare before troubling himself to discover what she had in mind, poor fool, and now he was stuck. He'd tried everything he could think of to change her mind, but once Bonnie had focused her brain on something that was an end to it. She'd made her plans, and he had promised. It was a *fait accompli*, and so she'd told him.

She waited until almost eleven o'clock before she slipped away. For her plans it would hardly be considered late in the evening, and yet it was long enough. She hadn't wanted to miss Harriet and Jasper's engagement ball, but it was likely her last chance for such a scheme. This way she could plead fatigue after having danced herself into exhaustion with no one thinking it suspicious. Smiling to herself, and with anticipation simmering in her veins, she hurried up the stairs to her room.

***

"There you are, old man. Been looking everywhere for you!"

Bonnie had to stamp on the urge to crow with laughter as Jerome jolted in response to her hearty slap on the back. He glowered at her, affronted by the temerity of the young man who'd taken such a liberty when they'd not been introduced.

"Who the devil are you?" he began and then stopped, the colour leaching from his handsome face as his gaze travelled over her, from tip to toe and back again. "B-Bonnie?" he stammered, quite obviously horrified.

"You didn't recognise me, did you?" Bonnie barely restrained herself from doing a little dance of triumph. She couldn't afford to draw attention to them.

"Hell and the devil, you'll be the death of me, Bonnie Campbell," he cursed, before his mouth fell open. She'd thought he'd seemed quite horrified enough before but now he looked like he might swoon. "Oh, Lord." His voice was rough, almost breathless. "Your hair! Bonnie, what have you done to your hair?"

Bonnie felt a tremor of regret as she lifted a hand to her shorn locks. She'd almost changed her mind when her maid had burst into tears, begging her not to make her cut off the thick, dark tresses. The sight of it piled on her bedroom floor had almost made Bonnie weep too, but what was the point? Jerome didn't think it her crowning glory. He didn't think of her at all in such a way. She was just one of his chums, not a woman whose appearance he admired, so what difference did it make if she cut it off or not? Except now, looking at his appalled expression, she wanted to cry. *Stop it,* she scolded herself. *You couldn't seduce him when you were all but naked and flat on your back. Cutting off your hair won't make him want you any less, you ninny.*

"It's fashionable to wear it short," she said defiantly. "And I can hardly pass as a man with long hair, can I?"

Jerome took her by the arm and hauled her into a quiet corner where he proceeded to scold her and do his best to wriggle out of his promise. Bonnie held firm and refused to budge. He'd promised her, and she was holding him to it. She didn't care if she was ruined. It wouldn't change anything. Morven had told her she'd marry Anderson, no matter what she did to try to get out of it. She believed him. All she could hope was that good old Gordy would be so disgusted with her that he'd refuse, dowry be damned.

Jerome muttered and cursed some more as Bonnie reminded him he'd not recognised her. This did not seem to appease him one little bit.

"Ah, don't be like that," she coaxed, reaching for his hand and giving it a squeeze. "We'll have fun, I promise."

Jerome stared back at her. "Oh, I don't doubt it, you little devil. I just wonder how long I'll be paying for it afterwards, that's all."

"It will be worth it, I promise."

Something in his eyes softened, and she knew she had him.

"I know," he said, before giving a short bark of laughter. "Well, then, if we're going to the devil, we may as well do it in style. What am I to call you, sir?"

"Bartholomew Camden, a distant cousin on your mother's side, Jerry, old man."

Jerome snorted. "Well, Coz, I'm very pleased to know you. Why don't we leave this place and find a bit of life?"

Bonnie grinned at him, wanting to hug him for forgetting his concerns and getting into the spirit of it. "I thought you'd never ask."

***

Jerome's heart had been lodged firmly in his throat for the past hour or more but, as he looked around the card table at the disreputable faces of some of his friends, it cautiously returned to the vicinity of his chest. Bonnie grinned at him, a cheroot clamped between her teeth, and Jerome had to bite back the desire to snicker.

Cholly or, more correctly, Lord Chalfont, Mr Gideon Newman, and The Honourable Algernon Fortescue—known appallingly and affectionately as Algae to his intimates, had all accepted Bonnie as his cousin Bart without so much as a blink. Admittedly, by the time Jerome had tracked them down through a variety of dubious drinking places, they had all been drunk as wheelbarrows, but nonetheless… were the brainless idiots blind? How could they possibly not see she was a woman?

Her skin was too soft, too perfect, and her heart-shaped face far too pretty. There were pretty lads about, he knew, but surely not with the lavish curves of waist and hips belonging to the dreadful girl across the table. Bonnie had bound her breasts so severely her shape had morphed into something that gave her the silhouette of a plump pigeon. It made him want to laugh every time he looked her. It also made his hands itch with the desire to unwind her like a spinning top, unravelling whatever was restraining her charms as his palms burned with the memory of having those generous mounds in his grasp. He rubbed a hand over his face, increasingly heated and agitated. Hell and the devil, he didn't even want Bonnie, not like that. He loved her company because she was impossible not to like, but he'd not given her a second glance when she'd turned up with her friends at Green Park, and would have continued to not glance her way if not for her outrageous sense of humour and devilish tongue. It was those things that had caught his attention, and held it too, but not her body nor her face. Here he was though, lusting over her breasts. He wanted to kiss and lick and soothe that tortured bounty once he'd freed them from the ridiculous cage she'd trapped them in, and then he'd….

Jerome cleared his throat and returned his attention to his cards. *Behave, Cadogan.* Grimacing at the inadequate hand he held, he threw it down on the table in disgust.

"I'm out," he said with a sigh.

"Bad luck, Jerry," Bonnie murmured as Jerome scowled at the tidy stack of counters before her.

Why he should be surprised she was wiping the floor with them, he had no idea. She was utterly diabolical. He watched as she took a draw on the cheroot and blew a perfect smoke ring across the table to him with a wink. He glowered back and snatched the brandy decanter from her vicinity before she could reach for it. She'd already had a generous measure, and he dared not think what might happen if he allowed her to get foxed. There were limits to his depravity. Allowing a virginal young woman to cut off her hair, dress as a man, and gamble in a low dive like the one they were at present inhabiting would put quite enough paving slabs on his personal road to hell for one night, thank you very much.

Bonnie returned an impatient glare but said nothing, instead spending the next half an hour relieving his friends of what remained of their coin. Algae groaned and put his head in his hands.

"Someone will have to pay my shot," he said, shaking his head mournfully. "I'm cleaned out."

"I say, Jerry," Cholly said, throwing down his cards with a grimace. "If you've any more cousins, do us a favour and leave 'em where ye find 'em."

"You need have no fear on that score," Jerome muttered. "Come on, Bart, my lad. That's enough excitement for one night. I'd best get you back, or we'll both be in the basket."

"Oh, but, Jerry—"

Jerome ignored Bonnie's complaints, knowing well enough what the rest of the evening would likely hold as Gideon crooked his finger at a comely serving wench. He watched, amused despite himself at the way Bonnie's eyes grew wide when the young woman sashayed over and settled herself in Gideon's lap.

"*Now,* Bart," he said, smirking a little.

Bonnie got to her feet and followed him out the door.

It was gone three in the morning by the time they got back to Holbrooke House. By some miracle, Jerome was able to put the curricle away and bed down the horse, waking none of the stable lads in the process.

"Well, then, you dreadful girl, I hope you're satisfied?" he asked, sliding the bolt across on the stall door and turning to her.

"Oh, yes, Jerome, thank you so much. It was fun, wasn't it?"

He laughed, shaking his head but unable to deny it. "I suppose so, once I'd convinced myself that my friends really are blind and even more thick-headed than I'd supposed. I thought I would have a heart attack in the first half an hour, I can tell you."

"You worry too much," she said, shaking her head at him.

"You don't worry enough," he muttered.

She rolled her eyes and then winced, her mouth tightening.

"What is it?" he asked, frowning at her obvious discomfort.

"It's the binding," she said, her voice tight. "It's really hurting now, and Mary will be abed. I'll have to sleep in the blasted thing, for I can't risk going to wake her. Not that I'll sleep, I can barely breathe."

"You fool girl," he said impatiently. "You'll do yourself an injury."

"Oh, Jerry, please help me get it off," she pleaded, shrugging out of her coat and letting it fall to the floor.

Jerome stared at her, his mouth growing dry as the visions he'd been lingering on earlier bloomed afresh behind his eyes.

No.

No.

No, no, no. Behave, Cadogan.

"I don't think…." he began, his voice creaking like a rusty gate, but her slender hands had already undone the buttons on her waistcoat.

"Oh, don't be so missish about it," she said, huffing with irritation as the waistcoat joined the coat in a heap on the floor. "It's not like you've not seen everything before, and you've made it plain enough you're not interested."

Not interested?

He blinked but said nothing, not that he could have. He was a man, and she was suggesting he unwrap her breasts like the best Christmas present a fellow had ever received. Also, he wasn't dead. Not interested? She was unhinged if she thought that likely in these circumstances.

Before he could find any way of stopping her—which, with Bonnie, would be as futile as trying to put out a fire with a decanter of brandy—she'd tugged the shirt over her head.

Jerome stared.

She was bound, mummy like, from her ribs to beneath her armpits, so tightly her skin was red and chafed where the edge of the wrappings had rubbed against her delicate flesh. He swallowed, heat climbing up his neck as she turned her back.

"The fastenings are in the back there somewhere. I can't do it by myself, so you'll have to undo them for me."

Just undo the bindings and walk away, he counselled himself as his heart began to thud in double time. *You can do that. It's not difficult.*

Jerome licked his lips and reached out to where the bindings had been tightly knotted, the ends tucked back under and out of sight. His hands trembled a little as he tugged the ends free and fumbled with the knot.

"Oh, do hurry," she pleaded.

"I'm going as fast as I can, curse you," he muttered. "And it's your own dashed fault, so don't go chastising me."

"I wasn't chastising," she retorted. "I was only asking you to hurry."

"Well, don't. I'll do it in my own good time." Except at that moment the knot came apart in his hands and he wasn't ready, hadn't steeled himself to say, *there you go, you're free. I'll leave you to it now.* He couldn't leave her half-dressed and alone in the stables in any case, he reasoned. Anyone might come across her and think her fair game for a tumble. No. No, he'd have to stay. Just to… to be on the safe side.

He tugged just as he'd imagined earlier and, just as he'd imagined, she turned around and around before him, her bindings unravelling along with his sanity. His breathing grew ragged as she turned and turned, and the tight wrappings tumbled to the ground as his pulse beat in his ears and his body grew taut with interest.

She was faced away from him as the last length of fabric fell and she let out a heartfelt sigh that he felt somewhere in the pit of his belly.

"Oh, thank heavens," she murmured. "That's better."

As though he was watching someone in a dream—some poor fool hellbent on destruction, no doubt—he reached out and traced one of the red lines across her back, where the bindings had left imprints in her soft skin.

"Look what you've done to yourself," he whispered, hearing the breathless quality of his own words. His finger trailed to her waist, and he put his hand on her at the point where the curve of her hips began.

She stilled beneath his touch and then looked back, over her shoulder at him. Her eyes were wide and dark, and she licked her lips.

"It's worse this side," she said, her voice low. "I wish you'd kiss it better."

Oh God, there it was: the toll of doom clanging in his ears.

Bonnie reached down and took his hand, guiding it to her breast.

"Bonnie," he said, shaking his head even as his body throbbed with desire. His heart was a drumbeat in his ears, his swelling cock pulsing in time with it, with need. Oh, good Lord, he was in deep trouble. "Bonnie, no," he said, though it was a pitiful effort to act the gentlemen as his hand curved about her breast and squeezed as he spoke.

"Your hands are so warm," she said, the words spoken on a sigh. "So big and warm."

She leaned back against his chest and he took it for the invitation it was, filling both his hands with her soft flesh, gently kneading and stroking and then pinching her nipples, rolling them back and forth between finger and thumb.

She gasped and tilted her head back, exposing the pale line of her throat.

Jerome stared down at it, willing himself to find the strength to move away from her, to stop, when the desire to kiss a path down that slender neck was so fierce he could taste it. She turned her head and looked up at him.

"It's all right," she said, and her eyes were clear, focused entirely on him. "I know we won't marry. I'm not trying to trap you. I want this. I want you."

"It's wrong…." he said, forcing the words out. "I ought not—"

"Nonsense," she said, smiling at him. "I want you. I want this night for myself, before my life is no longer my own. That's not so much to ask, is it? Unless… Unless you don't want to."

He watched uncertainty flicker in her eyes, saw the glimpse of vulnerability before she turned away from him, and he hated it.

"Seriously?" he asked, pulling her closer so that her bottom cradled his arousal. She let out a breath as he pressed against her. "Don't be so bird-witted."

"Jerome," she whispered, and turned in his arm, tugging at his neck, pulling him down and down into a kiss that drowned out good sense and any notions of gentlemanly behaviour.

After all, she wanted him, wanted this, her last chance to make her own decision about anything before she was married to a man she didn't even like. How could he refuse her?

Somehow, he guided her back into an empty stall, thickly bedded with clean straw, praise be to God. Not that he liked straw—it always ended up sticking you in the arse, blasted prickly stuff—but beggars couldn't be choosers.

They tumbled into it, the sweet scent of summers past and gone rising around them as Jerome found the buttons on the fall of her trousers and flicked them undone, sliding his hand beneath. His hand moved over the gentle swell of her stomach, over skin like satin until he found the feathery curls he sought and trailed his fingers through them.

Bonnie's breath caught and her hips arched, seeking more of the tentative touch his fingers teased her with. Jerome smiled at her impatience.

"Wicked girl," he crooned, nipping at her earlobe. "Always in such a hurry."

"I'm afraid you'll change your mind and leave me alone," she admitted, before tugging his shirt free and sliding her hands beneath. Jerome closed his eyes as her hands moved over him, the caress making him want to purr like a cat to announce his approval.

"I'm not that noble," he said, bending to swipe his tongue over her nipple and grazing the tender bud with his teeth, enjoying her soft cries and exclamations as his fingers slid through the curls between her thighs and caressed her intimate flesh. He groaned as he allowed his caress to slide deeper and found her hot and wet, wanting and needing him.

"Please," she begged him, clinging to his neck. "Please."

How could he refuse such a plea? It was the work of moments to shed his clothes and tug her legs free of the trousers she wore, easier still to take his place between her thighs, sliding his aching flesh against her until she cried out and he thought he'd go mad if he didn't have her. Yet she was a virgin and, though Jerome had never deflowered one before, he knew he must prepare the way to make it easier for her.

So he continued the glide of his flesh over hers, until she was writhing beneath him, her pale skin flushed and rosy as she clutched at him, grasping at his shoulders and holding him tight. He moved back then, returning his hand to that tender spot and sliding a finger inside as his thumb circled and caressed.

"Is this what you want?" he asked, as his finger moved slowly back and forth.

"Yes," she gasped, and then, "No, I... I don't know."

"Yes, you do," he said, smiling down at her. "Tell me."

"It's... It's... lovely," she managed, staring up at him from heavy-lidded eyes. "But...."

"But?"

"But it's not enough."

Jerome chuckled and moved over her, kissing her neck and then her mouth. "Greedy girl," he murmured against her lips. "Are you sure?"

"Yes," she said, the word long and drawn out into a decadent moan.

He crooked his fingers inside her, finding the tender spot that made her cry out again and again until she shattered beneath him and he swallowed her cries with his mouth. He didn't wait until the rapture had ebbed, thrusting inside as her climax still pulsed within her and she cried out again, pleasure and pain as she let him in.

"Bonnie," he whispered as euphoria and desire took over, sweeping him up with it. "Bonnie, you feel like heaven."

Chapter 3

I know I ought not have done it, but I love him, and it was wonderful, so perfect. I love him so much it hurts. What option did I have?

Oh Lord, I'm so unhappy.

— Excerpt of an entry from Miss Bonnie Campbell to her diary.

18ᵗʰ September 1814. Still the night of Harriet and Jasper's engagement ball. Holbrooke House, Sussex

Jerome stared at the stable roof overhead, a cold sensation settling in his guts. The knowledge he'd been a bloody fool was hard to refute. That he'd compounded his error by getting so carried away he'd not withdrawn in time to lessen the risk of putting a babe in her belly was beyond anything. He'd acted like some green boy with no idea of what he was about. That Bonnie had sent him careening over the edge so madly was something he was struggling to come to terms with, too. It seemed so unlikely as to be laughable, and yet… she had. She'd been so welcoming, so enthusiastic and bold, and… and he'd lost his bloody mind. There was no other explanation.

Beside him she was stirring, and it took him a moment to realise she was getting dressed. Belatedly, he realised he ought to have held her, comforted her and reassured her, told her it would be all right.

"Bonnie," he began, his voice sounding odd and rusty in the silence after their cries of pleasure had faded and gone.

"Oh, stop looking so anxious," she scolded him, pulling on her trousers. "You look like you're on your way to the gallows. I told you there's nothing to worry about. You don't owe me anything."

He stared at her, a little taken aback. "I might," he said. "I didn't... I mean I ought to have.... Oh, dash it all, Bonnie. We'll have to get married. You might be pregnant."

"Don't be ridiculous," she said, utterly calm, far calmer than he. "Your mother would never forgive you, and you'd hate me for trapping you, which was not my intention as you well know, so stop getting hysterical. That's supposed to be my job."

"I'm not hysterical," he objected, stung, though he didn't see how she was so bloody unmoved. "I'm just trying to do the right thing by you."

"Well, I don't want you to," she snapped, pulling her shirt back on. "I told you that from the start. There's no need. I doubt very much I'm pregnant, no matter how virile you think you are, and if I am... well, we'll worry about it then."

She shrugged on her waistcoat and coat and thrust her boots on, and would have walked away from him before he'd gathered his wits. He leapt up, pulling his trousers on as he hurried after her.

"Bonnie! Bonnie, wait."

She paused but didn't turn and he moved to her side, taking her hand in his.

"Bonnie," he said again, softer now.

"Don't," she said, and he heard the quaver in her voice as she tugged her hand free and ran out of the stables and into the dark.

***

19th September 1814. Holbrooke House, Sussex.

Bonnie fought for calm, fought not to cry as her friends chattered around her. She kept her eyes closed and pretended to sleep while focusing her entire being on keeping the tears at bay.

It was the afternoon after the engagement ball, and they all lounged on an elegant terrace overlooking Holbrooke House's splendid gardens. The girls were discussing love and childhood sweethearts, and the likelihood of the remaining unwed ladies finding anything like the marital bliss beckoning Harriet and Jasper.

"What do you hope for?" Matilda asked Ruth, and Bonnie tried not to listen, or to think, or to do anything other than exist.

She wished she could pack her feelings up in a box and bury them deep underground where they would no longer trouble her or anyone else.

"I hope to please my father and make him proud by marrying a titled man, to elevate the family as he dreams I will," Ruth said, sensible as ever. "I hope that man and I can be friends and allies and that we can make each other comfortable and perhaps even content. I hope to have children to love and a household to run and a position of respect and security. That is what I hope for. What about you?"

"I hope I can be satisfied with everything you just said," Matilda replied with a short, humourless laugh. "For I know it is also everything I should wish for, and it ought to be more than enough, more than I have a right to expect in my circumstances."

"It isn't what you want at heart though, is it?"

Bonnie could hear the understanding in Ruth's voice and her temper flared. Damn them for their good sense, for playing by the rules when the rules were unfair and unkind and the world about them was expressly designed for men, by men.

"Of course it isn't!"

Ruth and Matilda both looked up in surprise at Bonnie's outburst.

"How can either of you hope to be merely comfortable or content?" she demanded, too much emotion evident in her voice as she struggled to keep the tears back. "Perhaps that is the best reality will give us, but surely to goodness you *hope* for more than that? Don't you hope and dream and wish for love and happiness and a life that's full of all of those things, a life worth living, a life that touches others and leaves them changed by it?"

Matilda stared at her for a moment and then reached out and took Bonnie's hand, squeezing it tight.

"Yes," she said, holding on tight, the truth of her answer shining in her eyes. "Yes, I do. Of course I do."

"Me too," Ruth admitted, reaching out and taking Bonnie's other hand. "Though I am well aware it's a forlorn hope, I have to admit I do still dream of it."

"And me." Minerva got to her feet, put her arms about Bonnie, and kissed her cheek. "I dream of impossible things all the time, every day, and I shan't stop, though no doubt that makes me a fool."

"Not a fool," Bonnie said, more touched than she could say for the way they rallied to her. They didn't know what she'd done or why she was upset, but that didn't matter. They were here, they cared. That meant more than she could ever explain to them. "It makes you alive, and I refuse to live as though I've one foot in the grave. Not yet, at least. I'll not give in yet."

Of all the things life had given her and taken from her, she was most grateful for these women. She knew they would not condemn her for what she'd done last night. Oh, they'd be dreadfully shocked and think her a reckless fool, no doubt—and rightly so, she supposed—but they'd not shun her or call her a slut. She wondered if she *was* a slut. The world would think her so, she knew that much, but the world had always been out of step with her, or she with it. She belonged nowhere, had never been wanted anywhere, and so it was second nature to wait for rejection. It wasn't a matter of why, only when, because it always happened. For just a short time last night, she had belonged. She had belonged to Jerome, had found her place in his arms, and it had been every bit as perfect as she'd known it would be.

Until it was over, of course, but it was always going to be that way. She'd known it and had accepted it.

It was just as she'd imagined, watching the worry grow in his blue eyes as he realised what he'd done. She might have laughed at the predictability of it all, had she not been so heartbroken. Well, what was done was done. There was no point crying about it. He'd given her what she'd wanted, one night with him, one shining moment to remember a time when she'd lived for herself and her own dreams and no one could stop her. Ah, well. That was something. It was more than many could claim.

She looked up then and her poor abused heart constricted as she saw Jerome walking in the gardens with his brother and Harriet. St Clair looked stern, and she suspected Jerome had recently been on the receiving end of a lecture. Well, she knew the fact she'd come down to breakfast with short hair, when she'd gone to bed with acres of the stuff, had caused talk. No doubt St Clair was suspicious. She'd told them she'd cut it on a whim that morning, but she doubted they believed her. Oh, she would come clean to the girls later—she had to if she wanted to tell them she'd achieved her dare—but not while they were still at Holbrooke. She didn't want any of them scolding Jerome on her behalf. It looked as if St Clair had that well in hand in any case.

The ladies drifted away, some of them electing to go for a walk whilst others sought the cool of the house and a quiet corner in which to read. Bonnie stayed where she was. She didn't want company, didn't want to talk, only to reflect on what had happened last night and how she would bear it when Gordon Anderson came for her and hauled her back to Scotland. She'd likely never see Jerome again. The nearest she'd get would be reading the scandal sheets and hearing about his exploits. No doubt one day she'd read the announcement of his marriage to some fine lady of the *ton*, perhaps Lady Helena. It was clear Lady St Clair favoured her.

Bonnie's chest grew tight, and she squeezed her eyes shut, willing the tears back.

Whatever happened, she'd not marry Gordon Anderson. She'd go away if Morven wanted her to, which was likely once she told them what she'd done. Not that she'd mention Jerome by name, only that she'd fallen in love with a man who couldn't marry her, and that she was damaged goods.

"Bonnie."

She opened her eyes with a start, her heart thudding as Jerome's voice filtered through her agitated mind.

"What do you want?" she said, knowing she sounded unwelcoming and wary, but she didn't want to see him now.

Oh, what a ridiculous lie that was! Of course she wanted to see him. She wanted to wrap herself around him and cling like a limpet, never letting go, but that was out of the question. The only way she'd keep her pride and her sanity intact was by keeping her distance. Part of her wished Anderson would come for her now and get it over with. At least while she was rowing with him her other troubles would not be in the forefront of her mind—for they couldn't be in a room together without Bonnie plotting the brute's murder.

"We need to talk," Jerome said, his expression serious.

Bonnie rolled her eyes at him, even while her heart ached at his chivalry. He'd marry her, although he didn't want to, didn't love her, and despite knowing his mother would be furious and disappointed in him. There was a sweet boy buried under that devil may care exterior, though she'd known that from the start.

"No, we don't," she said, getting to her feet and walking away from him.

He caught hold of her arm, forcing her to a halt. "Bonnie," he said, and there was a thread of impatience in her name now. "You can't pretend nothing happened."

"I can, and I will," she said, trying to tug her arm free. "Let go of me."

"Not until you listen to what I have to say."

Bonnie glared at him, wishing she could tell him to go to perdition but there was such a look in his eyes, such determination to do the right thing, she hadn't the heart. So she steeled herself against his words, knowing it would be so tempting to let him play the hero and make a noble sacrifice on her behalf. She could make herself believe that he would grow to love her in time, that they could be happy, but she'd stopped believing in fairy stories when she was a very little girl. Some people got their happy ever after and some didn't, but you couldn't make it happen by wishing for it. She stopped struggling, and he released her arm.

"You were an innocent, Bonnie, and I took advantage of you," he said, his handsome face grave. "It's against the rules. I knew that, and I did it anyway."

She stared at him, at the vivid blue eyes and strong jaw, at the mop of golden hair glinting in the sunlight. He was so like his brother, the earl, and yet so different. That broken nose spoiled the perfection of his features and yet enhanced his appeal. It was visible proof of the devils that danced in his eyes, though they were missing now as he appealed to her to have some sense, to realise that she must marry him, for he'd ruined her and he must make it right.

Bonnie studied his serious expression with dismay. If she married him, she'd have killed that wicked spark for good, trapped it in a cage until it snuffed out. He'd come to resent her, perhaps even hate her, for what she'd done to him. For, no matter what Jerome told himself, last night had been her doing. She'd been pursuing him for weeks and last night he'd been just foxed enough to play into her hands. Not because he'd been dreaming of her, longing for her, but simply because she'd been warm and willing and there. Not very flattering, but it was the truth, and Bonnie always faced that head on. Better that than have it creep up on you when you weren't expecting it.

"Your brother has rung a peal over you, no doubt," she said, relieved that her voice was even and unemotional when her stomach had tied itself in a knot and she wanted to run away and cry.

"Yes," he admitted. "But that's not why—"

"Did you tell him?"

"Curse it, Bonnie, of course not! What do you take me for?"

"Good," she said, letting out a breath. That was something. "Swear to me you won't."

He glowered at her.

"It's my reputation at stake! Swear it, damn you."

He bristled at that, as she'd intended. "I may not be a very good gentleman, but I'm not a cad," he said stiffly. "Which is why I'm trying to do the right thing now. Belatedly I'll admit, but—"

"Oh, go away, Jerome," she said impatiently.

Tears were prickling her eyes and she had no choice but to get angry. She could get angry or she could cry. If she cried, he'd take her in his arms and tell her it would be all right and, before she knew it, she'd be married to him, and... oh, how she longed for it. Her heart ached at how tantalisingly close the dream was, images of him as her husband and golden-haired children playing at her feet choking her and closing her throat until she thought she'd pass out or go mad.

"I won't go away, you impossible girl," he snapped, keeping pace with her as she strode away. "Not until you see sense."

Bonnie kept going until it became clear he'd not let it rest. She stopped in her tracks, swinging round to face her. "Very well," she said, her heart beating too fast as hope flickered to life despite everything, despite knowing what his answer would be. "I'll marry you if you tell me, hand on heart, what I need to hear."

His thick blond brows knitted, and he stared down at her, so obviously perplexed she wanted to cry. "I don't know what you want to hear," he said, folding his arms.

She let out a long-suffering sigh and mirrored his stance. "I want to hear what every girl wants to hear when a fellow proposes marriage, Jerome," she said, speaking slowly and with infinite patience despite the fact her heart was trying to escape her ribcage. Was there a chance he'd say it? Was there the slightest chance he'd mean it?

He stared at her, blinked, and then his eyes widened. "Oh," he said, and a tinge of colour rose in his cheeks. He cleared his throat, looking increasingly awkward and any foolish hopes that had dared to spark to life instantly snuffed out.

"Bonnie, I…."

Bonnie turned on her heel.

"Bonnie!" he said, hurrying after her.

"I don't want to marry a man that doesn't love me," she said, weary now. "At least Anderson would get something out of marrying me, for he needs my dowry. You could do far better than anything I can bring you, Jerome, and you ought to, for your mother's sake if not your own. Go and find a pretty blonde heiress and fall in love, why don't you?"

"That's not fair, Bonnie. Perhaps I don't love you, but we're friends, aren't we? Lots of marriages start with less than that."

Bonnie paused and turned back to stare at him. "Then I must be very selfish, for I don't want half measures. I'll have a man who loves me, me alone and no one else, or I'll have no one at all."

"You're ruined, Bonnie."

"And no one knows that but you."

"You said Morven will force you to marry Anderson. He doesn't love you."

"No, true enough, but I don't love him either. If Morven forces the issue at least I won't care when my husband's unfaithful, and he won't care to interfere in my life. Perhaps I'll take a lover."

"And you'll not tell Anderson that his bride has been deflowered ahead of the wedding night?"

Bonnie's jaw tightened. "I'll tell him the truth, don't worry. I'm not a liar."

"Damn you, Bonnie, don't make me a villain."

"Oh, stop acting like you're the misunderstood hero in some Gothic adventure," she cried, needing this to be over now before her resolve faltered and she stopped fighting him. "I won't marry you. You've done nothing wrong. I practically threw myself at you, Jerome. Most any other man would tell himself I was no better than I ought to be and move on. Bloody well do the same thing and get over it. Just leave me alone!"

He jolted, and she wanted to curl up in a ball and weep at the hurt in his eyes, but she couldn't afford to let him see her pain, or to know how much his efforts to do the right thing had touched her. So she turned on her heel and left him.

Chapter 4

Everyone is so happy and excited for Harriet's wedding and I hate myself for how envious I am. What would it feel like to have Jerome's mother look at me with such affection as she shows Harriet, to know I was a welcome addition to the family and, most of all, that my husband loved me beyond reason? It must be a wonderful feeling, to be wanted.

What a wretched creature I am. I see the jealousy and despair in my own eyes as I look in the mirror, and I despise myself.

At least Jerome is not here to notice it. I've not seen him in ten days, since I told him to leave me alone. He's gone to visit friends, so it appears I got what I wanted. I should take more care in what I wish for.

— Excerpt of an entry from Miss Bonnie Campbell to her diary.

30th September 1814. Holbrooke House, Sussex.

Matilda closed her bedroom door behind her, tossed the armful of packages she held on to the bed, and sat down with a sigh. They'd been into Tunbridge Wells, shopping, and they'd walked so much her feet hurt, though it was her heart that ached the most.

There was something wrong with Bonnie.

Although the young woman loved shopping, she'd refused to come and when Matilda had looked in on her when she'd returned, it was clear the girl had spent the morning alone, and crying.

Matilda had known, as they all knew, that Bonnie had fallen in love with Jerome. Bonnie had hardly made a secret of it. Something had happened, though, and Jerome had left, apparently to visit friends. Matilda had tried to talk to Bonnie, to get her to confide in her, but Bonnie had assured her that she was fine, that she and Jerome were still friends, but that they knew it was best if they put distance between them. She'd sounded mature and level-headed when she'd explained it all, and Matilda had wanted to weep, for she knew she was heartbroken. All the spark had left her, all the fun and laughter chased from her eyes, and she was listless. Yet Bonnie did not want her sympathy or her interference. Matilda could only respect her wishes and pray it had been nothing more than a brief infatuation that would fade with time. She'd done her best to make sure Bonnie knew she was there if she needed her, but what else could she do?

Matilda flung her bonnet and gloves aside with a frustrated curse, rang for some tea to be sent up to her room, and paced to the window, then stopped in her tracks. There was a small leather box on the sill, tied with a blue silk ribbon. It had not been there when she'd left this morning.

"Oh, you wretched man," she whispered. "What have you done now?"

The last time something unexpected had turned up in her room, it had been a letter from the Marquess of Montagu. How he'd contrived to get it there she did not know, but no doubt he had lackeys who dealt with such matters, such as delivering letters to young ladies who ought not be receiving such things from an unmarried man. She ought to have thrown the letter on the fire, of course she ought. Not only had she not burnt it, however, she'd kept it, for reasons upon which she preferred not to dwell. Not that it had been a love letter, far from it. More like a warning shot, a confirmation of intent. Montagu's intent being to have her as his mistress, and she was all too aware his campaign was far from over.

Matilda's heart thudded as she moved to the window and picked up the little box. She ought to throw it away without opening it, or fling it in his face—also without opening it, —but curiosity was burning inside her, making her fingers itch with the desire to tug the ribbon aside and reveal the dreadful secret within, and it would be dreadful. Expensive, exclusive, horribly tempting, and dreadful.

"I want you very badly, Miss Hunt. I spend far too much time thinking of you, of how it would feel to take you in my arms. How is that for honesty?"

His words, spoken the last time she'd seen him, shivered over her, leaving a thrill of mingled excitement and terror in their wake. She was not beyond admitting to the thrill, to the knowledge that such a feared and powerful, desirable man wanted her so very badly. It was fear alone that held that excitement in check. Montagu was discreet in his affairs but his longest serving mistress had kept his interest for three years only. Then what? What if she gave into desire and temptation and put herself outside of respectable society for the chance to be with him for a brief affair? Her friends and family would still receive her, she knew, but they ought not, for they would be tarnished by association. She would be a pariah, more so than now even, where she still trod the fringes of the *ton* because of her brother's influence and her powerful friends.

For now, there was a chance for her still to marry despite her reputation, and have a home, a family, something that would endure for the rest of her life, rather than a handful of months or years. If she had an ounce of sense, she'd keep that in the forefront of her mind and cast temptation straight out of the window.

She opened the box, and her breath snagged in her throat.

It was a brooch, set with rubies and diamonds. A witch's brooch. Set in the shape of an open heart, the tail of the heart was crooked to one side and signified that the giver was bewitched. Matilda swallowed and lifted the brooch from its satin bed, tracing the heart with a fingertip before turning it over. On the back, at the tail of the heart was a tiny M set with rubies.

"Wicked, wicked man," she whispered, clasping the brooch tight as her fingers curled around it and she closed her eyes in despair. "Oh, Lord, what am I to do?"

***

Jerome stared down the hill towards Holbrooke House, his horse fidgeting below him, eager to get back to the stables where food and a rub down awaited it. Jerome stilled it, not ready to close the distance between him and Bonnie.

He still didn't know what he felt. When he'd left, he'd been bloody angry, not to mention hurt, that she had flung his efforts to do the right thing back at him with so much force. Why he felt so, he didn't know. He ought to be relieved. Marrying Bonnie was the last thing he wanted, the very idea of it made him go hot and cold in quick succession as he imagined the disastrous consequences of such a *mésalliance*. Not because he was a snob. He didn't give a damn that her family wasn't as illustrious as his, nor that her dowry was barely adequate, rather than the lavish fortune a match with the likes of Lady Helena could bring him.

No, that wasn't it.

The trouble with Bonnie was that she had the devil in her, the same devil that lived in him, and when they were with each other those two wicked creatures got their heads together, intent on mayhem.

Jasper's lecture was still ringing in his ears and for once Jerome had paid attention. Usually his brother's rants, whilst justified, left Jerome untouched. He'd listen—or pretend to—and nod and promise to do better and then go on his merry way. The morning after having relieved his friend of her maidenhead, however, guilt was already sitting heavy in his heart, and Jasper's words had struck hard. His brother was not in the least bit unreasonable either. He wasn't nagging Jerome to marry; at twenty-four Jasper felt he was young enough to wait a good few years yet. That he needed to grow up and start acting his age, however, was plain. Jasper had run through a variety of Jerome's recent exploits, reminding him of various scrapes he'd been hauled from: drunkenness, debauchery, a close shave with a married lady who'd been blackmailing him with telling the scandal sheets the intimate details of their affair, and not forgetting his finest hour, the courtesan for whom he'd believed he'd fallen head over heels for and had seriously considered marrying. Admittedly, this last had been over two years ago, but the experience had clearly scarred his big brother for life. Jerome's lovely petticoat had cost Jasper a small fortune to get rid of, and he wasn't about to let him forget it.

That the girl had skipped off without a backward glance had hurt too, though not as deeply as it ought to have. Not too many weeks later, Jerome had been forced to acknowledge it hadn't been love he'd felt, or if it had, it was a shallow, fragile variety, for he'd not pined for her. He didn't know what love was, he supposed, though he wanted to, more than he'd ever admit.

Running through his recent escapades, which when listed one after the other did not create a pretty picture, had given Jerome pause, as his brother had no doubt intended. Then, Jasper had started in on Bonnie, and not for the first time. She was a lovely girl, a great deal of fun, his brother said, telling Jerome he quite understood the appeal, but she was an innocent and clearly in love with Jerome, and it was cruel of him to pay her such attention when he had no intention of offering for her. The girl would be hurt and her reputation damaged if Jerome didn't stop encouraging her. If he cared for her at all, he'd keep away. If, however, he continued to put her heart and reputation at risk, Jasper would be forced to take action and stop Jerome's allowance. He'd already threatened this once before, a threat which Jerome had taken with a pinch of salt as Jasper really wasn't a bad fellow and wouldn't throw his weight around and play the lord and master if he didn't have to. Now, however, his intent was obvious. He meant it.

It wasn't the threat that had made him think, though. Jerome's heart had felt raw and exposed, the pain of guilt and responsibility so heavy he couldn't breathe as he realised how right Jasper was. Bonnie loved him, and he'd ruined her. What kind of man was he, what kind of *friend* was he, to treat her so badly?

He'd met her in Green Park, the night of the fireworks on the first of August and liked her at once. Was it really only two months ago? Yet she'd been at Holbrooke House since the middle of August and, until he'd run away from her, they'd spent nearly every day in each other's company. Other than his family—and, he supposed, his fellow pupils at school—he didn't think he'd ever spent so much time with one person. He'd certainly never spent so much time with a female.

If Jasper had had the slightest inkling of all the times they'd snuck out of the house to meet each other too, he'd have been a damn sight more furious than he had been.

Jerome had been uncharacteristically penitent in the light of that scolding, and he'd meant it too, with all his heart. He'd sworn to Jasper that he'd change, that he'd grow up and behave himself. No more drinking and carousing, no more scandals, no more getting into trouble. He'd put his hand on his heart and sworn to do better, to make his brother proud. It was hardly surprising that Jasper had looked sceptical, but Jerome was determined to do as he'd said and put things right. With that in mind he'd gone straight to Bonnie and proposed, only to have his offer thrown back in his face.

It had hurt more than he liked to admit.

So now he was back, after having taken to his heels and run away, rather than being forced to look into Bonnie's eyes every day and face the truth of how badly he'd let her down. He'd ruined their friendship and ruined her, and she wouldn't let him make it right in the only way he knew how.

"Oh God," he moaned, rubbing a hand over his face.

He didn't know what to do. Perhaps if it weren't for his brother's wedding he'd have played the coward and kept away, no matter how much he hated himself for doing so. Missing the wedding was out of the question, however, and Bonnie would be there so… so, he damn well needed a plan.

Except he had no idea where to start. Bonnie didn't want to marry him unless he was in love with her, and he could hardly pretend he was when he wasn't. So, where did that leave them?

With another groan of despair, he urged his horse on, and rode on to Holbrooke.

By the time he entered the house, everyone was gathering for lunch, and he met Miss Hunt in the hallway.

"Have you seen Bonnie?" she asked, her expression one of such anxiety his heart clenched in anticipation of the worst.

"No," he said, aware of his guts twisting with guilt, a sensation with which he was becoming far too familiar. "I've just arrived. Is she missing?"

Miss Hunt shrugged. "I saw her an hour ago, and she said she'd see me at lunch but now… well, she's not here and…."

She paused and gave Jerome a hard stare, apparently weighing him up. To his horror, he felt a flush of heat climbing up the back of his neck.

"I know it's none of my business," Miss Hunt said, lowering her voice though there was a sharp glint to her blue eyes. "But Bonnie is hardly discreet in these matters and you've been keeping away and…."

"And…?" Jerome prompted as she paused, wishing she'd just get on and accuse him of being a bastard and a cad. It would almost be a relief. They'd make Bonnie marry him then.

"She wouldn't come out with us this morning," Miss Hunt said, and for a moment Jerome thought she'd strayed from the topic. "When I came home, it was clear she'd spent the morning crying."

Jerome swallowed around the lump that was now lodged securely in his throat. It didn't budge. "I'll find her," he said, his voice rough, before turning on his heel and heading out of the door again.

He hurried back to the stables to enquire if anyone had seen Bonnie. She loved to ride, and whenever he was blue devilled his first thought was to ride off into the wilderness and get some peace.

Sure enough one of the lads told him that Miss Campbell had taken Magnar, a huge bay stallion, out of the stables over an hour ago.

"Magnar?" Jerome repeated, horrified. "What bloody fool let her take that great brute out alone?"

The groom blushed but stood his ground. "I seen 'er on a horse, Mr Cadogan, and beggin' your pardon but she's a bruising rider, else I would never 'ave let her choose the big fella, but she was set on 'im and I reckoned they'd get along well enough."

Jerome cursed and muttered. Though he knew the fellow was right—Bonnie was a fine horsewoman, as she'd proven to him before now—it didn't mean she ought to be riding out alone, reckless creature that she was. So, he demanded someone bring him a fresh horse at once, before discovering what direction Bonnie had taken and setting out after her.

***

Bonnie drew her mount to a halt and took a moment to admire the scenery. It was a fine afternoon, not as warm as it had been, with the faint scent of autumn and a cooler edge to the day than the past weeks had held. The sun shone, however, though it disappeared from time to time as fluffy white clouds obscured it before drifting on their way. The horse shifted beneath her and she patted his powerful neck. He was a lovely beast and very well-mannered, after an initial set to about who was in charge. Having proved her worth, he'd settled down, and she felt they'd come to an accord.

The big animal turned his head and took a half-hearted nip at her toe and Bonnie laughed. "You big fraud, you're not half so scary as you make out."

She drew in a deep breath, feeling a small part of the tension she carried ease a little. This had always been her escape, to ride out far from anyone and be on her own. Better that way. Better to be by yourself than surrounded by people to whom you were a burden and a bother.

Bonnie's mother had died when she was five, following two older sisters and a newborn son to the grave in a matter of days. Her father had no notion of what to do with a grieving child and Bonnie had been passed back and forth among various relatives, none of whom had been cruel, but none of whom had wanted her much either. Once her father died, three years later, she'd gone to the Earl of Morven's estate, as the earl wanted to keep the promise he'd made her father, who'd been a close friend. Morven had promised to keep her safe and see her wed, even providing the dowry her feckless father had not been able to supply.

Bonnie had been well fed, well dressed, and utterly alone. Morven was a fierce and uncompromising mountain of a man, with a ferocious temper that could even reduce a rugged Highlander to a trembling morass of nerves. He was not a cruel man by any means, however, and had done his best to be kind to Bonnie, but he had no time for her, and she'd been lost among the myriad of responsibilities by which such a man was burdened. His own children were grown and long gone and the nanny he'd employed to look after Bonnie was not unkind, but lackadaisical at best. Not that Bonnie was complaining. She'd enjoyed a great deal of freedom, more than any young lady ought to be allowed, that was for certain. By the time Morven had realised that perhaps his ward ought to have been given a bit more attention and guidance, Bonnie had become wild and ungovernable, and very used to the idea that nobody wanted her.

Her boldness had shocked Morven, who was used to grown men cowering at his feet. It had also impressed him. Over the next years he'd spent a little more time with Bonnie and come to like and respect her, as much as she made him want to tear his hair out and lock her in one of the farthest dungeons. Her rows with him over the subject of Gordon Anderson were legend. He'd relented and allowed her two seasons to catch herself a husband, sending her off to London with the grim reminder that no sensible man would marry a hoyden, and that good old Gordy would be waiting for her on her return.

Well, her two seasons were well and truly over, and Morven had been proved right. No one wanted Bonnie. It wasn't as if it was a surprise, only a confirmation of everything she'd always known. After her mother had died, she'd tried so hard to be a good girl so that her father wouldn't send her away from him. She'd tried to be quiet and well behaved and not to cry for her mama and sisters, but it was hard. How could she help the fact that she looked so like her mama and the sight of her made her father sick with guilt? For it was his fault his wife had died and, young though she was, Bonnie knew it.

If Mama hadn't been so weak from so many lost pregnancies, trying and failing to deliver the boy that her father longed for, she might have been strong enough to care for Bonnie's sisters. If they'd had her care they might not have died, and Mama might have been strong enough to fight the disease herself, rather than following them to the grave with the sickly son she'd just delivered in her arms.

Well, she had, and they had, and Bonnie had been a bother and a nuisance and always in the way ever since. She swallowed hard, forcing back the sorrow and burying it down deep. Perhaps she should just marry Gordon Anderson and have done with it. At least she'd have children to love, and perhaps they'd love her too. Children had to love their mamas, didn't they? If she wasn't too stern and cross—which she never was with children—perhaps they'd like her and want her around them.

Blinking away tears, she put a hand to her belly and wondered if Jerome's seed had taken root there. There was a wicked, selfish part of her that hoped it had, for then she'd always have a part of him for herself. Oh, what a horrid creature she was, wishing for a child that would have no name, but surely Morven would protect them? She knew he thought her a blessed nuisance—who didn't? —but he'd not leave them to make their way alone.

Scolding herself for wallowing in self-pity, Bonnie dismounted and led the horse to the stream she'd discovered, letting him drink his fill before tethering him and leaving him to crop the grass whilst she unpacked the picnic she'd brought with her. She sat beneath the heavily laden boughs of an apple tree and tried to find some enthusiasm for the slice of pie and other tasty morsels cook had given her, but everything tasted like sawdust and stuck in her throat. At least she'd lost a bit of weight. She supposed she ought to be glad of that. All the other girls were always fretting about their waistlines, and Bonnie's proportions were far more generous than any of them. With a sigh, she packed the food away again, curled up under the apple tree, and went to sleep.

Chapter 5

My Lord Montagu,

It is the strangest thing, but this parcel seems to have been delivered to Holbrooke House by mistake. I return it to you now in the hopes it can be given safely to its rightful owner.

— Excerpt of a letter from Miss Matilda Hunt to The Most Honourable Lucian Barrington, the Marquess of Montagu.

30ᵗʰ September 1814. Holbrooke House, Sussex.

Jerome watched the huge horse lumber towards him, tugging at its tether. It huffed and tossed its head, for all the world as if it were standing guard over the sleeping girl.

"It's all right," he said, tugging an apple from the tree and holding it out to him. "I don't mean her any harm." Any *more* harm, he amended silently as Magnar took the apple from him and crunched it with enthusiasm before giving Jerome a warning push with his head that made him take a few steps backward. "All right, point taken," Jerome grumbled.

Good Lord, even the bloody horse knew he was a worthless scoundrel.

He turned back to Bonnie and felt his chest grow tight. She might have been some manner of fae creature, curled up asleep under the old apple tree, the afternoon sun dappling her face. He knelt beside her and reached out a hand, tracing the curve of her jaw as her skin slid like warm silk beneath his touch. He frowned as a surprising thought filtered through his stubborn brain. She really was lovely. Not blonde, no—not slender and fragile as a reed either—but no less beautiful for all that. He remembered the mad joy of that night in the stables and the heat of desire so fierce he'd thought it might burn him up. The moment he'd touched her he'd been lost, out of control. Being with her was like nothing he'd ever experienced before. The idea that nothing would ever match it gave him pause as that same burst of heat surged through him again. His breath caught as he stared down at her. It would be no hardship to wake to such a vision every morning.

As if she'd heard his thoughts, her eyes flickered open, blinking in disorientation before they focused on him. For just a moment he saw a burst of happiness, and then it was snuffed out and she sat up, moving away from him. Jerome felt the rejection as a stab to the heart, though he knew he deserved far worse. What damage he'd done by being an unthinking cad.

"What are you doing here?" she asked, one hand reaching up to touch her hair, a self-conscious movement that made his throat ache.

"Looking for you," he said. "You had everyone worried, disappearing like that."

"Well, here I am," she said, giving him a forced smile with none of her usual joy showing in it. "So you can report back that I'm safe and well."

"Bonnie," he said, exasperated that she'd brush him off again and so quickly.

"There's nothing to say, Jerome. There's no need to fuss. I've had my monthly courses so you're off the hook. There's no need to keep fretting yourself to death about me."

He stared at her, an odd, hollow sensation in his chest he couldn't quite identify.

"Oh," he said, at a loss for what he ought to say, let alone feel. "Well, that's… that's good news, then."

She nodded and got to her feet, moving back to Magnar, who whickered softly as she approached.

"At least let me help you mount," he said as she untied the horse and led him to stand beside an old tree stump.

"No need," she said curtly as she stepped onto the stump and got herself into the saddle with impressive ease. "I'm used to doing things for myself," she added, arranging the skirts of her riding habit.

"I'll ride back with you," he said, hurrying back to his own mount. Perhaps they could talk on the way, though his greeting so far was not filling him with hope.

"I'm not going back yet," she said and rode off without waiting for him.

"Bonnie!" he yelled, to no avail as she guided the horse out of the little orchard and back onto the track. "Damnation," he cursed as he mounted, and set off in pursuit.

***

Bonnie looked over her shoulder, infuriated if not surprised to find Jerome was following her. What was wrong with him? She'd told him he'd had a lucky escape, hoping that would ease his mind, even though she'd lied and had no idea if it was true. Her courses weren't due for another couple of days yet, but she needed him to stay away from her. If he didn't, she was in danger of making a fool of herself over him, and she'd done enough of that already. She'd had enough sympathy and understanding from her friends. They were all very sweet and kind, but there was only so much pity a girl could stand.

To know Jerome pitied her too, and pursued her because he felt guilty for what he'd done, was more than she could bear. If she allowed him to be nice to her, she'd crumble and fall into his arms, and then they'd both be sunk. He'd persuade her to let him do the honourable thing and sacrifice his future for her, and she'd have to bear the dismay in Lady St Clair and the earl's eyes, and know that she'd tied herself to another family who didn't want her.

Well, she was done being unwanted. If she was destined to be alone, so be it. She'd do it on her own terms, though, and never again would she stay where she was not welcome, lonely among people who wished her elsewhere.

"Come along, Magnar," she said, leaning forward to speak to the great stallion. "Take me away from all this."

She urged the horse on, catching her breath as the powerful beast thundered across the hillside as the track gave way into open countryside. She heard Jerome hailing her but ignored him. The lively mare he was riding was fast and nimble but no match for Magnar, who ate up the ground beneath him as if he was Pegasus flying across the fields. How wonderful to fly this fast, the illusion of freedom allowing her to slip free of the burden of sadness that weighed her down. It was only in moments like these, with a surge of recklessness, that she found some measure of respite from a world where she didn't fit.

Bonnie laughed despite herself and gave a whoop as the horse jumped a high hedgerow as if it was nothing at all. For a brief time she allowed her misery and despair to fall away, to live in the moment and find happiness in the thundering of hooves and the wind on her face as the countryside flashed past. Her heart was beating with exhilaration, the excitement of riding so hard and fast a burst of joy that she couldn't contain.

Glancing over her shoulder, she found Jerome gaining on her and caught his eye. Despite everything, she grinned at him, unable to keep her delight from bubbling over. He laughed and shook his head, and she knew he felt it too. He delighted in the same things she did, in adventure and fun and in living for the moment, snatching at happiness.

Jerome understood; it was why she'd fallen so hard for him.

All at once, the fields gave way to thick woodland and forced Bonnie to slow Magnar. She brought him to a halt by the edge of the woods. She was laughing still, tears in her eyes, though she could not tell now if they were from joy or misery. Before she could decide, Jerome was there. He leapt down from his horse, grinning like a fool as he ran to her and hauled her from her mount.

"You mad, diabolical girl!" he exclaimed as he lifted her down. "I thought my heart would give out when you took that second hedgerow, it was so huge. Good God, but you can ride."

He gave a bark of laughter and lifted her again, high in the air, spinning her around before setting her down. His hands were still at her waist and he gazed down at her, his eyes serious now.

"Ah, Bonnie," he said, and then he pulled her into his arms and kissed her.

If he'd asked her to marry him again, she could have fought it. If he'd tried to persuade or cajole her into being sensible, she'd have known what to do, but she couldn't fight the touch of his lips upon hers when her entire being lit up like a firework the moment she was in his arms. She clung to him, wishing she wasn't so weak, so desperate to belong to him, to belong somewhere. His lips were warm and increasingly hungry as he deepened the kiss. His hunger fed her own, and Bonnie's appetites did little by halves. His kiss was like a spark against dry timber and up she went, lighting up the sky and flying beyond good sense and what was right and proper. All those things were distant concepts now, drowned out by the roar of flame as it consumed her, desire scalding her blood, intoxicating her mind until she was drunk on the heat, the wanting, and the all consuming passion.

Before either of them knew what they were about, they were lying under the shelter of an ancient oak, its boughs so low they touched the ground and hid them from view, not that they were anywhere near a track or road this far out into the countryside.

"Yes, yes," she murmured as Jerome's hand slid beneath her gown.

You fool, you fool, whispered a voice in her head, but it was too faint, too feeble to be heard over the thunder of her own heart and the pulse of desire that beat in her ears, in her chest, between her thighs, wanting him, needing him. Her hand smoothed over him, to his waist, to the fall on his trousers and the little buttons there.

"Bonnie, oh, saints preserve me, I'll go mad…. Stop, stop, we must… yes, no… no… don't… don't… *don't stop*, Oh God."

***

Jerome was lost, insane, out of his damn mind. What was it that happened when she touched him? He couldn't account for it, couldn't account for the wild, untamed thing that flared to life inside him when her hands were on him.

He'd always loved women, loved the intimacy and honest joy in the way it felt to thrust into the silken heat of a willing female, but he'd never been so lost to his baser nature as to lose control. He'd not lost control with the most exclusive and skilled of courtesans, and even when he'd believed himself in love, he'd never been so powerless in the face of his own desire. Yet Bonnie, who knew nothing but what she'd learned at his hands that one night, had the power to turn his brain to mush and melt what little remained to a puddle on the floor. There was no thought in his head past the need to be inside her, to lose himself in her. The where and the why, the right and wrong of it was so beyond his comprehension it might as well have been a long dead language chiselled in stone, buried and forgotten for centuries for all the chance he had of understanding all the reasons he must stop.

For all she had run from him and told him to leave her be, she clung to him now, urging him on, begging him to hurry as he lifted her skirts and sank into her with a shout that joined with Bonnie's exalted cry of pleasure and lifted the birds from the trees with angry squawks and chattering.

There was only the exquisite pleasure of her body, her generous curves moulded so perfectly to his, cushioning him and welcoming him like the most long awaited home coming. She'd tugged his shirt free and her slender hands were on his skin, her nails scoring his back as she arched beneath him, clutching at him as he sought her mouth and stole the soft moans of rapture she made with his kiss. The thick and copious material of her riding habit was nothing but an irritation, impeding him when he wanted her lush body exposed to his hungry gaze and questing hands, wanted to put his mouth upon her and kiss every inch of that satiny landscape as she quivered and trembled and murmured his name.

She cried out as they crested the peak together, calling for him as her body tightened around him and sent him spiralling into a place he hardly recognised, so far removed was it from any other experience he could compare it to. Pleasure rippled through him in ferocious waves, claiming him and tumbling him under until he thought he'd die of it.

At length, the tumult quieted and Jerome collapsed on top of her, wrung out both physically and emotionally. He was honest enough to acknowledge his emotions were raw and exposed, uncertain and all in a muddle as he came back to his senses by degrees and realised what he'd just done. *Again.* Good Lord, what the devil was wrong with him? What did she do to him?

They were like brandy and fire, intoxicating and combustible, and whilst it might be an uncomfortable mix for a marriage, he had to persuade her it was for the best. He'd just been given another fine opportunity to get her with child and, like the unthinking bastard he was, he'd leapt at it.

Aware that he must be crushing her, Jerome rolled to the side, but having learned his lesson the last time, he took her with him, holding her close.

"Well," he said, once he had breath enough to say anything. "Well, that…." He let out a soft huff of laughter. "You should have a warning sign tattooed on your forehead, you impossible female. *Dangerous, do not touch.*"

She stiffened in his arms and he cursed himself for having made a joke of it. Usually he knew better, but he'd never had to watch himself with Bonnie before. He'd said what he thought, when he thought it, but he ought to have known she was feeling as raw as he was, more so.

He turned a little, looking down at her, and cupping her face with his hand. "Ignore me," he said. "I didn't mean it how it sounded, only I seem to lose my mind when I lay my hands on you. I never meant for this to happen, Bonnie. Not like this, at least. Not until we were married."

"Oh!" she exclaimed and pushed at his chest, fighting to get free of him. "Don't start that nonsense again."

"It's hardly nonsense," he retorted, struggling to hold on to her in case she bolted again. "No, stop that, listen to me. You may have escaped getting pregnant the first time, but that's twice now, and it's clear we can't be in the same place at the same time without taking each other's clothes off."

"Oh, don't look so perplexed," she said, giving him another hard shove. "You know I want you, I'm female, willing and available and you're a man. It's hardly a difficult equation to figure out."

"You don't have a very high opinion of the male of the species, do you?"

His tone was dry and humourless, and this time he allowed her to get up, uncomfortable with holding her to him against her will, no matter his desire to make things right between them.

"Goodness, how astonishing, when I've been provided so many sterling examples of masculinity during my life," she spat back with surprising bitterness. She glared at him and then took a deep breath, pinching the bridge of her nose. When she spoke again, she was contrite. "Forgive me, that… that was very unfair. You are a good man, Jerome, a kind one, and I'd no business comparing you to anyone else. I know you're trying to protect me as best you can and… and I'm touched, truly I am, but… no," she said simply, giving him a tiny smile. "No, I won't marry you. It would be a mistake, for both of us, and you know it as well as I do."

"I'm not sure I do know it, Bonnie," he said, frowning now as he considered it again. They had passion, after all, and they liked each other. They were friends. There really were worse ways to start a marriage.

She stared at him for a long moment. "Just imagine taking me to your mother and brother and telling them we're getting married, Jerome." He flinched before he could stop himself and Bonnie returned a sad smile. "There you go," she said.

He watched as she rearranged her clothes and strode away from him.

"Wait," he said, stumbling to his feet and doing up his buttons as he hurried after her.

"No."

"This isn't over, Bonnie."

She gave a little derisive snort. "It never even began, Jerry. Just let it go. Help me up, will you?"

Cursing, Jerome moved to her and helped her into the saddle, watching as she covered her ankles with the thick layers of her gown.

"You will not get away from me, Bonnie," he warned her.

She gathered the reins in her hands and then turned to look down at him, reaching out a hand and touching a finger to his lips. "Stop trying to act the hero, you sweet fool. We're neither of us suited to good behaviour. I'm a bad girl and I'll likely make a bad end, but that's my affair, not yours. I'll not drag you down with me. Go and marry Lady Helena. She's rich and beautiful, a duke's sister no less. You'll make your mama proud then. Isn't that what you always hoped for?"

He watched as she smiled at him and then rode away, and he wondered how it was that Bonnie saw him like no one else did. Jasper had always been both his parents' favourite. Not that they'd ever said so, not that they'd ever deliberately snubbed Jerome in his brother's favour, but he'd known all the same. When Jasper behaved badly, he'd be hauled before his father and lectured about the responsibilities of the earldom and what was expected of him.

When Jerome behaved badly, they rolled their eyes at him and shrugged their shoulders, as if they'd expected no different. Everyone adored Jasper, of course; he was better looking than Jerome, and he could disarm a crotchety dowager, a gruff military man, or a virtuous miss with equal ease, his charm was so irresistible. Even when his reputation as a libertine had been at its worst, the marriage minded mamas had still welcomed Jasper with open arms. Not so Jerome. Eligible he might be, but he was a loose cannon, unpredictable, and no one knew quite where or in what manner he might go off. Wherever he went, trouble of one kind or another inevitably followed, whether or not he meant it to.

Jerome sighed and watched as Bonnie rode out of sight. It was best they didn't arrive back at the house together. It would look suspicious. People might think they'd been up to no good. With a groan, Jerome put his head in his hands. Damnation.

What the devil was he to do?

Chapter 6

Why is it every man I meet is so terribly dull?

Even the ones I <u>know</u> aren't the least bit dull, do nothing for me. I've met every eligible man there is to meet and can't muster the least bit enthusiasm for any of them. No matter how handsome or charming they are, I feel nothing. Even the wicked ones don't stir my interest, which I don't understand in the least. What is it I'm looking for, I wonder? When will I feel that spark of attraction that will make everything clear to me?

I do wish he would hurry up whoever he is I'm waiting for to set my soul alight. I'm so dreadfully bored.

— Excerpt of an entry from Lady Helena Adolphus to her diary.

2nd October 1814. Holbrooke House, Sussex.

The wedding was an informal affair, though the small family chapel seemed full to the rafters with Jasper and Harriet's closest friends. The Peculiar Ladies, or whatever they were called were out in force and Jerome was disquieted to acknowledge something disturbingly close to jealousy as he watched his brother and Harriet exchange their vows. Whatever had caused such animosity between them over the past years was well and truly dead and buried, and it was apparent to everyone that this was a love match.

Their happiness was tangible, infecting all present judging from the laughter and smiles of all the guests.

Jerome glanced over at Bonnie to see her laughing at something her friend Alice said to her. Alice was with child, according to the gossip, and going on adoring way her husband saw to her comfort, they were both well pleased with themselves. Alice and her husband did not see the look in Bonnie's eyes as she turned away, though. They didn't see the effort it took her to compose herself, to force the sorrow from her expression and put another smile in its place. They didn't see, but Jerome did.

He made his way through the crowd to her, ignoring her warning look.

"Marry me," he said in an undertone, not bothering to list all the reasons they must. She knew them as well as he did.

She jolted at his words and then glared up at him.

"Did you not see the way your brother looked at Harriet?" she asked him, low enough not to be heard by anyone else but still fierce and angry. "If ever you look at me like that, I'll marry you in a heartbeat, but you never will. That's not your fault, and I'm not blaming you for it, but I'm tired of being where I'm not wanted, can you not understand that? If I marry, I want it to be because my husband can't live without me, not because he's tumbled me once or twice and feels he ought to. For once in my life I want to belong somewhere, and if I can't have that, I'll belong to myself, at least. Now go away before we cause another scene and make your mother cross."

He watched her stalk away, torn between hurt and guilt. Looking up, Jerome caught Jasper watching him, concern in his eyes, and heat prickled over him. It was Jasper's wedding day; the least he could do was behave as he ought and not cause any further worry.

"Jerome, darling, look who I found."

Jerome looked around at the sound of his mother's voice and wasn't the least bit surprised to find Lady Helena being thrust under his nose again. His mother had decided the two of them would deal admirably together, and she would do her best to make it happen. Jerome could see why she'd think they'd go well together, too. Helena was an exquisite girl, bright and vivacious. She seemed a restless creature, always in motion, and no doubt his mother thought such a woman would suit him as he was easily bored. Jerome could tell she wasn't interested in him, though, and couldn't summon the will to care. Now, in the light of yet another rejection from Bonnie, he wondered if perhaps he ought to try harder.

"Lady Helena," he said, smiling as he greeted her. "How lovely to see you again."

***

Bonnie did her very best to endure the wedding breakfast with a smile on her face. Harriet was her friend, after all, and Bonnie was so pleased for her. It was a joy to see the happiness shining from her and yet it only made Bonnie ache with sadness. The temptation to just accept Jerome's offer had become so fierce that she'd had to force herself to sound angry and storm away, hoping to offend him enough that he'd stay clear. What she'd said had been the truth, though, and every time she thought of facing Lady St Clair on Jerome's arm when he told her they would be married, Bonnie flushed hot and cold in quick succession. His mother would know why they were marrying and believe that Bonnie had set out to trap him, and she'd hate Bonnie forever for having done so. No more than Bonnie would hate herself though.

Yet now, after refusing him again, she had to endure the sight of Jerome and Lady Helena in animated conversation. They'd been seated beside each other—naturally, as his mother had arranged the wedding herself. She was a very beautiful girl with thick dark hair and the most extraordinary green eyes. They were a deep, dark green, like a pine forest, not the pale uncertain colour of Bonnie's.

Helena's eyes and dark colouring showed her kinship to her brother, the Duke of Bedwin, but there the resemblance ended. Helena was slender and elegant and wherever she went her adoring entourage of male admirers followed her. Soon, it appeared, Jerome would be added to their ranks.

Bonnie gritted her teeth and looked away, telling herself not to be so stupid and fickle. Hadn't she told him to marry Helena? What did she think, that she could keep telling the man no and telling him to leave her be, and that he'd keep running back for more? No. No, she thought nothing of the sort, because she knew he didn't love her, and he didn't really want to marry her. Oh, she was good enough to take his pleasure with if she offered him, he was a man after all, but still… it would have been nice to have been proven wrong for once.

For the rest of the day Bonnie endured, laughing and smiling and doing her best to appear happy and carefree. The newlyweds had slipped away, not that Bonnie blamed them one bit, and all the guests were in good spirits, so they had moved the furniture back and the rugs were rolled up. Alice had offered to play piano and now an impromptu dance saw everyone celebrating the day with a great deal of amusement. Lady St Clair kept the champagne flowing, and her eye on her son and Lady Helena. Jerome was dancing with her now, the two of them making a handsome picture with his golden hair and her dark beauty.

"Hasn't it been a lovely day?" Matilda said, slipping her arm through Bonnie's.

"Oh, yes, lovely," Bonnie agreed, though she wanted to shake her head and cry and tell Matilda that it had been the worst and longest day of her life. That, however, would be churlish and inappropriate. As she watched Jerome whirl Helena around the floor, Bonnie knew she had reached the limits of what she could endure. "Would you excuse me, Tilda?" She smiled at her friend. "I'm dying of thirst. I must just get myself a drink."

Matilda nodded and Bonnie ignored the concern in her eyes. Matilda was such a lovely woman, always concerned with all of them, mothering them all and wanting them to be happy, but there was nothing she could do. It was a stupid situation, and one of Bonnie's own making. She'd known from the beginning Jerome was out of her reach, and yet they'd had such fun together that she'd let herself forget. Well, it had been wonderful while it lasted, and now it was over.

She hurried over to the refreshments table and helped herself to some lemonade. Strangely, she didn't feel like champagne tonight. The thought of drowning her sorrows and allowing the alcohol to numb everything was an appealing one, but her stomach rebelled at the idea. Once she had a drink in hand, so Matilda didn't think her a liar, she escaped from the room and wandered out into the hallway.

What a vast place it was. Though she'd been here for some weeks, Bonnie had only seen a fraction of the palatial building. Jerome had taken her exploring a couple of times, but the weather had been so fine they'd both preferred to be out of doors. He had shown her the picture gallery, though, and told her stories of some of his ancestors, playing the fool for her before a portrait of a very sombre looking old man who had glowered down from the walls at them, as though he knew full well they were up to no good.

The illustrious heritage Jerome could claim had only magnified the gulf between them, but she'd been too happy in his company to worry. Goodness, had that only been a few weeks ago? Why had she spoiled their friendship by seducing him? Yet, despite everything, she couldn't find it in her heart to regret it, nor the fierce coupling under the great oak tree. Those were memories she would cherish when she was alone and far away, and no one could take them from her.

Well, then. Bonnie shook off such maudlin thoughts and returned her attention to discovery and adventure. She would explore and take her mind off the wretched mood she was in, like a character in some Gothic novel. Perhaps she was no waiflike heroine, but she was an orphan and in something of a pickle as they often were, and maybe there were no mad monks or evil villains pursuing her, but she had imagination enough to cope with that. The rather intimidating atmosphere of the vast house would provide plenty of inspiration.

She remembered then what Harriet had told her about there being a ghost. St Clair's great-great-grandfather had rebuilt the west wing and put a kitchen over the original chapel. The story went that he'd been punished for it by being forced to walk the corridors on stormy nights. It wasn't quite dark yet, a glorious sunset lighting up the sky beyond the windows, and there was no sign of a storm, but soon enough the light would fade, and the house would be full of shadows.

The sombre tale and the gathering gloom rather suited Bonnie's mood, and so she set off in search of a spectre.

***

Jerome watched Bonnie climb the staircase and frowned. He knew full well that she was unhappy, and he was miserably aware that it was his fault. Perhaps she had thrown herself at him that first time, but she'd not held a gun to his head, and he'd not had to give in. She'd been full of excitement after their adventure, not to mention having had a glass of brandy. Not drunk, perhaps, but she was unused to strong liquor and he ought to have allowed for that. It had been up to him to act the gentleman. He was the experienced one, he ought to have known he was opening Pandora's box the first time his lips had touched hers, but he'd been helpless to resist. God, how feeble that sounded. Yet, when the two of them were together, something combustible happened. Though he knew he ought to keep away, as she'd asked, it was killing him to see the spark that had drawn him to Bonnie in the first place snuffed out. It was suddenly imperative that he make her smile, that he make her laugh and bring that wicked glint back to her eyes.

Hurrying up the stairs after her, Jerome pursued Bonnie, realising she was heading to the west wing, far away from her own room. No doubt the curious cat had gone exploring.

Grinning to himself, Jerome decided he had just the thing.

By the time he'd ransacked the linen cupboard and found what he was after, Bonnie had long gone, and it took him some considerable time to track her down. She'd picked up a candle somewhere along the way and now crept about with it, peering into rooms and starting every time a floorboard creaked. Jerome padded after her and opened a door which gave a shrill squeak of protest. Cursing softly he propelled himself out of the corridor before Bonnie caught sight of him.

He heard her cursing and telling herself not to be such a scaredy cat as she regarded the empty corridor and had been hard pressed to smother his laughter. Yet, she'd come to the west wing—which everyone knew was supposed to be haunted—with the express purpose of scaring herself witless. He'd not be much of a friend if he didn't help her out.

Jerome, like his brother, had spent many, many wet afternoons exploring all the secret passages and hidey holes that such a huge and ancient building possessed, and so it was not such a hard thing to get ahead of Bonnie and set a trap.

He heard the faint tread of footsteps farther along the corridor and held his breath, lying in wait in the alcove until the dim glow of a candle touched the surrounding gloom. With a bloodcurdling howl, he leapt out at her, the sheet he'd thrown over himself billowing out in the darkness.

The scream nearly deafened him and was closely followed by a crash as Bonnie flung the nearest thing to hand in his direction. By the sound of the smash as it hit the wall, it had missed his head by a hair.

"Bonnie, Bonnie, it's me!" he exclaimed, fighting his way out of the sheet and flinging it to the ground. By some miracle, she was still holding the candle, and he had a brief glimpse of wild eyes before she flung herself at him, hitting him with her free hand.

"You beast!" she cried. "You stupid, stupid, horrible boy!"

Jerome ducked away and backed off, grinning. "Sorry. I'm sorry, but I couldn't help myself when I saw you skulking about like you were in some lunatic Gothic novel. It was too delicious to resist."

"Oh, I could kill you," she said with feeling, still breathless as she leaned back against the wall and put a hand to her heart. She slid to the floor and put her head against her knees. When she spoke again, her skirts muffled her voice. "I thought I would die, swear to God."

Jerome snickered and, as she looked up again, he saw her lips twitch.

"I hate you." She glared at him, but there was an upwards turn to her mouth, and he could tell she wasn't cross any more.

"I wish I could have seen your face," he said, shaking his head with regret as he moved to sit beside her. "I couldn't enjoy your expression of terror from behind the sheet." She snorted then, and he chuckled. "My ears are still ringing, mind you."

"You're lucky I didn't have something heavier to hand," she muttered. "I'd have knocked your brains out, what little you have of them. Then you'd be sorry."

"Ah, come on, Bonnie," he said, bumping his shoulder against hers. "You'd be sorry too, wouldn't you? Just a little bit?"

She shrugged. "A very little bit," she allowed with a huff. "I hope whatever I threw at you wasn't some priceless antique."

"If it was, it was my fault for scaring you to death. Don't fret about it."

They sat in silence for a moment, the candlelight flickering on the floor beside them.

"I'll be going back to stay with Ruth for a bit," she said, her pale fingers pleating and smoothing the skirts of her gown as she spoke. "We're leaving tomorrow."

Jerome frowned, turning to look at her. "So soon?"

She smiled and nodded. "Yes. Just think how relieved your mama will be to be rid of me." Her voice was just a little too bright to be convincing.

"I don't want you to go."

He reached out and took her hand, entwining their fingers together, and Bonnie put her head on his shoulder.

"Ah, well. It's for the best," she said, her voice soft. "We both know it. Besides, I must go back to Scotland soon."

"To marry Gordon Anderson?"

Jerome felt an odd, uncomfortable sensation flicker in his chest at the idea. It was unsettling, but of course he would be unsettled. Bonnie was his friend, and she'd gone on at some length about how awful this Anderson fellow was. It troubled him to think of her married to a man she disliked so much, that was all. It was perfectly normal that he should worry for her.

She shrugged. "Maybe."

He turned to look at her then. "Maybe? I thought it was a foregone conclusion, that Morven would make you marry."

There was a long silence, and he studied her face as she stared into some distant place. "I don't want to marry him, and he only wants me for the dowry. He badly needs the money to repair his home. It's falling down around his ears. He's a man, though, and a proud one. Once he knows I'm no longer a virgin bride... well, he might change his mind." She turned towards him then and flashed a smile which revealed the dimples in her cheeks. It always gave him the urge to touch the little divots whenever he saw them, though this time he was too struck by her next words. "I can only hope."

A cold sensation rolled over him and he frowned, that odd feeling flickering inside him again.

"What?" she asked, shifting around to study his face.

Jerome hesitated, unsure if he wanted to ask, only…. "Is that why you did it?"

"Did what?"

"Is that why you gave yourself to me? In the hope you wouldn't have to marry Gordon Anderson when he found out?"

Bonnie stilled for a moment before looking away from him. "Sure," she said lightly. "Why not?"

Pain, sharp and bright as a blade, lanced through him, taking his breath away. He reached out, taking hold of her chin and turning her face back towards him.

"Truly?" His voice was unsteady and suddenly the answer was terribly important.

She stared at him, studying his expression, and then let out a breath. "No," she said with a sigh. "No, of course not. Don't be a fool. You know it's not true, though I can't pretend to hope it works that way all the same." She gave a soft laugh and reached out to cup his face. "Do you feel better now? Male pride all back in one piece?"

Jerome swallowed, disturbed by the churning sensation in his guts. He couldn't cope with this… this *upset*. He was used to tumbling in and out of love, but it had always seemed a simple affair. There would be some weeks or even months of dizzying happiness and physical pleasure, and then a few days or weeks of melancholy. It was something he had grown accustomed too and was quite capable of handling, but this…. Why did Bonnie make him feel so jumbled up? There were too many messy *feelings* involved, and none of them were simple. Everything had become a tangle of complications and he didn't like it. Not one bit. This was what came of tumbling a friend.

"Jerome?"

She was staring at him still, her expression one of concern, and he knew he ought to answer.

"Good as new," he said, smirking, though his face felt stiff and uncomfortable.

"And don't worry. I won't tell him or Morven who it was, so you needn't worry about having anyone come after you to defend my honour. Not that I think they would," she added with a chuckle. "I doubt it will come as a surprise to either of them. They always assumed I'd ruin myself."

"You should tell them," he said, surprising himself with the force of his words. "And they damn well ought to come after me. For God's sake, what kind of men are they?"

Jerome knew her eyes were on him, but he didn't meet her gaze. He felt stiff and angry and as if he wanted to hit something, or someone, but he couldn't figure out who or why or… God, what a bloody mess!

"Thank you."

Jerome closed his eyes and tightened his grip on Bonnie's hand. "I don't want you to go. I'll have no one to get up to no good with."

He sounded like a sulky child but there was no help for it.

"Ah, you'll still have Cholly and Algae and Gideon," she said, squeezing his fingers. "You managed well enough before I came crashing into your life. I'll expect to see your name every week in the scandal rags, so don't go disappointing me."

"Not the same," he grumbled.

"I should hope not."

She laughed and bumped his shoulder again, and he tried to do the same but his chest was tight and he still felt angry and… and… he didn't know what it was he felt, but he didn't like it. He didn't like it at all. Maybe it was best that she was going away, then. He could get back to normal, get back to his life, without this madcap girl making everything so dashed complicated. His throat ached.

"I should go," she said, shifting as though she would move away from him.

Jerome tightened his grip on her hand and she paused, smiling.

"If I stay, we will end up naked again, and as lovely as that is, I'm not sure it's a good idea."

Desire lit under his skin in an instant and he forced it back. Damn, but he wasn't such a scoundrel as that, was he? She was leaving tomorrow, and he'd likely not see her again. Just because he ached to be inside her again was not a good enough reason to take his pleasure. Christ, she might already be pregnant.

"Bonnie, if anything happens, if—"

"Stop worrying," she said, shaking her head at him. "Everything will be fine."

"But…."

"I know," she said, leaning in and pressing a kiss to his cheek. "You are a good man, Jerome Cadogan, and any woman ought to be proud to marry you. If things were different, I know I would be."

"Bonnie," he said, his voice rough.

She pressed a finger to his lips and smiled again, her eyes very bright. When she spoke, her voice quavered. "Don't make me cry," she begged him, moving her hand away to stroke his face.

He stared at her, torn, not knowing what to do or say except "I'll miss you." He had to tell her that much. It was nothing less than the truth.

A fat tear rolled down her cheek and his heart hurt.

"Now look what you've done, you wretch," she complained, dashing the tear away, laughing and crying at the same time.

"I will," he insisted, feeling very much like weeping himself, which was ridiculous. He never cried, not even when he'd believed himself heartbroken because a love affair had ended badly.

"Stop," she wailed, and leaned in, pressing her mouth hard against his.

Heat bloomed in an instant and his arms went around her, pulling her to him, deepening the kiss as his body reacted at once.

This time, however, she broke the kiss and stared up at him. He knew they couldn't. It was over. If she wouldn't marry him, it had to be.

He took a deep breath, trying to calm himself and holding her to him just a little longer. There was a sweet, sad ache in his chest, and it was hard to breathe.

Bonnie shifted in his arms and hugged him tight, pressing another kiss to his cheek.

"Goodbye, Jerome," she whispered. "I'll never forget you. Not as long as I live."

She moved to get up and this time he let her. "There's only one candle," she said, giving him a sceptical look as she picked it up and the flame wavered, casting mad shadows around her.

"It's fine," he said. "Not the first time I've walked the place in the dark. I'll find my way."

Bonnie nodded then and stood looking at him for a moment more. "Be happy," she said, softly, and then she walked away.

It was a long time later before he stirred himself to move, and when he did, it was with no idea of what he would do next. Go back to town, he supposed, pick up his life where it had left off before Bonnie had crashed into it. He smiled to himself, knowing that this summer would forever be engraved in his memory as one of heat and sunshine, and more laughter than he'd ever known.

"Be happy, Bonnie, my girl," he whispered to the darkness, before finding his way back to his room.

Chapter 7

Oh, Jerome,

I'm in such a fix. Whatever shall I do?

— Excerpt of an entry from Bonnie Campbell to her diary.

22nd October 1814. Upper Walpole Street, London.

It was three weeks since she'd seen Jerome. Three weeks since she'd bade him goodbye and told him to be happy. Three weeks since her monthly courses had failed to make their appearance.

During that time, there had been plenty of mention of Mr Jerome Cadogan in the scandal sheets. It seemed he was back with his friends and, though there was no terrible behaviour to report, he'd been seen in the company of one Lady Helena Adolphus often enough for it to have been remarked upon. Good, Bonnie told herself. That was good. She'd set him free as she'd promised she would, and he would marry Lady Helena and make his mama proud and live happily ever after... and... and....

Bonnie buried her face in her pillow and sobbed, though she despised herself for doing it. It wouldn't change a thing. She was ruined, and now Morven would be ever more determined to get Anderson to marry her to save her from shame. Not that she had any intention of doing so, but she knew how difficult it was to stand up to the earl. He was a formidable man, and he played dirty. It would be hard enough to keep quiet about who the father was, but she knew he'd try to persuade her the babe needed a name. How could she deny it? She didn't want to condemn the child to being a bastard, but she didn't want to marry anyone but Jerome and she'd not trap him into it in such a way. She only hoped that Anderson had more pride than to take on another man's bastard. She supposed it depended on just how badly he needed her dowry. If he refused to marry her, though, Morven would support her. He'd send her off somewhere quiet and let her raise her child in peace. He'd not like it, but he'd do it.

Despite everything, Bonnie could not regret the babe that they'd made between them. She would forever have a part of Jerome now, and that meant the world to her. She'd always loved children and had hoped for a big family. As a girl, she'd dreamed of a husband who adored her, and a gaggle of children for them both to love and fret over. She was so tired of being alone, but she'd come to realise being alone was not as bad as being among people who did not want you around. She knew she was not a perfect young lady by any stretch of the imagination and, whilst she might doubt her own worth, she still knew she deserved better than that.

At least she would have a son or daughter to love, and to love her. She would be such a good mother, she would try so hard and do her very best, and the child would love her and want her around. Wouldn't they?

She'd have to tell Jerome, she supposed. It wasn't fair for him never to know he had a child with her, but not yet. If she told him now, he'd feel honour bound to do the right thing, and she doubted she'd be able to persuade him otherwise again. She doubted she'd be able to hold to her principles in truth, when the idea of facing the future alone was so very daunting. How easy it would be to run back to him, confess everything, and let him take care of her. It seemed such an inviting idea until she considered how he might feel a year or two from now... when he was well and truly trapped. He'd loved her company because she was fun and went off on mad adventures with him, but when they were married with children that would be at an end, and he'd see that he'd made a mistake. It was hard enough to make a marriage work when both parties wanted it and there was love involved. Without it, things could go very bad very fast. She couldn't bear for him to look at her with resentment or regret, nor live with the recriminations that his mother would be bound to heap on her, whether or not she spoke them aloud.

No. She'd tell him one day. In the future. When she was settled, perhaps.

Wiping her eyes, Bonnie scolded herself for being such a wet blanket and sat up in bed. At once she was assailed by nausea and groaned. She'd not actually been sick yet, which was a blessing, but she felt utterly wretched and had completely lost her appetite. It seemed a very odd and unfair thing that she should be with child and losing weight for the first time in her life, but there was no denying it.

A knock at the door preceded her maid, who bustled in and set a cup of tea and a biscuit on the bedside table.

"Miss Stone is going shopping this morning, miss, and wishes to know if you'd like to accompany her?"

Bonnie reached for the biscuit and took a cautious bite, chewing slowly. "No, thank you, Jenny. Please, apologise to Miss Stone, but I have some letters to write."

"Very good, miss. Shall I lay out the blue sarsnet?"

Bonnie nodded her agreement and picked up the teacup. The morsel of biscuit seemed to have lodged itself in her throat. She would have to leave. It wouldn't be very long before her condition became apparent. Jenny would guess before anyone else and then it was only a matter of time. Morven had employed the young woman, and Bonnie didn't doubt she'd tattle on her in no time at all. Bonnie went hot and cold as she realised Jenny would likely guess who the father was and be just as keen to unburden herself of that little nugget, too. Oh, good Lord. Well, she'd just have to deny it. She'd tell them it had been another man, a guest at the engagement ball, perhaps? She could say she'd been drunk and didn't know who it was. It wouldn't reflect well on her, but she doubted it would surprise anyone. She was a bad girl, everyone had always thought so. No doubt they'd be pleased to be proven right.

Anyway, there would be a tremendous scandal and it would be too bad of her to bring such a horrid mess down upon poor Ruth. She'd been so very kind to Bonnie, and her own chances of making a good match were fragile enough with her vulgar father to contend with, no matter her vast fortune.

Terror struck at her heart, but there was no point in putting off the inevitable. She could not embarrass Ruth, and so she could not stay. She would not face the indignity of being hauled back to Scotland by Gordon Anderson, and it was only a matter of time before he appeared on her doorstep. No, she'd return to Scotland, but when she was good and ready and… and she wasn't ready.

Perhaps she was a coward, but she needed a little time to get used to the idea of being an unwed mother before she looked Morven in the eye and confessed all. Well, that was easily enough dealt with.

***

"Why are we here?"

Jerome looked around, jolted out of his abstraction by an impatient voice.

Lady Helena Adolphus was staring at him, arms folded. She looked quite a picture, all dressed in a deep green pelisse that brought out the colour in her eyes. A charming chip bonnet, trimmed with green velvet leaves, completed the ensemble and Jerome had noticed that she'd received many admiring looks as they'd strolled down Bond Street, with her maid and a footman walking discreetly behind them.

"Er… shopping?" Jerome suggested, though he suspected that wasn't the answer she was looking for.

With an exasperated sigh, Helena rolled her eyes to the heavens, and he congratulated himself on being right.

"Yes, but why are *you* here?" she demanded.

Jerome opened and closed his mouth, uncertain of how to best answer that. The outing had been arranged a few days ago and, although he'd agreed to it, he couldn't for the life of him remember how it had come about.

"For the pleasure of your company," he ventured, with an uneasy smile.

Helena made a very unladylike noise and sent him a look that would have made small children cry. He wasn't a small child, he reminded himself fiercely and forced back the urgent desire to tug at his cravat.

"Oh, please," she said with a sigh. "You have no more interest in me than I have in you. It's your blessed mother who keeps arranging all these outings, as we both know, and for what purpose I cannot fathom. Surely she can see you'd rather be anywhere else, and I've not the least intention of marrying you, either."

Jerome stared at her for a long moment and then let out a breath. "Oh, thank God," he said.

"Well, really!" Helena said indignantly. "There's no need to be insulting."

"Oh, Lady Helena, I do beg your pardon... I...."

She snorted and shook her head. "Oh, stow it," she said with a short laugh, rather taking him aback. "It's not as if I care." She gave a heavy sigh and then glanced at him, her mouth quirking. "The trouble is, I wish I did. I've got my brother and his wife billing and cooing all over the house and I'm dying to fall in love with someone, but it simply won't happen. It's so annoying."

"I know," Jerome said, nodding as he guided her around two gaudy macaronis, simpering and giggling and taking up most of the pavement.

"You do?" she said in surprise, clearly taken aback.

"Yes." He returned a rueful expression. "I've fallen in and out of love a half dozen times in the past couple of years, but the one person I want to fall for...."

"Oh." Helena flushed and Jerome realised his mistake.

"Oh, no," he said in a rush. "I don't mean you."

Her eyebrows shot up at that and Jerome felt his own colour rise as he realised he'd unwittingly insulted her again.

"I beg your pardon," he said with a groan. "Perhaps I'll just keep my mouth shut."

"Safest," she agreed tartly. "But a deal less entertaining." She grinned at him and Jerome let out a breath.

"Well, it's good to know my entertainment value is still high, if nothing else."

"Oh, no it isn't," she said with a mournful sigh. "You've been the model of propriety these past weeks, and deadly dull. What *has* got into you?"

"I don't know." Jerome shrugged and obediently turned as Helena drew him over to look in a shop window. "My brother rang a peal over me recently and I promised him I'd do better, so there's that, but...."

"But?" she asked, dragging her gaze from a rather bizarre confection of lace and frills that seemed to be the latest thing in ladies' bonnets.

"But... I don't know," he admitted. What else could he say? That he felt adrift? That his life was an endless succession of grey days, each one blending into the next as boredom stifled him to death? That he missed his friend?

A pair of laughing eyes and the wicked flash of dimples flickered in his mind and he sighed. He felt Helena studying him.

"*Ennui*," she said, diagnosing him with a quirk of her lips. "I should know. I have a terminal case myself."

"What do we do about it?" he asked, praying she had an answer for him.

She rolled her eyes again and Jerome suspected any fellow seriously wanting to court Helena Adolphus would need a strong personality and a vast ego, or he'd be a broken man within a week.

"If I knew that, I'd not be here with you, now would I?" she retorted.

Jerome laughed. Though he'd rather stick pins in his eyes than marry her, he rather liked Helena Adolphus. She was good company, in a brutal, rather painful way.

"Fair point."

She grinned at him and turned back to the bonnet. "What do you think of it?" she asked, turning her head this way and that.

"An abomination," he replied.

"Yes," she said with a heavy sigh. "I thought so too."

"What now, then?"

He waited while she considered, pursing her lips. "When in doubt, eat large quantities of cake. Take me home. I have it on good authority that cook made scones this morning and her blackberry conserve is a thing of beauty. We shall smother our boredom with cream and jam."

"I can do that," Jerome replied, relieved that he didn't have to pretend to court her anymore. As they walked on, the thought drifted into his mind that he would have liked to take Bonnie to Gunter's. Goodness, but she liked cake and sweet things. He could just see her expression when faced with all the delicious confections that the elegant shop offered.

She would….

He stopped himself before the daydream could take hold. That was over. She'd said so, and she'd been right. He'd known she was right.

And yet….

***

24th October 1814. St James, London.

"What the devil is it, Thomas?" Jerome muttered, as his valet woke him from an uneasy dream. It had taken him hours to fall asleep last night and now he felt heavy eyed and irritable. "Good Lord, man. What time is it?"

"Beg pardon, sir. It's not yet eight o'clock but there's a young lady downstairs who's demanding to see you right away. She says how it's an emergency."

Jerome was awake in an instant, his heart pounding. *Oh, Lord. Bonnie.* "What young lady?" he demanded, throwing back the covers.

"A Miss Stone, sir."

Jerome paused, frowning and trying to place the name. Damnation. Ruth Stone. Bonnie was staying with Ruth. "Hurry, Thomas," Jerome instructed as both he and his valet flew into action.

Ten frantic minutes later, still buttoning his waistcoat, Jerome ran down the stairs and into the parlour, where he found an agitated Miss Stone waiting for him.

"What's happened?" he demanded, with none of the niceties a gentleman ought greet a lady with.

Miss Stone nodded at her maid. "Please wait outside, Rachel."

The maid, an older lady with a fierce expression, glowered and sent a disapproving look in Jerome's direction.

"You may leave the door ajar," Miss Stone added, returning an equally fierce look as the maid subsided and did as her mistress bid.

Jerome waited impatiently as the woman left before turning back to his guest.

"What's happened?" he asked again, clenching his fists against the need to shake the information out of her. "Is it Bonnie?"

Miss Stone nodded. "She's gone."

"Gone? Gone where?"

"If I knew that, I should not be here at this unreasonable time of the morning," Miss Stone snapped at him before realising how rude she sounded. She took a breath and a moment to gather herself. "I beg your pardon, Mr Cadogan...."

Jerome waved her apology away. "No apology needed, Miss Stone. Tell me what you know. Did she say anything? Leave a note?"

Miss Stone nodded. She reached into her reticule and went to hand the note she withdrew to him, but then her fingers tightened on the paper as he began to pull it from her grasp. Jerome looked at her, the letter held between them.

"What is written here is private, Mr Cadogan. I would do my utmost to find her myself, only I am supposed to be going away with my father for a few days and I'm already cutting it very fine. He'll kick up such a fuss if I'm not ready on time, and then he'll want to know why I was late. If there's anything even vaguely resembling a scandal, he'll never let me out of his sight again."

Jerome could well understand why Miss Stone would rather not have her father hanging around. He'd not met the fellow, but he had a reputation for vulgarity which did not aid Miss Stone's chances of marrying well.

The young woman took a deep breath and ploughed on. "I am only here because… because I believe you were a *particular* friend of Bonnie's and I hoped…."

Jerome felt a dull flush creep up the back of his neck at the woman's words. Oh, Miss Stone knew exactly what kind of *friend* he'd been to Bonnie and that was why she was here.

"I understand," he said, interrupting her. "I would rather die than see Bonnie come to harm. Whatever the problem is you may rely upon my help and my discretion."

Miss Stone let out a breath and nodded before releasing the note and Jerome opened it with hands that were not entirely steady.

My dearest Ruth,

I hope you will forgive me for causing any worry or distress, but I have decided that I must go away. I am increasingly aware that Mr Anderson is likely to arrive on your doorstep at any time and I am not ready to return to Scotland. I will go, I promise. I just need a little time to myself before I resign myself to my fate. I beg you not to worry on my behalf. I have not taken Jenny as I know she spies on me for Morven, but I shall engage another maid and take lodgings in a respectable neighbourhood. I just want time to think and be by myself without the spectre of Morven or Mr Anderson breathing down my neck. It will only be for a few weeks, perhaps a month or two at most, and I will be quite all right. I have money enough to look after myself and I'm really not quite as hen witted as some people would like to believe.

I must thank you, my dearest Ruth, for being such a kind and loving friend to me, and I hate myself for causing you a moment's worry, but I can see no other way of giving myself the time I need.

I will write again soon, once I am settled, to reassure you of my safety.

Your friend,

Bonnie.

Once Jerome was done, he looked up to meet Miss Stone's eyes.

"I know what you're thinking," she said, twisting her hands together. "You're thinking that it seems a perfectly sensible letter and that I should respect her wishes."

Jerome hesitated. "In part," he said, though it was only a small part of it. "My first instinct is to tear London apart, looking for her. A young lady ought not be alone in the city, maid or no, but Bonnie is not a fool, not by any means."

Except for being foolish enough to fall in love with him, Jerome thought with a surge of misery.

Miss Stone nodded. "I know that. For all her madcap ways, she's got a brain in her head. I do know that, believe me. It's only—"

Jerome's heart twisted in his chest. "Only?"

"Only I've been with her since we left Holbrooke and... and she's not been herself. Not at all. I—" Miss Stone broke off, a tinge of high colour in her cheeks.

"You may speak plain, Miss Stone," Jerome said, steeling himself. "No matter if it reflects badly on me. It *ought* to reflect badly on me, I'm afraid. I know I'm responsible for her unhappiness even... even if I did not intend to hurt her. Far from it," he added in an undertone.

Miss Stone's expression softened just a little. "It's only that I rather felt that... her heart had been broken. She's been so unhappy and, despite what she's put in the letter, I'm frightened. I can't help worrying that she's not being entirely honest and that perhaps she has no intention of returning to Scotland." She took a step closer to him, fear for her friend written starkly in her eyes. "What if she intends to disappear for good? What if we wait and she never gets in touch? If we try to find her then, and it's too late? We might never pick up the trail."

Jerome nodded. "I'll find her, Miss Stone. You have my word. If I discover what she has said is true and there is no cause for concern, I will leave her be until she is ready to return. If, however, it appears she's in distress or…."

He faltered. Of course she was in distress. Hadn't Miss Stone just told him he'd broken her heart? Oh, God. What a bastard he was. He had to make things right.

"Thank you, Mr Cadogan."

Jerome snorted and shook his head. "Don't thank me, for God's sake," he said in disgust, running a hand through his hair and wanting to pull it out by the roots. "This is all my fault."

Miss Stone smiled at him then and shook her head. "I think perhaps you're being a little hard on yourself. Bonnie is something of an irresistible force. Being in her company is akin to being swept up in a whirlwind of laughter and mischief, and she's very persuasive. From the first time you met it was clear to me that you were kindred spirits."

"You're too kind, Miss Stone," Jerome said, wondering if it was possible to hate himself any more than he did. "Now, is there anything else you can tell me about Bonnie's departure?"

Chapter 8

Dear Mr de Beauvoir,

I hope you are not angry with me for getting in touch again. Although you suggested it wise that we keep a distance from each other, you did invite me to correspond with you, so I have taken the liberty. I cannot, after all, <u>try my wiles</u> on you with mere ink on paper so surely you must be reassured that you are perfectly safe. If my charms in person are not enough to have you fall at my pretty feet, then my fine penmanship is unlikely to accomplish the task.

In any event I wanted to let you know how very much I loved "Conversations on Chemistry," by Mrs Jane Marcet. I had assumed the subject would be far beyond my meagre intelligence, so imagine my surprise to discover that I not only understood every bit of it, but enjoyed it thoroughly too. I have since discovered that Harriet - the Countess St Clair, who lent me the book, was given it by your good self.

You have whetted my appetite, Sir, and even having done so by proxy I believe it would be monstrously unfair if you do not give me something else with which to continue my education.

Yours in admiration,

Miss Minerva Butler.

— Excerpt of a letter from Miss Minerva Butler to Mr Inigo de Beauvoir.

24th October 1814. Church Street, Isleworth, London.

Inigo de Beauvoir glared down at the letter in his hand and toyed with the idea of consigning it to the nearest flame, or possibly dousing it with acid. Maybe he could blow it up? The problem was, no matter how thoroughly he destroyed the blasted thing, his mind had already committed the words to memory. Short of dashing his brains out on the nearest blunt object, he was stuck with them. Just as he was stuck with the memory of that provoking creature, dressed all in yellow like some innocent daffodil — ha! —pressing her sinful mouth against his.

"Perfectly safe," he muttered, rubbing a hand over his face.

Good Lord, a fellow wouldn't be safe from the likes of Miss Butler if he established a laboratory somewhere near the centre of the earth, though in his current state of mind the idea was one he imagined with longing. Yet her image, the scent of her, and more precisely the soft press of her lips against his, had been etched upon his brain for all eternity, to the detriment of his work, sleep, and peace of mind.

"What are you muttering about?"

Inigo scowled and looked around, only then remembering the presence of his friend, Baron Rothborn. Solomon, or *Solo* as he was more commonly known to his intimates, was one of the few people whose company Inigo could tolerate. Mainly because Solo was even more antisocial than him. Forced to come to London to attend to some business matter or other, Solo often sought refuge in Inigo's laboratory, as it was a place he was assured of some peace and quiet. At least, it usually was.

Solo put his book aside with a sigh. "You've been pacing and muttering from the moment you opened that bloody letter. Who is she, that the chit has got you in such a lather?"

Inigo opened and closed his mouth and then stood a little straighter, indignant at the implication even though the blasted fellow was spot on. Solomon was always a damned sight too perceptive for anyone's comfort. "It's not from a woman," he retorted. "It's... from a colleague, and I'm irritated because he's talking rot."

Solo arched an elegant eyebrow at him.

Inigo did his utmost to return that implacable look but gave in with a groan.

"I've known you too long, Inigo," Solo said, his lips quirking. "You may be a brilliant natural philosopher but, for the love of God, don't ever play cards. I can read you like a book."

"You've certainly had enough practise," Inigo shot back. "Instead of spending your life with your nose rammed against the dusty pages of some ancient tome why don't you *do* something... other than irritate me that is?"

"Stop trying to turn the subject," Solo said, unperturbed by his friend's ill-temper. He was used to it by now. "Who is she?"

"I told you—"

"Oh, give over," Solo said, rolling his eyes. "If it was a colleague or a scientific conundrum, you'd be making my ears bleed trying to make me understand what it was all about. As you've not said a word but have clearly worked yourself into a lather, it's obviously a woman. As that's a subject I actually know something about, you might as well unburden yourself."

Inigo folded his arms and glowered but Solo just returned his look with one of quiet patience. Inigo sighed.

"I have an... admirer," he admitted, with much the same enthusiasm he would admit to having a boil on his arse.

Solo shrugged. "That's hardly news."

That was true enough. For those in the scientific community Inigo had attained celebrity status, and not just among men. From some of his talks given at the society president Joseph Banks' *conversazioni,* he had gained quite a following among the wives and daughters of his contemporaries. He now had his fair share of female admirers, and some of them had been remarkably... persistent. Inigo had viewed them as a minor irritation. Not one of them had claimed his attention, and he'd brushed off advances and flirtation with no more thought or effort than batting away an aggravating bluebottle.

Yet Miss Butler was no bluebottle. In his mind, Miss Butler had not only claimed his attention, she held it, rather in the manner of a ferocious dog he didn't dare take his eye off. No matter which way he turned to make his escape, she was there, holding him captive, daring him to ignore her and threatening dire consequences if he did; and even worse ones if he didn't.

He wondered if Miss Butler would be dismayed by his unflattering comparison to a rabid canine, and rather thought she'd not turn a hair. The appalling female was bold as brass and he still hadn't gotten over the shock of being kissed by her. The worst thing about it was that he wasn't sure he *wanted* to get over it.

"Good heavens, she has got you confounded. I've never seen you in such a passion."

Bearing in mind Inigo hadn't moved or said a word, he well knew that Solo was amusing himself at his expense. Sadly, however, the wretched fellow was right, and they both knew that, too.

"She kissed me," Inigo said in a rush and then, to compound his mortification, he felt colour rise on his face. He turned away before he could see his friend dissolve into hysterics.

"Well," Solo said, and Inigo could hear the laughter in his voice, damn him. "That's one way of getting your attention. Short of laying herself out on your laboratory table and requesting you dissect her, that's probably all the poor girl could think to do."

"I'm a natural philosopher, not a biologist," Inigo muttered, folding his arms.

"Was it a nice kiss?"

Though he tried very hard not to, his mind immediately returned to the moment Miss Butler had leaned in and pressed her petal soft lips to his. She'd been telling him of a man she was infatuated with, and how it would be terribly easy for her to fall in love. Her eyes had been impossibly blue, He'd imagined at once that some wicked, handsome rake had been trying to seduce her and implored her not to do anything foolish.

"Too late," she'd whispered, and then she'd kissed him.

It could only have lasted a second—less, and yet in that moment his heart had stopped beating, he was certain of it. He was a man of reason and science, but for that suspended moment he would have sworn that the world had stopped turning. Prussian blue; that was the only thought in his head in the moment before she'd closed her eyes and kissed him.

Impossible, of course, and yet he'd never seen a shade quite that dark, quite that intense. Her lips, though... oh, her lips.... His heart sped in his chest as he considered that soft pink, the lush, sweet curves as tender as a rose bud....

"Inigo? Good heavens man, what did she do to you? Was there opium in her lip salve?"

Inigo jolted and cursed Miss Butler, then himself, then Miss Butler a bit more.

"A nice kiss?" he repeated, aware that he sounded vague as he tried to recall and understand the question. *Nice* did not seem an appropriate word to use in conjunction with Miss Butler. Apocalyptic, maybe? Cataclysmic? A panicked voice echoed back and forth in his head like a frantic oracle, shouting danger, beware, here be dragons… even if that dragon did look like Aphrodite dressed in sunshine. Oh, God, how nauseating. What *was* wrong with him?

The next thing he knew Solo was standing before him, studying him as if he was one of the revolting looking specimens kept in jars in the biology labs. "Are you quite certain it was just a kiss?"

Inigo gave a slightly hysterical laugh. "Just a kiss," he repeated nodding, and then shook his head in despair. "But not *just* a kiss."

Solo's eyebrows shot up. "I see," he said, though he clearly didn't. No one could. "Well, old fellow, I'd say you were in trouble. Deep, *deep*, trouble."

***

By the time Jerome arrived at the sixth servant registry office, it had gone noon and he was ready to tear his hair out, but his tenacity paid off. Yes, a dark-haired young woman with a Scottish accent had hired a Mrs Agnes Lacey to act as her companion and maid. She had been engaged at once. It appeared the young lady was going under the name of Macdonald. Getting the address from the suspicious matron at the desk, however, was a deal more awkward and vastly more disquieting. She'd looked Jerome over with the air of a woman who knew a libertine when she saw one and clearly believed he was up to no good in hunting down an innocent young lady. To his intense discomfort, Jerome had struggled to gainsay her, knowing she had it entirely right. He'd been reduced to shamelessly bandying his brother's name before her, an act he'd usually rather cut his own throat than resort to. It had the desired effect, naturally, which only soured his temper further, and by the time he was back out on the street he was beside himself with frustration and annoyance, all of which he knew was fuelled by the sickening anxiety that was twisting his guts into a knot.

The address he held was a respectable one, much to his relief, and it was only this that allowed him to keep his patience as he endured the journey to Dulwich Common.

The Oaks was a handsome stucco villa with a slate roof and deep eaves. It was attached to an identical villa on its right side both with two bays each and a trellised porch. Upon knocking and giving his card, he was shown inside by a disapproving looking woman who introduced herself as Mrs Morris, gave him the cutty eye and left him to cool his heels in the parlour. It seemed to be his day for being disapproved of, though he supposed he'd earned it in full measure. At least he had the correct address, he thought with a sigh.

A few moments later he heard raised voices outside the door. Curious what the fuss was about, he crept closer, only to hear Mrs Morris reprimanding Bonnie in severe tones.

"I thought you were a respectable young lady, Miss Macdonald, but you've hardly set foot in my house a moment before you have gentlemen callers."

Jerome winced and then braced himself, which Mrs Morris would have done too if she'd known Bonnie a little better.

"*Gentlemen?*" Bonnie retorted. "I thought you said there was a Mr Cadogan awaiting my attention. If you'd said there were a host of fellows expecting me I'd have made greater haste, for surely it's an orgy I have planned in your front parlour, madam, or could it possibly be that a friend of mine, who happens to be the Earl of St Clair's *brother*, has taken the liberty to see I arrived safely at my lodgings?"

Well, his brother's name was certainly getting an airing today. Bonnie didn't wait to see what effect this tirade had on her victim and, a bare moment later, she swept into the room, dark eyes flashing with fury.

"Jerome Cadogan, I could wring your blasted neck!"

Jerome cleared his throat. "Afternoon, Bonnie."

Then, to his appalled astonishment, she burst into tears.

"Bonnie! Oh, love." He hurried to her, slammed shut the door which she'd left discreetly open, and pulled her into his arms. "There, there, I'm here now," he said, holding her tightly, only to be thrust away a moment later.

"Yes, you great l-lummox, and you've ruined everything. Now that awful woman will think you're m-my l-lover and turn me out," she stammered in between sobs as she flung herself down in a chair.

Jerome crouched down in front of her and took her hand. "I am your lover," he said gently. "No getting away from it."

She stared at him for a moment and then began crying harder.

Good heavens.

He thrust a handkerchief at her and waited until the storm subsided a little. "Bonnie, what is it? What's wrong, love? Why did you run away?"

"I didn't run away," she said indignantly. "And I told Ruth why I was going. It's too b-bad of her to come running to you and tattling."

"Oh, come now, sweetheart. She's your friend, and she was worried sick."

"Well, there's no need," she said, wiping her eyes and gathering herself together. "I'm perfectly all right."

"Of course you are," Jerome said with a sigh. "That's why you burst into tears at the sight of me."

"Because I didn't want to see you, for heaven's sake!" she cried, throwing up her hands. "I just wanted a bit of peace away from everyone. I've only just unpacked my bags!"

"Well, I'm sorry for it," he said, and then changed his mind. "Dash it all, no. I'm not the least bit sorry. What the devil are you doing out here, all by yourself? What is so bad that you ran away from your friends? If it's this Anderson fellow you're frightened of, you need only say so, love. I'll not let him haul you back to Scotland if you don't want to go."

She stared at him for a long moment and then gave a wan smile. "That's sweet, Jerome, but I'm used to being by myself. It really isn't so terrible."

Jerome felt his heart clench at her words. How much of her life had she been alone? The loss of his father had utterly devastated Jerome when he was nineteen. Bonnie had lost everyone but her father at five years old, and then he had promptly abandoned her to relatives she didn't know from Adam. She'd not spoken much about it, but it occurred to him now to wonder just what her life had been like.

"But you hate to be alone," he said, and saw her eyes widen. He reached out and took her hand. "I know you, Bonnie Campbell, and I know you can't abide silence and solitude."

"That's not true," she countered, but her voice quavered a little.

"Perhaps, if there's no one you want to be in company with, but you adore your friends, and you'd always rather be with me than alone."

She flushed then, putting colour in her cheeks, which were far too pale. He realised now that she'd lost weight too, and he felt his heart ache. All the life and vivacity that he'd adored had vanished, the sparkle gone from her eyes. Had he done that? Had he caused so much damage? Was he only making things worse for her, seeking her out like this? Yet, what else could he do? Friends did not forsake each other when they knew the person they cared for was unhappy and alone, no matter if their attentions were unwelcome.

"I wish you hadn't come," she said, the words so forlorn he wanted to weep himself.

"But I have, and I'm not going to abandon you. Besides, that starched up old tabby will want you out of her house now you've been alone in her parlour… *with a man.*" He leered at her and twirled an imaginary moustache like a theatrical villain and, to his relief, she grinned at him.

"You're a devil and no mistake, Jerome Cadogan," she said with a sigh. "But Ruth's gone away to her father's, and I can hardly come and stay with you."

"What about Miss Hunt?" he asked, knowing full well that the young woman had appointed herself mother hen of their particular—*peculiar*—group of friends. "She'd be pleased to see you, I think?"

Bonnie sighed and nodded. "I suppose so."

"And we'll not tell anyone you're there if you prefer, so you'll have the peace and quiet you need and, if Mr Anderson comes to town, I'll tell him to sling his hook."

She snorted at that. "Oh, that I would pay to see," she said, and he was more than relieved to see something of a glimmer return to her eyes.

Jerome squeezed her hand. "Are you all right, love? Was it really only that you didn't want that brute coming after you?"

Bonnie brought his hand to her face and kissed his knuckles. "Mostly," she said, not looking at him. "And because I have some decisions to make about my future."

That strange, aching sorrow rose in his chest again and it felt stronger this time, tinged with panic. "Bonnie," he said, knowing he had to ask her again, but she reached out and pressed a finger to his lips.

"No," she said. "Don't. Don't say it. Not again."

The panicky feeling rose and expanded, making it hard to breath but he obeyed her. What choice did he have?

"All right," he said, though he was unsettled and unhappily aware that he didn't like the fact she'd cut him off so automatically. "Well, you'd best go and pack up again, and hurry. It's a good couple of hours back to Mayfair and we must leave soon to have any chance of arriving before dark."

Bonnie huffed at him but got to her feet. "You're a blessed nuisance," she muttered.

"I know," he agreed.

"More trouble than you're worth," she added, shaking her head now.

"Undoubtedly."

"I don't know what I ever saw in you."

"Me either," he said, meaning it, though the words were light. "But you love me anyway, don't you?"

She stilled, staring at him, and Jerome realised she'd never actually told him she loved him, not in so many words. Neither of them had ever acknowledged her feelings, though he'd known, and she'd known he knew. At least, he'd thought so. Had he been wrong? Had it only been lust and desire, the excitement of it? Now his heart was thudding in his throat and he knew there had been too much emotion in the words, too much anxiety, and he desperately wanted to hear the answer to the question.

"I'd best hurry," she said, and rushed from the room.

Chapter 9

Miss Butler,

*Please find enclosed an extensive list of reading
material. I believe there is enough here to keep
you occupied for the foreseeable future.
Certainly enough to avoid any need for further
contact with me.*

I hope you find the contents satisfactory.

De Beauvoir.

P.S. Do not underestimate your penmanship.

**— Excerpt of a letter from Mr Inigo de
Beauvoir to Miss Minerva Butler**

The evening of the 24th October 1814.

Minerva stared down at the terse note in her hand and then
squealed, clutching it to her chest. She cast the lengthy list of
reading material to one side and instead looked at the horrifically
untidy scrawl before her, and most especially the postscript. The
writing on that delicious little PS was worse still. Consigned to the
very bottom of the page and, unlike the note, it had obviously been
dashed off in haste and as an afterthought. It wouldn't have
surprised her if he'd crossed it out before sending it to her, so
begrudging were those words.

Not that she cared. Those few near illegible scratches of ink could have been dragged from him at gunpoint and it wouldn't have made a jot of difference. It gave her a glimmer of hope, no matter how faint and fragile, and she would cling to it for all she was worth.

"What's that, Minerva?"

"Oh, nothing, Mama," she said, hastily stuffing the note and the list into her reticule. "Just a shopping list. Are you ready to go?"

"Yes, quite ready. We mustn't keep dear Robert waiting. I know how he gets if he doesn't get his dinner on time."

Minerva suppressed the desire to roll her eyes. Though her mother had been desperately disappointed that Minerva had failed to catch the Duke of Bedwin for herself, the next best thing was for him to have married her cousin. Now she insisted on referring to him as *dear Robert*—though never to his face—and would namedrop shamelessly at every opportunity. Tonight they were dining with Robert and Prue and, to her great relief, Minerva would stay with them whilst her mother visited a sick friend in Bath. If her dear mama had the slightest idea that her only daughter, for whom she had such lofty ambitions, was infatuated with a lowly natural philosopher of all things, well, she'd likely expire of shock.

Minerva was sorry for it too, but it had taken her a long time to fight her way free from the weight of her mother's expectations and realise that she didn't want any of the things her mother wanted. Oh, not that she was averse to being wealthy or titled; it just wasn't on her list of requirements. No. What she wanted was to be wanted. She wanted love and romance and to be desired beyond reason. Why then, she'd become so smitten with Inigo de Beauvoir, who hadn't given her a second glance, she couldn't fathom. Perhaps *that* was why, she considered, as his grace's luxurious carriage bore them off to Beverwyck, the duke's London home.

Perhaps it was the challenge of capturing the attention of such a clever man? For surely, clever as he was, he'd not be foolish enough to fall head over ears in love with a pretty ninny like Minerva. Except she was coming to realise she wasn't quite as stupid as she'd feared, and Inigo de Beauvoir didn't believe in love. He'd said so.

Minerva smiled and clutched her reticule tighter, dreaming of eyes that were an odd grey-green, and a man who didn't want to want her.

***

25th October 1814. South Audley Street, London.

Bonnie made her way slowly down the stairs, clutching at the banister so hard her knuckles were white. Why, oh why had she allowed Jerome to bring her back to Matilda? Her friend was too observant, too concerned with Bonnie's welfare not to notice that she was ill. It was only a matter of time before Matilda put two and two together and came up with an answer she wouldn't like. Yet, Jerome had been right. Being alone had solved nothing. When she'd seen him standing in the parlour waiting for her, she'd wanted to launch herself into his arms and beg him never to leave her again.

Pathetic, she scolded herself. She'd not be that woman, throwing herself repeatedly at a man who didn't want her. Yes, she had done it, she knew that, and now she was paying the price, but it was her price, not his.

"Oh, good morning, Bonnie," Matilda said, beaming at her as she entered the breakfast parlour. It was clear Matilda had been up for some time and had finished her breakfast. At once the scent of bacon and kippers and a dozen other things that Bonnie usually loved, rose around her and her stomach lurched in protest. "Are you quite well, dear?"

Bonnie forced a smile to her face.

"Oh, yes. I'm fine. Just a little tired and… and I think the fish I had for lunch yesterday was not as fresh as it might have been."

"Oh," Matilda said, her lovely face screwed up in a grimace of sympathy. "How vile. Poor you. Is there anything I can get you?"

Bonnie shook her head. "I'll just have a bit of toast and some tea. I'm sure I'll feel much better then."

"Oh, and it's such a shame too," Matilda said with a sigh, passing her the toast rack. "I was going to Madame Lanchester's. My new gowns ought to be ready and I was hoping for your opinion."

"Sorry, Tilda. I really couldn't."

"Oh, no. That makes me sound too dreadfully selfish. I wanted your company above all things, love, but you must stay and rest. I had planned to call in on Prue and Minerva in any case. I'm sure Minerva will come with me."

"Oh, yes," Bonnie said, almost sagging with relief at having the day to herself. "Minerva will love to come with you, and she has such a marvellous eye for fashion."

"Well, I shall leave you to your breakfast and a quiet day. I do hope you feel better soon. Shall I send for some willow bark tea for you?" Matilda asked, getting to her feet and leaving the table.

"Oh, no, this will do fine, thank you. Don't worry about me. I shall have a peaceful day reading and look forward to hearing all about your new gowns once you return," Bonnie said, giving Matilda what she hoped was a reassuring smile until her friend was satisfied she would be all right, and left her alone.

Once Matilda had taken herself out, Bonnie settled herself before the fire in the elegant parlour and perused the stack of books Matilda had left for her. With a sigh, she selected one at random and stared at the first page for a good five minutes before realising she would never make it past the first word. She put the book back with the others and reached instead for the scandal sheet, which had been delivered that morning. Perhaps she could distract herself with other people's folly and misfortune, she thought with a sigh. She'd certainly had her fill of dwelling on her own.

With little interest she scanned each story before a familiar name caught her eye.

Mr C. younger brother to the E. of S. C. has oft been seen of late in the company of Lady H. The two certainly made a lovely picture, shopping together arm in arm on Bond Street, says our source. We predict an announcement in that quarter soon, and wedding bells before Easter.

Bonnie's stomach lurched and the nausea she'd fought back all morning rose with a vengeance. *Stupid, stupid*, she scolded herself. *You knew this would happen. If you won't marry him, someone else will. His mother will see to that.*

She got to her feet, flinging the paper down in a crumpled heap on the floor. Her eyes blurred with tears and she felt ill, and more miserable than she'd ever done in her life before. The discreet knock and the appearance of Matilda's butler was not, therefore, a welcome sight. His announcement of Lady Helena Adolphus and the sight of the dark haired beauty sweeping into the room as if she'd just stepped from a fashion plate was a blow Bonnie could well have done without.

"Forgive me for interrupting your morning, Miss Campbell," Lady Helena said, with an overabundance of cheer that made Bonnie want to throw things. "I came to visit Miss Hunt but, on finding her absent, I hoped I could foist my company on you for a while. I declare, I'm bored to tears this day and in desperate need of some lively conversation. I felt sure you were just the person to provide it."

She beamed at Bonnie, her smile faltering only a little when Bonnie just stared back at her.

They'd met, of course, at various parties. Indeed, Bonnie had liked the woman and admired both her beauty and her dry wit, and especially her sharp tongue. Right at this moment, however, she wanted to ram the scandal sheet between Lady Helena's perfectly white teeth until she choked.

Helena glanced down at the crumpled paper on the floor and coloured a little.

"Oh," she said.

"Oh," Bonnie mimicked, folding her arms.

The two women stared at each other.

"It's not true," Helena said, after a long, uncomfortable moment. "He doesn't want to marry me, and I don't have the least intention of marrying him even if he did... which he doesn't," she repeated.

"What's wanting got to do with it?" Bonnie asked dully. "His mother wants the match. No doubt Jerome will do as she wishes."

Helena frowned, her elegant dark brows knitting over deep green eyes. "Do you really think he's so easily managed? That's certainly not the impression I got, but I dare say you know him better than I do."

"What's that supposed to mean?" Bonnie snapped, clenching her fists.

The young woman's eyes widened, clearly surprised by the animosity. Bonnie was being rude and hateful and horribly unfair, and she well knew it. She could not, however, seem to stop herself. Lady Helena was everything that Bonnie wasn't, the epitome of an elegant young lady. She was poised, beautiful, witty, and slender, and her manners were quite perfect, Bonnie didn't doubt. Not to mention, she was a duke's sister. No wonder Lady St Clair was so desperate to make the match.

"Only that you and Jerome are good friends," Helena said carefully. "I know he thinks the world of you."

Bonnie snorted and turned away to stare at the fire before she lost complete control, either of her temper or the tears that were threatening to spill.

"Miss Campbell, if you wish for the unvarnished truth, I have no interest in Jerome Cadogan, nor he in me, and even if his mother were to move heaven and earth, my brother will never agree to the match. Firstly, Jerome is a second son and I am the daughter and sister of a duke. It's hardly a great match from my perspective but, putting that aside, my brother would never force me to marry a man I neither love nor desire. Is that plain enough?"

Though she knew she ought to turn around and beg Lady Helena's forgiveness for her appalling behaviour, Bonnie could do nothing. The tears were streaming down her face and she could not stop them. Suddenly she was trembling and helpless to stem the ugly tide of emotion battering her on all sides.

"Oh, my dear."

Bonnie turned her head, horrified but resigned as she saw Lady Helena at her side. The young woman put her arms around her and hugged her tightly.

"Oh, you poor thing. I'm so sorry. Good heavens, I must be the last person on earth you wished to see this morning. I wonder you didn't attack me with the poker. I think I might have in your position."

Bonnie gave a hysterical laugh and then the storm she'd tried so valiantly to keep at bay broke. To her astonishment, Lady Helena held her while she sobbed her heart out, stroking her back and her hair and murmuring reassurances. Though she had no idea how long the tears and the tide of misery flowed, by the time it had abated it was replaced by a swell of nausea that made Bonnie first hot, then cold, and sent her rushing from the room at a run.

She abandoned her poor abused guest and flew up the stairs, just reaching her room in time to grab the chamber pot and empty the contents of her stomach.

Through the retching and moaning, Bonnie was only dimly aware of the door opening and closing, of a cool cloth being pressed into her hand, of the vile chamber pot being taken away and a glass of water held out to her. She looked up then, into deep green eyes filled with sympathy and dismay.

"Have you told him?" Lady Helena asked her, and to Bonnie's shame she could detect no victory or malice in the words, despite searching for them.

She had been hateful to this woman because of her own jealousy, and yet Lady Helena gave her nothing but kindness in return. Her shock at being so easily discovered must have shown on her face.

Helena smiled at her. "Prue is increasing," she said. "Though don't tell anyone. You have the exact same look she has worn this past month or more."

Bonnie closed her eyes and shook her head. "I can't," she whispered. "I won't trap him. He doesn't love me. I knew that when…." She glanced at Helena and blushed, shamed further. "I got myself into this mess. There's no one else to blame."

"Nonetheless," Helena persisted.

"No!" Bonnie cried, wrapping her arms about herself. "You must swear to me you'll not tell him. Nor anyone else, but especially not Jerome."

"The child is as much his responsibility as yours," Helena said, surprisingly fierce now. "It will be his son or daughter too. He has a right to the knowledge."

Bonnie nodded, knowing that was true. "I'll not keep it from him forever, I swear, but I'll not have him forced into a situation where he's honour bound to marry me. He's already offered his hand for having ruining me, when the truth is I threw myself at him repeatedly, but he is my friend, and I will not destroy his life and our friendship by tying him to me forever. I love him too much for that. Can't you understand?"

Helena stared at her and, to her surprise, Bonnie saw tears in her eyes. "You would face ruin and shame, rather than save yourself, to ensure his happiness?"

Bonnie nodded.

Helena reached out a hand and tousled Bonnie's short curls. "I wish I had gotten to know you sooner, Bonnie Campbell, but all is not lost. You may count me a friend. I must tell you I disagree with your decision, but... I will not tell Mr Cadogan that you carry his child."

All the air left Bonnie's lungs in a shuddering breath. "Thank you," she said.

Helena smiled, but Bonnie knew she was unconvinced and worried for her future. Well, she thought wearily, she was certainly not the only one.

Chapter 10

Dear Mr de Beauvoir,

I have compelled myself to wait a whole four days before replying to your note. I shall not call it a letter, as you were so terribly grudging with words that I was forced to sigh with longing over that terse little postscript. Did it hurt very much?

You will note that I have taken extra care with my writing today. Look at all those curly ascenders and descenders and those neat little tittles – yes, the dots really are called tittles, I looked it up. Aren't you proud of my enquiring mind?

Is your heart beating just a bit faster?

Though I long to tease you further, I shall spare you the horror, though I am imagining the horror on your face all the same. Instead, I will tell you simply that I am enjoying the Royal Society Journal, Philosophical Transactions. I hope you will not be too disappointed to discover that my favourite work has been 'An Account of the Remains of a Mammoth, found near Rochester'. Perhaps I am a biologist at heart? (Or are you going to scold me and tell me I mean Palaeontologist?) Does this distress you? I beg you not to be jealous. My devotions and infatuations are still, wholeheartedly, yours.

— Excerpt of a letter from Miss Minerva Butler to Mr Inigo de Beauvoir.

The evening of the 28th October 1814. Lady Manning's Rout Party, Bruton Street, London.

Matilda peered through the crush of people and wondered if she might have done better to have stayed at home. Bonnie would certainly have preferred it, she thought with a sigh, regarding the young woman's rather wan countenance. She was speaking to Lady Helena, the two women having become remarkably close in a very short time. Matilda was surprised, especially in the light of the rabid gossip surrounding Helena and Jerome, but they were thick as thieves, and Helena seemed to regard Bonnie with a proprietary air which Matilda found both odd and just a little vexing. The realisation that she was somewhat jealous Bonnie had confided her troubles to Helena—for surely she had—was not one of which she was proud.

What a wretched busybody she was becoming. If she didn't watch herself, she'd become an interfering old woman, always sticking her nose into other people's business. That was what came of having too much time on one's hands, she supposed. Really, she had troubles enough of her own to think on. Mr Burton had written to tell her he would be in London next week and would call on her as soon as he arrived. Though he didn't say so explicitly, the implication was clear enough. He wanted permission to court her publicly, and he wanted it now.

Matilda smothered the panic that made her heart hammer in her chest, took a large swallow of orgeat, and tried to pretend it was brandy. It didn't work.

Though the night outside was cold and wet, Mrs Manning's luxurious home was verging on tropical as the servants kept the fires roaring and the press of so many bodies added to the furnace-like temperatures. Easing her way from those thronging the front parlour, Matilda escaped into the grand entrance hall where the temperature was a few degrees below sultry and tried to determine whether one of the card rooms or the music room held a greater or lesser appeal.

"Dithering, Miss Hunt? How unlike you."

Matilda spun around, knowing at once to whom the languid, teasing voice belonged.

"Oh, it's you," she said with a sigh, for all the world as if she was heartily disappointed when her heart was skipping about in her chest with its usual combination of terror and glee.

Contradictory as the emotions were, it was entirely normal when in the presence of the Marquess of Montagu. Any sane young woman would be gibbering with fear and doing her utmost to make her escape to safety. Sadly, the man made Matilda act like a lunatic and she could never quite decide if she wanted to hit him with a heavy blunt object or kiss him senseless. She couldn't help but think the only safe way to kiss Montagu would be if he was unconscious. Perhaps she could consider it as an option? Then she might get him out of her system without risking further damage to her virtue and her sanity. Laudanum, perhaps? She could spike his champagne.

Having reviewed the idea, Matilda couldn't help but decide her sanity was beyond saving.

"Yes, indeed, I am dithering," she admitted, fanning herself, for surely the temperature had just climbed past tropical to hot as Hades. Or perhaps it was just her? She hoped it wasn't in reaction to the sight of the marquess in evening attire. After all, she'd seen it before… and no, that didn't shield her from his magnificent face or form one little bit. A mere mortal woman could never get used to a celestial vision of a man who looked like a fallen angel. "I shall seek your assistance, my lord. Which room do you think I should visit next? A hand or two of cards, or some music in the drawing room?"

"Oh, no, Miss Hunt. I am not so foolish as to give an opinion, for you will choose to do the opposite of what I decide upon and I shall not see you again all evening." He held out his arm to her. "Please allow me the honour of escorting you."

Matilda regarded his arm and then looked into his silver eyes. They were as changeable as smoke, revealing nothing. They seemed darker in this light, almost grey.

"I won't bite," he said.

"I don't believe you," Matilda retorted, but she took his arm all the same, too aware of the hard muscle beneath her gloved hand and struggling to contain the wash of heat that upset her equilibrium and made her want things she ought not even know she desired. She repressed a sigh as he guided her to the drawing room. Naturally. He'd struggle to torment her sufficiently during a game of cards, but he could whisper his wickedness into her ear during a recital.

"You returned my gift," he said once he had settled her in a chair as far back in the drawing room as he could get.

"Why, naturally," Matilda said, trying to ignore the fact that he sat close beside her, which was akin to pretending there wasn't a sabre-tooth tiger draped across her lap. "It was quite clearly delivered to me in error, for a gentleman would never presume to send a gift of such value and intimacy to a lady unless they were betrothed. Not if he had any respect for her."

She felt the weight of his gaze on her face and forced herself to concentrate—or at least to appear to concentrate—on the musicians' performance.

"I have the greatest respect for you, as I'm certain you are aware. I might add that your scruples were not in evidence when I sent you the orchid. I'm told it sits by your bed."

Matilda could not repress the flush that swept up her neck. Oh damn the man. "I cannot believe you have sunk so low as to snoop about my room," she raged, though she spoke low, barely above a whisper. "Will you break into my house next?"

She could not help but turn and glare at him, despite knowing she ought not look into his eyes. He was just like the cobra to which she'd once compared him; surely those eyes were hypnotic for she felt dazed whenever she looked at them. Now they held a glint of amusement, and something that might have been reproach.

"I could hardly have the letter or the gift left in plain sight, now, could I?" he said reasonably. "If the person who left the gift on my behalf noticed the orchid was by your bed as they passed through your room; it was nothing more than any maid in the household might have remarked. If you think my obsession has sunk me far enough to rifle through your drawers, then I must disappoint you. Bewitched I may be, but not entirely without pride."

"Bewitched," Matilda repeated with disgust. "You're not bewitched, you're sulking like a little boy who's been denied a treat. You're spoilt and greedy and unused to being told no. The more I tell you *no* the more determined you are to have your own way."

"Spoilt *and* greedy. My, my, Miss Hunt, what are you to do with me?"

"I wish I knew," she said in exasperation, meaning it. "And of course I kept the blasted orchid. It was the most beautiful thing I'd ever seen in my life, drat you. I couldn't bear to give it up, even though I've cursed myself ever since. With the sole exception of the man who gave it to me, it's the most troublesome, capricious thing I've ever come across. Not to mention that I live in constant terror of killing it."

"Was the brooch not beautiful?" he asked, his voice soft now, lingering like silk as he leaned in and spoke close to her ear.

His breath was warm against her neck and Matilda shivered with the longing to turn and press her mouth to his. Oh God, his mouth... his mouth, that terrible, sinful, wicked mouth. Damn her for a fool, why did she want him so badly when she knew what it meant for her?

"Of course it was beautiful," she said, forcing the words out. "It was also quite inappropriate. If I'd worn it, I may as well have written your name across my skin for you'd have taken it as a sign of ownership. I will not be bought, my lord. You may not pay me to lift my skirts for you like some common strumpet."

She thought she heard a slight hitch in his breathing as she spoke, but that was ridiculous. Nothing ever discomposed Montagu, everyone knew that. Certainly she wasn't capable of it, though wanted to be. She wanted to torment him as badly as he tormented her. She wanted to keep him from sleep and invade his every waking thought as well as his dreams. She wanted him mad for her, a sweet, terrible madness that would destroy them both in the inferno of their insanity.

"You have an inflated impression of what a common strumpet earns, my dear," he said, and he sounded as infuriatingly composed as ever. God, how she wanted to ruffle him. "Though," he said, and his voice dropped to something impossibly low and dangerously dark, "I admit I am now captivated by the notion of my name written across your lovely skin."

Despite herself, her eyes snapped to his, and there was the cobra she feared, the intensity of his scrutiny hypnotising. Matilda was aware of her own breath, harsh and ragged, her breasts pushing against the confines of her corset as she fought to drag enough air into her lungs. Her skin was on fire—so hot, too hot—

every part of her ablaze, the private place between her legs hottest of all and aching with need. The silver grey smoke of his gaze seemed to burn away the layers of fabric, the silk and the lace and muslin, all of it reduced to cinders in the heat of that proprietary look that imagined his name written across her naked flesh. He wanted to see it. He was imagining it right now, and God help her, but her body throbbed with desire in response.

"Stop it," she said, her panic audible as she tore her gaze from his.

"I can't."

Matilda's head snapped about once more, and she stared at him in astonishment. That had been honesty, a confession. She'd heard the frustration, and something else too, something that might have been bewilderment or even... fear.

Too late. In the moment it had taken to turn back to him, he'd looked away, staring straight ahead, his expression as unreadable and cold as always, but she'd heard. She'd heard.

"Miss Hunt?" Matilda jolted as a feminine voice broke the spell and she turned to see Lady Helena staring at her.

"Lady Helena," she said, trying to find something resembling a smile, desperately trying to moderate her voice, so she didn't sound every bit as breathless and flustered as she might if the man beside her had his hands under her skirts. He may have well as done for the effect he had on her with a few words, a look.

"Forgive me, Miss Hunt, but...." She shot a look at Montagu, who was apparently absorbed by the music, before bending to whisper in Matilda's ear. "Bonnie is not well. She needs to go home at once."

That, if nothing else, doused her with cold water and brought her to her senses. One of her friends was in trouble. Bonnie needed her. She got to her feet, barely giving Montagu the civility of a curt goodbye before she swept away.

It was the work of a moment to order her carriage be brought around and then she followed Helena to Bonnie. She was pale and quite obviously miserable.

"Oh, my dear. You should never have come. I thought you still looked peaky. Oh, how I wish we'd both stayed at home," she said, meaning it with all her heart.

"Nonsense," Bonnie said, forcing a smile. "It's a lovely evening and I feel wretched for spoiling it for you. I insist you stay, or I shall feel terrible. Lady Helena will come with me."

"Indeed, I wonder if we have not both caught the same malady," Helena said gravely. "I have the most dreadful headache and should be glad to get out of this infernal heat."

Matilda looked at Helena and felt certain she was lying, though she could not fathom why. Helena was as cool and lovely as always, and though it was possible she really was ill, she hid the signs well. She appeared to be the picture of health.

"Very well," Matilda said, resigned. She would have liked to have escaped too, but she did not want to force her company on the young women if they didn't want it, and instinct told her they'd prefer her to stay and leave them be.

Once they were safely away, she stood dithering in the entrance hall again. The temptation to return to her place beside Montagu was beyond anything, but she would not. She was not so lost to reason that she would invite a cobra into her bed, and that's what it would amount to if she went back to him now.

I can't.

His words rang in her ears and she told herself to cease being foolish. He couldn't stop because he was a man, and she'd wounded his male pride by telling him no, and no, and no again. He was not only a man, but a marquess, and they were a breed apart. How it must provoke him to discover something he could not buy or force to submit to his will. Had anyone ever denied him? Had he ever not had his own way? Well, it was good for him to learn the lesson then. Someone must teach him what his parents, guardians, and tutors had all failed to get into his obstinate, arrogant head. Some things could not be had for a price. Some things belonged to people other than the Marquess of Montagu. He was not God Almighty, and she would tell him no and keep saying it until he understood.

Matilda worked herself up into a fury of righteous indignation as she stalked towards the card room. Sadly, that fury did not diminish the ache beneath her skin, the clamouring need inside her that made her feel weak and empty. She was still trembling with the effort it had taken not to reach out and touch him there in the dim light of Mrs Manning's drawing room, where anyone might have seen and recognised her for the besotted fool that she was.

"Miss Hunt."

"Mr Cadogan," Matilda said, hurrying towards him as though he held out a lifeline. Yes, anything, anything to take her mind out of the mire of foolish longing that was dragging her down. "How do you do?"

"I'm well, Miss Hunt, and yourself?"

The two of them exchange the usual polite nothings until he took a step closer, his expression serious. "I'd hoped to see Bonnie here," he said, looking somewhat sheepish as he turned the glass in his hand back and forth. "I've wanted to call only... well, she asked me to stay away."

Matilda nodded. "It's for the best. People were beginning to talk and... and you know as well as I do how easily a woman's reputation can be ruined."

He blanched and Miss Hunt regretted her reproachful tone. It was unfair that the two of them could not be friends, that the world judged them so harshly, but that was the way of things. If Mr Cadogan did not intend to offer for Bonnie, he could only hurt her by paying such close attention. Especially when they were so wild and unheeding of consequences when they were together.

"In any case, I'm afraid you've just missed her," Matilda went on, softening her tone. "She's not well. Oh, nothing too serious, I'm sure," she said at the anxious look that sparked in his eyes. "She's been rather unwell ever since she came to stay. Something she ate, I believe. I think she had persuaded herself it had passed, but it appears she was too optimistic."

"She'... s-sick?"

Matilda smiled at him and laid a comforting hand on his arm. He appeared very concerned, and she was relieved that Bonnie wasn't alone in her unhappiness. As cruel as it was, it seemed even worse when the woman was the only one heartsick and lonely. "I shall have the doctor call on her tomorrow, no matter how she protests this time. How stubborn she is about that! I can't help but wonder if she convinced herself she was well just to avoid his visit. In any case, Lady Helena has taken her home, so you need not worry yourself. She's in good hands. The two of them seem to have become great friends."

"Lady Helena?" Mr Cadogan seemed astonished by this piece of news.

"Why, yes. She visited the morning after Bonnie came to stay and they have been inseparable ever since. I declare, Helena spends more time at South Audley Street than she does Beverwyck. Not that I mind, of course," she added with a laugh, lest he should think she was complaining. "But I wonder if there is something going around. Mr Cadogan, you're most dreadfully pale. Do tell me you're not coming down with the same malady?"

"N-No... I.... That is, yes. Yes, I think perhaps I shall step outside for a moment and... and get some air. If you would excuse me, Miss Hunt."

Chapter 11

Miss Butler,

I beg of you, stop writing to me. Go and turn your attention to the handsome dukes and noblemen who must surely lay their hearts at your pretty feet if you would only put half the effort into winning them as you do to the business of driving me out of my mind. At the very least, could you have pity and not send letters that bear only the faintest hint of jasmine. It's never strong enough to be certain, just elusive enough to drive me mad, wondering if I only imagine your scent lingers on the paper.

I am a man of science and I know what this is. It is lust and desire and no good will come of it if you persist.

For the love of God, leave me be.

— Excerpt of a letter from Mr Inigo de Beauvoir to Miss Minerva Butler, never sent.

29th October 1814. South Audley Street, London.

Jerome hurried down the street towards Miss Hunt's home. It was far too early for callers, but he didn't give a damn. He'd break the bloody door down and rouse the entire household if need be. It had taken all his self-control, such as it was, to force himself to wait this long. He'd not slept. What had begun as a terrible suspicion had grown into certainty in the long, dark hours of the new day, and he had to see Bonnie.

He ran up the stairs to the front door, raised his hand to knock, and then paused. If his assumption was correct and Bonnie really was pregnant, he'd be a brute to come thundering at her door and distressing her at the crack of dawn. She'd been unwell last night. If she was carrying his child, she needed her rest, not to be woken at some unreasonable hour of the morning. Damnation. He stood, wavering, uncertain of what to do. He could hardly breathe, let alone think, and much as he wanted to ascribe it to having almost run the short distance here, he'd felt the same way since last night, when Miss Hunt had told him Bonnie was unwell. It had knocked the air from his lungs as efficiently as a fist to his solar plexus. It had shaken him, too. It had shaken him from the stupor he'd been in ever since Bonnie had left him sitting in the dark corridor of Holbrooke House.

She was his. Whether or not either of them liked the idea, he'd made her his. It didn't matter whose fault it was, who had instigated it or who had given in. They'd both been there, the two of them had shared that passionate coupling, and now they faced the results. A child. She was carrying his child. He forced the terror away, the panic that made his chest grow tight and the little voice inside scream *I'm not ready*. It was too late to consider such things. He hadn't had a gun to his head; he could have withdrawn and not left his seed to take root inside her. Except he couldn't have done. He'd been out of his senses, mindless with desire and need, frantic and out of control, the same way Bonnie always made him feel when he put his hands on her.

Hell and the devil, he couldn't be seen kicking his heels on her doorstep. The talk about the two of them had only just begun to die down, replaced now by those ridiculous rumours of him and Lady Helena. Cursing himself and life in general, Jerome took himself off the nearest chop house to find some breakfast and wait out the morning.

***

Ruth made her way up the steps to Matilda's home and knocked on the door. She was a little early for good manners, but she was eager to see Bonnie and knew neither she nor Matilda would give a fig for propriety.

The way Bonnie had run away had shaken Ruth, and she could not help but fear there was more to her friend's flight than she had originally supposed. During the recent trip with her father she'd had plenty of time to think whilst he was shut away in various business meetings for hours on end, and she no longer accepted Bonnie's explanation.

Surely if it had been only the imminent arrival of the dreadful Mr Anderson, then she would have confided as much to Ruth? Though they were perhaps not bosom bows, she had believed that they were close, that Bonnie trusted her. Yet she'd not confided whatever this problem was. There was an awful suspicion gnawing in the back of Ruth's mind, to which she did not want to give credence, but once she'd thought it she could not unthink it. It had kept her awake all night and now she felt she must see Bonnie at once. If the girl was in the kind of trouble Ruth feared, she would need all her friends. Perhaps Bonnie would still not confide in her today, but Ruth needed her to know that she was here, that she would stand by her and not judge or condemn her. How to get that across if Bonnie did not reveal her situation, Ruth wasn't entirely certain, but she hoped she'd figure it out when the time came.

"Good morning, Baines," Ruth said to the immaculate butler, who smiled warmly at her as he took her hat and gloves.

Ruth prided herself on remembering the names of the servants she met regularly. Though she was trying hard to fit into the *ton*, and most of the upper classes disregarded servants entirely, she refused to believe that good manners ought to diminish with rank.

Quite the opposite, in fact. In many houses this would cause the servants themselves to despise her, for they could be even worse snobs than their masters and mistresses, but happily Matilda's staff suffered no such airs and graces.

"Good morning, Miss Stone. I'm afraid Miss Hunt left the house a few moments ago; you've just missed her. However, I believe Miss Campbell is in the breakfast room, if you would like to follow me."

Ruth followed the man along the elegant entrance hall to the breakfast room. It was a light and cheery space, decorated in a sunny lemon yellow, but the effect seemed to have been lost on Bonnie, who was staring into her teacup with an expression of abject misery.

She started in surprise as Baines announced her guest and at once rearranged her features, smiling at Ruth.

"Ruth, how lovely to see you. I'm so glad you've come."

The ladies waited while a footman supplied Ruth with tea and laid another setting for breakfast, before both he and the butler withdrew.

"I'm so sorry, Ruth," Bonnie said, reaching out and taking her hand. "Jerome told me how worried you were. I never meant—"

"Oh, stuff," Ruth said, waving that away with impatience. "Never mind that now. I only wanted to know you were safe, and you are, so that's in the past. What I do want to know is why you went, Bonnie. What was so terrible you couldn't confide in me? And don't go telling me you were frightened of Gordon Anderson. From everything you've ever told me, as dreadful as the man obviously is, you've never had a problem standing up to him. My word, if you can shout down the Earl of Morven—who's supposed to be an absolute ogre—you'll not make me believe Mr Anderson holds terror enough to send you running."

To her dismay, Bonnie's eyes filled with tears, and Ruth clutched her hand harder.

"Bonnie, you are my friend, surely you know that? You are my dear friend, and I would never let you down. *Never,* " she added fiercely. "No matter what."

Bonnie gave a choked sob.

"Oh dear," Ruth said, her own throat tightening. "Oh, I had so hoped I was wrong, but I'm not, am I? You're… You're…."

To her dismay, Bonnie's eyes went wide as she realised what Ruth was implying, and she promptly turned the ghastliest shade of sickly green. "No," she breathed, so horrified Ruth feared she would swoon. "*No!* How… How did you know? Oh, my Lord, everyone will know before long, if they don't already. I must leave."

She sprang to her feet, but Ruth clung to her hand, forcing her to stay put.

"You're going nowhere," she said, surprising Bonnie with the force of her words.

Ruth bit her lip. She knew well enough she was a managing creature; indeed, bossy would not be too strong a term to apply to her. Though she did her best to hide such dreadful character flaws, it was in her nature to take charge, especially when people were being so obviously thick-headed.

"But Ruth," Bonnie pleaded, her voice quavering. "I ran away because I dared not bring such shame to your door. I only came to Matilda because Jerome insisted, and I meant to leave in a few days but… but if you and Lady Helena have already guessed—"

The two women jolted as the door opened once again.

"Mr Cadogan to see you, Miss Campbell."

The butler went out again, and at once Ruth saw the look in Mr Cadogan's eyes. Bonnie jumped to her feet, her expression one of sheer panic.

"Bonnie," he said, his voice so tender Ruth almost sighed with relief.

"Oh no," Bonnie said, and swayed.

Mr Cadogan moved before Ruth could even speak a warning and caught Bonnie up in his arms. Ruth rushed to get up and pull out a chair so that he could set her down. Bonnie slumped into it and Mr Cadogan sat before her, chafing her hands as Ruth searched out a vial of sal volatile from her reticule and waved it under Bonnie's nose.

"Thank goodness you've come," Ruth said, her relief palpable as Bonnie began to revive. "She was going to run away again. I was terrified I wouldn't be able to stop her."

"I'll stop her," Mr Cadogan said firmly. "I'm going to marry her."

Ruth let out a sigh of relief. "Oh," she said. "Oh, thank heavens, though I should have known you'd do the right thing."

He snorted. "I have no idea why," he muttered, giving Bonnie his full attention as she came around.

She sighed, her eyes flickering, and then a sob escaped her as she found Jerome on his knees before her, holding her hands.

"Oh, love," he said, his voice aching with sorrow. "Oh, Bonnie, why didn't you tell me?"

Ruth stood and turned away as Bonnie burst into tears.

"Oh, Jerome, no," she sobbed. "D-Don't be n-nice to me. It's all my fault...."

"Don't be such a goose," he said, sounding amused now, though the words were full of tenderness. "Shall I beat you for letting me get you pregnant?"

"B-But you don't w-want to marry me," she wailed, sobbing harder.

"Oh, Bonnie, don't take on so. I had to marry someone, and I'd rather marry someone I liked than some starchy lady with a vast dowry. At least you don't expect me to behave, because you're worse than I am."

Bonnie stared at him for a long moment and then her lip wobbled, and she began to cry again.

It would seem Ruth's company was suddenly *de trop*, and so she tucked the little vial back into her reticule and was halfway to the door when it opened yet again, and the butler appeared once more.

"Mr Gordon Anderson," he intoned, betraying not a flicker of interest at this flurry of activity, whilst within the room the name was greeted with frigid silence and as much welcome as the knell of doom.

Ruth froze as the man strode in… at least, she thought it was a man. On second thought, it might have been a mountain.

She looked up, and up, and her breath caught in her throat. Ruth was very tall for a woman and solidly built. She always felt rather clumsy and somewhat Amazonian around most of her friends, who'd been made to much more delicate proportions. Beside this man she felt like a fairy nymph.

Never in all her days, had Ruth seen such a blatant representation of the male animal, and there was something undoubtedly animal about him. He appeared barely tame, with a mane of deep brown hair and eyes the colour of a cat's. There was a day's stubble darkening his strong jaw, and his presence seemed to eat up all the space in the room, shrinking it with the sheer force of his bulk.

Oh, my, thought Ruth. *Oh my.* Her knees felt distinctly odd.

He was magnificent. His face appeared to have been chiselled from rock, and he was so big. His eyes were beautiful, and his skin tanned and weather-beaten, and he was so big. His shoulders were massive and those powerful arms and surely the thighs beneath his kilt would match and he was so, so… *big*.

Her heart gave an erratic thump in her chest as the man's furious gaze swept the room and landed on the pale young woman in the chair.

"Aye, Bonnie Campbell, ye wee hellion. I've tracked ye down at last. Pack yer things, ye infernal female, for I've better things to do that waste another moment in this misbegotten city."

Ruth gasped. As Bonnie had clearly lied through her teeth about all of Gordon Anderson's physical attributes, in the moments before he'd spoken, Ruth had harboured a flickering flame of hope that she'd treated his character just as cavalierly. Apparently not.

"She's going nowhere," Mr Cadogan growled, surging to his feet. He was vibrating with tension, his face white and his fists clenched. "And I'll thank you to keep a civil tongue in your head when addressing my fiancée."

"Oh, Jerome, no," Bonnie pleaded, grabbing hold of his hand.

"Hush, love," Mr Cadogan said, smiling at her. His expression had changed at once, the look in his eyes so tender Ruth felt for certain that everything would be all right if Bonnie only did the sensible thing.

"And who the devil may you be?" Anderson demanded, his deep voice reverberating around the room as the burr of his Scottish accent made Ruth ignore his appalling manners in favour of staring at him as if he was the last cream cake and she was the only one in reach.

Catching herself a little too late, she snapped her mouth shut and tried to rearrange her face into something less revoltingly smitten. He was only a man, she chided herself. A huge, virile, beautiful, glorious specimen of a man, yes, but … oh, what was the use? She gave up trying not to come unglued and gazed at him in wonderment, watching the scene unfold before her.

"I am Jerome Cadogan, and Miss Campbell has done me the very great honour of agreeing to marry me."

"Oh, aye?" said Anderson, his strangely golden brown eyes settling on Bonnie. "And why would ye do such a thing, Bonnie lass, without writing to tell me of it? Eh? I could have saved myself a God awful journey, could I nae?"

"We're not engaged," Bonnie said tightly as Jerome blanched at her words. "But I'd rather die than marry you, and you know it, so you've wasted your time all the same."

"I dinnae reckon so," Anderson said, his expression uncompromising. "Morven wants us wed. If ye dinnae mean to honour the arrangement ye can tell himself."

"No. I won't go back," Bonnie said, getting to her feet, and now the colour was back in her cheeks, her eyes flashing with fury. "Certainly not with you. You can find yourself another dowry to wed, for you'll not have mine."

Mr Anderson's expression darkened and there was something like desperation edging the harsh growl of his words. "I need that money, Bonnie. For the love of God, woman, ye know I do. I've waited this long. I gave ye the time ye begged for to find another, and ye've not done so."

"Yes, she bloody well has!" Jerome shouted, stepping in front of her. "She's to be my wife, and I'll see you in hell before I give her up."

"Oh, aye, and why does she not say so, then?" Anderson demanded, taking one pace closer to Jerome and covering damn near half the room in the process. Ruth tried not to stare at his knees, visible between the thick socks and the edge of the kilt. She failed.

"Because I didn't have time to get the proposal out of my damned mouth before some lumbering great caveman barged in and started shouting the odds!" Jerome retorted furiously.

Ruth could only admire his pluck. She'd always thought both the Cadogans large men, though the earl was certainly more refined and elegant than his brother. Yet even the room seemed to shrink before this hulking Highlander. Nonetheless, Mr Jerome Cadogan's reputation was one that told tales of brawling and troublemaking—*among other things*—and the fact that the man opposite him was built like a mountain range didn't seem to faze him one little bit.

The thought came into her head as she stared at the huge, unruly Scot who seemed to vibrate with tension, that this Mr Anderson needed managing. Someone with as much pig-headed determination as he had needed to take him in hand and teach him not to act like a bull in a china shop.

"Well, ask her, then," Anderson said, his eyes narrowing as Ruth returned her attention to the scene before her.

Jerome shook his head. "No," he said. "There's no asking now. She must marry me. She's carrying my child."

Ruth gasped as Bonnie groaned and put her head in her hands.

"I'm sorry, love," Jerome said, gently, turning back to her and taking her by the shoulders. "But you need looking after, and I'm tired of your determination not to trap me. I trapped myself and there's no one else to blame, certainly not you. We'll marry as soon as I can arrange it. I won't have any son or daughter of mine growing up with no name, and that's an end to it."

Bonnie burst into tears and Jerome pulled her into his arms, clasping her to him as though he feared she'd still try and run away.

"The devil take ye both!" Anderson exclaimed, clearly furious, or perhaps it was more than that, as he raked a massive hand through the disorder of his thick dark hair. "What's to be done now?" he said, though so low he must have been speaking to himself. There was a definite air of desperation to the words now, like a man who'd reached the end of a long, hard road only to find it carried on into infinity.

Ruth felt a swell of compassion stirring in her heart as she stared at him, and something very much like longing tugging at the pit of her belly. She wanted to go to him, to sit in his lap and make him lay his head on her shoulder while she smoothed the furrow from his forehead. The image made her breath catch. He looked up then, as if noticing her for the first time and, the moment his eyes met hers, Ruth felt any last hold on her sanity disappear in a puff of smoke.

"You n-need to m-marry a woman with money, Mr Anderson?" she asked, trying hard not to stammer but knowing it was an appalling thing to say aloud. It was exactly the kind of vulgar thing the *ton* expected a woman born into trade to say, of course, but she didn't care. The words of her dare were ringing in her ears and the urge to act on it was making her heart skitter about in her chest like a day old foal. She'd lost her mind. If it hadn't gone in that puff of smoke it must have been when she'd seen his bare knees.

He looked incredulous for a moment and then he gave a bitter laugh.

"Aye, what of it?" he asked, suspicion glinting in his eyes. "I suppose a fine English lady like yerself will despise me for it?"

A fine English lady? Ruth blushed.

"N-No," Ruth squeaked, shaking her head with vigour. "Not in the least. Am I right in believing you are heir to the Earl of Morven?"

The suspicious glint deepened, and he folded his arms. "Aye."

Ruth stared back at him, stared at that cleft chin and clenched her fingers against the desire to reach up and touch it, to slide her palm over the coarse, rough stubble along that uncompromising jaw. Her heart was beating so hard and fast she felt dizzy with it, and she took a moment to wonder if there was any insanity in her family. If there was, it was about to make a spectacular reappearance.

"How... old is the earl?" Ruth asked, wondering how she dared. She was trembling now with the enormity of what she was doing, the dare clamouring in her ears, over and over.

Say something outrageous to a handsome man. Say something outrageous to a handsome man....

He folded his massive arms and Ruth's knees threatened to buckle as she saw the heavy muscle of his biceps strain against the fabric of his coat and imagined those same arms closing around her. "Ye're mighty inquisitive, Miss...?"

"Miss Stone," she said, aware that she sounded breathless. "Yes, it's awfully rude of me, I know, but I assure you, I do have a very good reason."

"Morven's sixty-nine, by my reckoning," he said, watching her with interest now.

Ruth nodded, trying her damndest to be calm and clear-headed when the weight of this man's full attention was making her hot and giddy. Sixty-nine. That seemed acceptable odds in favour of her father living to see her gain a title. She'd heard from Bonnie that the earl had been a hard living kind of fellow, so he'd unlikely go on forever. Ruth took a deep breath, knowing she was about to bypass vulgar and go straight to hell.

"How much is Miss Campbell's dowry?"

"Oh, Ruth! No!" exclaimed Bonnie, suddenly paying attention to the conversation. She pulled away from Jerome and ran to her. "No. Whatever you are thinking, Ruth, no. Don't do it. It's not worth it for a title. He's not got a brass farthing, the castle is practically in ruins and miles from any society and, what's more, he's a dumb brute with as much sensitivity as a rock, and not a civilised bone in his body."

124

Not a civilised bone in his body. Ruth looked the man over and something hot and lewd turned her insides to liquid.

Anderson glowered a little as he looked between her and Bonnie, clearly bemused. "Five thousand pounds," he said after a taut pause.

Bonnie groaned.

Ruth closed her eyes for a long moment and then opened them again. She took a deep breath and looked the man straight in the eye. "Mine is fifty thousand. Why don't you marry me instead?"

Chapter 12

My dear Kitty,

I hardly know where to begin. I only went out for an hour, yet in that brief interval everyone seems to have run quite mad.

— Excerpt of a letter from Miss Matilda Hunt to Mrs Kitty Baxter.

29th October 1814. South Audley Street, London.

Ruth was vaguely aware of the door opening as she made her perfectly outrageous request. Somewhere in the dim recesses of her mind, she also registered Matilda's sharp gasp of shock. None of it mattered, though. Her entire being was riveted on the man in front of her.

His eyes had gone wide with astonishment and he was staring at her as if she'd just sprouted horns and a tail.

"Did ye nae hear what she said, lass?" he asked, talking slowly as though she'd taken leave of her senses. It was a fair point. "I have nae money, and I live in the wilds of the Highlands. Ye'll never change that, so don't go thinking ye can reform me. I dinnae like society, and though that one's a saucy wee hellcat," he added, jerking his head at Bonnie. "I cannae pretend she's said a word that's nae true."

Ruth swallowed and tried to find her voice. "I understand," she said, wishing the words didn't sound so faint and unlike her.

Mr Anderson let out a breath. "Aye, well, nae harm done. I'll not speak of it—"

"No, Mr Anderson, you misunderstand me," she said, rushing towards him in a panic as he made to leave the room. In her anxiety she reached out and took hold of his arm, and then gasped at the feel of the heavy muscle beneath her fingertips. She let him go at once as though he'd burned her, and then stared up at him to see a look of utter shock in his catlike eyes. "I meant that I perfectly understand that you have no money, that you dislike society, and that you will have no intention of changing in that regard and spending time in town. I accept all of this."

"Ruth!" Matilda and Bonnie exclaimed unison, but Ruth's attention never wavered. She *wanted* him. It was perhaps a form of temporary insanity, but she was in its grip and helpless to deny it. Her whole life she'd done her best to please her father, to be a good daughter, to catch him the kind of husband he wanted, i.e. one with a title attached. She'd never once stopped to complain or explain what she wanted; she had a duty to perform, to drag the family into society by marrying a title. Yet she didn't really like society, and had never wanted to be a part of the *ton*. The only thing she'd ever hoped was that the title came with a country estate and that she could bury herself there once her duty was done. This, though... this was perfect. An heir to an earldom! She'd never dreamed of aiming so high. A baron or a viscount was the most she'd dared hope for and she'd never even gotten close. Her father was too vulgar, her looks too... *challenging*, she supposed, and her temperament... well, she was blunt and forthright and found it impossible not to have an opinion on... on just about anything.

"What say you, Mr Anderson? You need my money; I need a husband with a title."

"I dinnae have a title yet, Miss Stone," the man said, never taking his eyes from her.

"Is there any reason you might fail to inherit?" she asked, blunt as ever.

She thought his mouth twitched but she couldn't be certain. It was a very long way away.

"I might die, I suppose," he said, rubbing his hand over his chin as he stared at her. It made an odd scritching sound that made her want to put her hands on him too. Ruth fought the urge to stare and concentrated on his words instead. Frankly, it seemed unlikely that death would dare to come for Gordon Anderson. He'd frighten it off.

"But if you had sons when you died, the eldest would inherit?"

His eyebrows went up. "Aye."

Ruth felt the heat sweep her from her head right down to her toes, but she never wavered. She'd likely never have a chance like this again, and she'd not lose it now.

"And would you leave the running of the household to your wife and not interfere in her decisions?"

He considered this for a moment. "Aye, so long as it dinnae interfere with my life."

"Of course not. A well run household ought only add to your comfort. And the children, they would also be her affair?"

"Daughters certainly," he said, dismissing this as if it were of little importance. Ruth bit back her irritation; she was too used to the idea that females were of no use or value other than their ability to marry well. "Sons, however, they'd need to learn from their da."

Da. This man could give her fine, handsome sons, no doubt. He'd be their father. Her breath quickened.

"But you would allow your wife a say in their upbringing, their education?"

He rubbed the back of his neck, considering her. "Aye. Reckon I would."

Ruth took a deep breath and then gave a businesslike nod and held out her hand.

"A deal then, Mr Anderson."

"Oh, Ruth, no!" Bonnie exclaimed. "Jerome, do something!"

Jerome gaped, looking as though he'd had quite enough shocks for one day without sorting anyone else's problems out.

"Ruth, darling," Matilda said, coming over and taking her hand before Anderson could shake it. "Don't you think this is all rather sudden?"

"Sudden?" Ruth said with a bitter laugh. "Matilda, this is my sixth season. I'm prepared to do my duty by my family, but the only offers I've received so far have been so distasteful to me that I simply could not countenance them. One must face facts, and the fact is...." She turned back and looked once again at Mr Anderson, taking him in from head to toe. All six feet and quite a bit more of him. She fought the urge to sigh. "The fact is," she said, wishing her voice hadn't gone all faint and reedy, "he'll suit me very well."

She turned back to the man in question, who'd been watching the proceedings in silence, removed her hand from Matilda's grip and offered it once again. "Well, Mr Anderson, what say you?"

He reached out and Ruth's breath snagged in her throat as his warm, callused hand engulfed her own. "A deal, Miss Stone," he rumbled, though there was a wary look in his eyes now that suggested he wasn't certain he hadn't lost his mind too. She could hardly blame him. Bonnie might have a lot less money, but she was far prettier than Ruth and, though voluptuous, she wasn't as big and cumbersome either. Still, hopefully he'd get used to her.

"Good," she said, trying hard to smile when she rather felt a large brandy and a lie down in a dark room was what she needed.

"You'd best go and pack then," he said, sending all her hopes for a moment's peace shattering as she jolted in alarm.

"P-Pack?" she said, striving for calm. "N-Now?"

"Aye, lass," he said, his eyes glinting with amusement and challenge. "I leave tomorrow morning. We'll be wed as soon as we get to Scotland. I'd make haste if I were you."

"Anderson, you brute," Bonnie exclaimed, rushing over in an absolute fury. "You can't expect her to leap to do your bidding. I know you're an unfeeling beast, but if the poor fool has lost her senses enough to agree to marry you, the least you can do is give her a few weeks to get used to the idea and for her friends to see her off."

"What, and give her time to think better of it?" he said, shaking his head at her. "I'm nae so foolish as all that, lassie."

"No, it's quite all right, Bonnie," Ruth said, astonished by how calm she was now, or perhaps that was shock setting in? She felt rather numb. "Mr Anderson is right. There's little point in dillydallying, though my father will want to speak to you about the dowry, no doubt."

"Lass, if the fellow will give me fifty thousand pounds there's little I will object to, so long as I keep control of where and how it's spent."

"I have my own money and property," Ruth said warily. "That will not be a part of the dowry."

Anderson waved this off. "I'm nae greedy. What's yours will remain yours, ye'll spend it as ye see fit, though I wish ye luck trying at Wildsyde."

"W-Wildsyde?" Ruth stammered.

"Wildsyde Castle," Bonnie said, the anxiety shining in her eyes. "That's where he'll take you. Oh, Ruth. It's such a long way away. Are you sure you haven't made a horrible mistake? You can make him wait, you know. For fifty thousand pounds he ought to spend a month on his knees thanking you from the bottom of his black heart," she added, glaring at the towering Scot.

Anderson shrugged, unconcerned, though something dark and wicked glinted in his expression for just a moment as he caught Ruth's eye. "Ach, I've nae objection to getting on my knees for my wife," he said, suddenly the picture of innocence.

Why then, the words turned Ruth a searing shade of scarlet, she wasn't quite sure.

"Tomorrow morning will be acceptable, Mr Anderson," she said, seeking sanctuary in her best businesslike tone. "I think we have taken up enough of my friends' time, however. If you would care to come with me, I shall take you to my father. The sooner the details are tied up the better."

Having said her piece, she embraced Bonnie and made her swear to write to her, kissed Matilda and said the same, and swept out of the room before she entirely lost her composure.

***

Bonnie watched Ruth go with Gordon Anderson following behind and promptly burst into tears.

"Oh, love," Jerome said, and tugged her back into his arms. She buried her face in his cravat and sobbed.

"I-I'm s-sorry," she stammered. "I can't seem to stop crying. I'm n-never usually such a watering pot."

"It's the baby," he said, his voice reassuring as he stroked her back in soothing circles. "I hear it makes women very emotional."

Suddenly you could have heard a pin drop and Bonnie looked up at him at the precise moment he too remembered Matilda was in the room. She was staring at them both, wide-eyed.

"I'm sorry, M-Matilda," Bonnie said, mortified and ashamed that she'd brought this scandal into her friend's house.

"Oh, Bonnie. You little fool," Matilda said with a sigh, before opening her arms to her. "Whyever didn't you tell me?"

Jerome took himself off and pretended to be terribly interested in something outside the window whilst Bonnie and Matilda hugged and sobbed. Once they seemed to have gotten a grip of themselves, he came back and Bonnie felt her throat tighten again as he took her hand.

"Well, love. Ruth's not the only one who must pack. I'd like to be married in the chapel at Holbrooke, if you've no objection?"

Bonnie shook her head, too miserable to say a word. She was ruining her best friend's life. He wasn't ready to marry and become a father, she knew that, but he'd do it because it was the right thing to do. Misery welled up inside her and she'd never hated herself more.

"Will your m-mother be there?" she asked, knowing she was a coward but wanting to put it off as long as possible.

"No," he said gently, understanding in his eyes. "She's come up to town, and Jasper and Harriet won't be back from honeymoon for a while. We'll have the place to ourselves, for a few days at least. Then we must come back and face her."

Bonnie nodded. He wouldn't risk speaking to her first, not knowing just how hard Lady St Clair was likely to take the news. Once it was done, she'd have to accept there was no undoing it. Then she'd hate Bonnie forever. Oh well. It wasn't as if she was unused to being unwanted. She'd survived this far, hadn't she? So long as no one ever made their child feel less than wanted, never made them feel they didn't belong, or weren't good enough, well, then Bonnie could stand the rest.

"I should come with you," Matilda said. "It's not right for Bonnie to be alone on her wedding day. She should have a friend with her. I'll not stay," she added. "But I don't want her to feel alone, because she isn't." She turned and faced Bonnie. "They'd all come, if you asked them to."

Bonnie smiled, knowing it was true. "I know," she said. "And that helps a great deal, but I don't want anyone there, Matilda.

Perhaps, when we come back to town, we could have a little celebration, like we did for Aashini. That would be nice."

Matilda frowned, her blue eyes troubled. "But, Bonnie..."

"Please, Matilda," she said, her voice cracking. She didn't know how to explain that she wanted no one there to witness what she'd done, to see firsthand the trouble she'd caused the only man she'd ever loved, would ever love.

"Very well," Matilda said, though Bonnie could tell she was a little hurt.

Bonnie hugged her tightly. "Thank you," she said, meaning it with all her heart. "You've been so kind to me, all of you. Please tell the others how... how very foolish I've been. I'd rather not have to explain it myself."

"Oh, love." Matilda hugged in return, just as tightly, and then let go. "Well, then," she said briskly. "We'd best see about packing your things."

Matilda hurried out of the room, leaving Bonnie alone with Jerome once more.

"Bonnie?"

Bonnie turned to look at him, and fixed a smile to her face. The poor man was sacrificing his future to marry a girl he'd never wanted, and to saddle himself with a child he didn't want either, not yet anyway. The very least she could do was look pleased about it.

"Are you all right?"

"Of course," she said, forcing her voice to sound bright and cheery. "We're to be married. I'm the happiest girl in the world."

Chapter 13

Dear Jasper,

*I thought I'd best write and tell you at once.
I've gotten myself into a dreadful fix, just as
you warned me I would. There's no getting out
of it, Jaz. I've been such a bloody fool…*

**— Excerpt of a letter from Mr Jerome
Cadogan to Jasper Cadogan, The Earl of St
Clair.**

30th October 1814. Holbrooke House, Sussex.

They travelled to Holbrooke House the same day and were
married the following afternoon. Jerome was everything that was
kindness and charm and Bonnie did her utmost to be her usual self.
She ought to be happy. It was everything she'd ever dreamed of.
She was marrying the man she loved, and they had a child on the
way. It would be the beginning of the big happy family she'd
always longed to be a part of. Yet, how could it be? How could
their family be built on love and happiness when Jerome didn't
want her? Not as his wife, at least. She was unsuited to his life, she
knew that. His interest in her had been an aberration; she'd been a
novelty among all the slender blondes who'd captured his heart as
she'd failed to do. Even all those prettier girls hadn't been able to
hold him for long, but at least they'd had his love for a short while.
He was famous for falling in love at the drop of a hat, yet he'd
never fallen for Bonnie. Not even close. It wasn't as if she hadn't

been given the chance, either. She'd tried and failed, because she wasn't what he wanted.

If she hadn't come along, he'd still be free and enjoying life. Once his wild oats had been sown, he would have settled down with a charming young lady who knew how to entertain, to please his mama and make him proud when they were out in public together. Bonnie couldn't do that. She was too loud and uncouth. She was too much in every sense. Even her body was vulgar. Her curves were the generous proportions desirable in a woman of easy virtue, the kind you tumbled and forgot about, not an elegant lady you made your wife.

Bonnie struggled to imagine attending dinner parties with him and making polite conversation instead of putting her foot in her mouth. She tried to imagine a life where he wasn't always on edge, waiting for her to say or do something outrageous and put him to shame.

She'd seen the letter he'd written to his brother. Oh, she hadn't meant to snoop, but she'd come across it, the top section not properly folded over, and she'd seen the opening lines. She'd not pried further; it wasn't as if she needed to read any more. It was nothing she hadn't known.

There's no getting out of it, Jaz. I've been such a bloody fool...

Her heart constricted.

"Come on, wife," Jerome said, snapping her out of her thoughts. "I want to have my wicked way with you."

He leered at her like a theatrical villain and she laughed, for what else could she do? He was trying so hard to be kind, to act as though he wasn't sorry, as though he wished he had never laid eyes on her.

"You've hardly eaten a thing," he said, looking around at the lovely spread the housekeeper had put out for them. They'd set the poor woman on her ears, arriving as they had and announcing their imminent marriage. Bonnie had done her best to ignore the stares and the whispers from the appalled staff. She knew what they thought, and they were right. She'd trapped him. Perhaps she'd not meant to, but she had, and so now she must bear the gossip.

"I'm not hungry," she said, pushing her plate away. "It's been such a lovely day and I'm too excited."

His expression softened, and he took her hand. "Truly, love? I know it can't have been what you dreamed of, but it seemed like the best thing to do. If you conceived the first time we…." Bonnie smiled to herself as a tinge of colour rose to his cheeks. How funny to see Jerome blush, of all people. "Well, the thing is, that's over six weeks ago and I'd rather not make things too obvious."

"Oh, I think they're quite obvious enough," she said and then looked away as his smile faltered. The words had sounded far more bitter than she'd intended. Oh, Lord, she must watch her mouth. Whatever happened, Jerome must believe her wildly happy. He'd sacrificed so much for her; it was the least she could give in return. "But didn't you say something about having your wicked way with me?"

She flashed him a naughty grin and got to her feet, running from the room. He caught her before she made it to the door, pulled her into his arms, and kissed her.

Oh.

At least there was this. Perhaps as long as this fire blazed between them he wouldn't regret every aspect of their marriage. She hoped it didn't fade too quickly. Bonnie melted into his embrace, truly feeling as though her bones had become molten with desire.

"Oh, Bonnie," he breathed, kissing a path down her neck before returning to her mouth. "Oh, love. I've thought of nothing but this, of you… since the last time we were together. God, how I missed you."

Bonnie closed her eyes against the prickle of tears. How good he was, how sweet and kind to say such lovely things. He sounded so sincere she could almost believe him. Almost.

There's no getting out of it, Jaz. I've been such a bloody fool...

Jerome broke away from her, breathing hard. "We need a bed," he said, a devilish glint in his eyes now. "It's our wedding night and I'm not about to scandalise the staff by having you on the dining table, and I shall if we don't get a move on." He grabbed hold of her hand and towed her from the room, pulling her towards the staircase.

Bonnie laughed and ran after him, wishing with all her heart that he was as happy as he pretended to be, but if he could pretend, then so could she. She would pretend to be happy, pretend to be the perfect wife and mother, and pretend she didn't know that her husband regretted marrying her, and his family were ashamed of her. There were worse things, she was sure. Only right at his moment, she couldn't think what they were.

***

Dear Jasper,

I thought I'd best write and tell you at once. I've gotten myself into a dreadful fix, just as you warned me I would. There's no getting out of it, Jaz. I've been such a bloody fool in my life until now, and I know you won't understand this, but I thank God for it.

If I hadn't acted so badly, I would never have ruined Bonnie, would never have gotten a babe on her - yes, do you despise me? - and she might have gone back to Scotland and married Gordon bloody Anderson before I realised the truth.

I went to get her, to do the honourable thing and marry her and all the way there I felt like a lamb to the slaughter, such a burden of responsibility weighed me down. How appalling to have a wife I'd not wanted and a child too. A child? Me? I wanted to weep with terror I was in such a panic.

And there I was, proposing to her, when this huge bloody Highlander comes barging in and threatens to take Bonnie away from me, because she'd been promised to him by Morven.

Jasper, I've never been so afraid in all my life.

Suddenly it was so clear to me, what my life would be like if Bonnie was not a part of it. It was bleak and empty and devoid of life and laughter. I've been wretched these past weeks without her, but it was only in the moment I feared I would lose her that I understood why. I love her. I love her with all my heart, and I beg that you will forgive me for the scandalous way I've gone about this but if you must punish someone, punish me.

Bonnie is not so tough as she appears. She's been so alone her whole life and she's desperate for a family. She needs to be loved and accepted, and if she feels you are ashamed of her, it will hurt her terribly, more than you can realise, and that would kill me. Please make her welcome, no reproaches, I beg of you. This is all my doing, not hers, and I want to make her happy more than anything.

Forgive me for rambling on so, and for talking of feelings may God forgive me. Wish me happy Jaz.

Your ever dreadful brother,

J

Jerome slammed the bedroom door behind them and pulled Bonnie into his arms, staring down at her. There was anxiety in his heart, though how there was room for it he couldn't understand. How stupid he'd been for such a long time, how blind. He'd longed for her company all the time they'd been apart, but he'd thought he'd just missed his friend, missed their madcap adventures. None of his other friends amused him like Bonnie did, none of them made him glad to be doing whatever it was they were doing, whether it be one of her diabolical schemes or just sitting, talking and laughing. God, she made him laugh like no one else ever had. He'd never realised, though, never even suspected that she'd been stealing into his heart a little farther every day.

He'd not realised it right up to the moment she'd told Gordon Anderson that they were not engaged to be married. She'd not wanted to marry him either, of course, though Jerome could hardly blame her; the fellow was barely civilised. Yet, the man knew Bonnie well, and she him, and terror had struck Jerome's heart at the dreadful possibility that she might run back home and be among those she knew.

He'd been an utter bastard to announce her condition in front of Anderson, the man she'd been promised to by her guardian, but he'd not been about to risk losing her. She was his, his child was even now growing inside of her, and the thought of that made tenderness well up inside him until his throat grew tight. They'd made a child and, though the idea still made his heart thud with fear, it was not the same now. It was fear of failing to be all that he wanted to be for his child when he felt such a swell of love for them already, a wave of protectiveness sweeping over him so fierce his vision blurred.

"Bonnie," he said, pulling her to him and kissing her with everything he had, everything he felt, fighting to keep his emotions in check as happiness and desire rose inside him. He'd already made a mull of this. A shabby hole-in–the-wall affair of a wedding when she'd no doubt dreamed of a church and a pretty dress, and her friends wishing her well. He'd do better from now on, he swore it. He was to be a husband and a father, and he'd make certain he could be relied upon. Not that he was about to become dull and boring, Bonnie would hate him if he did that. His father had been both a charming rogue and a loving husband and father. Now, there was a fine example of a man. Jerome's heart ached with the need to speak to his father. He'd know just what to do, what to say, but never mind. He wasn't a boy any longer; he'd figure it out a bit at a time. No doubt he'd make a lot of mistakes, but Bonnie would forgive him because she loved him.

Yet there was a tiny corner of his heart that doubted it. She wasn't happy. He knew it, despite the laughter and the way she looked at him with her heart in her eyes. She was pretending, and he didn't know why. Was it simply the baby? No doubt she was terrified. He certainly was. Being a father was daunting enough, but thinking of all the things that might go wrong during the birth made his blood run cold. What if he lost her?

He held her tighter, as if he could keep the world at bay and protect her from everything with his embrace.

"Oh, love, you're mine. There's no getting away now." He pulled back and grinned at her, holding her sweet face between his hands. "Mrs Cadogan," he said, kissing her nose. "How well that sounds, and how lovely you are, but you're wearing too many clothes."

"Well, help me do something about it, then," she said, saucy as ever.

Jerome spun her around and began unbuttoning and unlacing and throwing garments hither and yon until she was naked before him. His breath caught as he stared down at her, and he placed the palm of his hand over her stomach.

"My son," he said, his voice reverent.

"Your daughter," she corrected, and he laughed and then frowned as he saw the change in her.

"You've lost weight."

She grinned and turned in a circle for him. "I have. At least I'm slim for my wedding night, but you'd best make the most of it. I'll be fat as a whale soon enough. Well, more so than usual."

"Bonnie," he said, grabbing hold of her wrist and tugging her closer. "You're beautiful, and you ought not be worrying about such things. Certainly not now, and never on my account." He cupped one full breast and his body tightened with anticipation at the soft, warm weight against his palm. "I love your curves. You're gorgeous. Perfect."

She laughed and shook her head. "Stop trying so hard. We're married, for heaven's sake, and you never felt the need to woo me before, so there's no reason on earth to bother now."

"I mean it," he began, disturbed by her manner, but then she pressed her body against his and tugged at his neck, pulling his mouth down to meet hers, and anything he might have said was lost in the frantic thundering of his heart and the need to be inside her, now, at once.

This, his heart cried as they tumbled to the bed, this was what love felt like. It was so easy with her; no pretences, no games. She'd given herself to him fully and unashamedly from the start, but he'd been too stupid to recognise what he held in his arms. No longer. It had taken him a while to come to his senses, but he was alert now and he knew how rare this was, how real this was, how different from anything else he'd ever known.

He joined them together and the pleasure of it was so fierce he wanted to weep and to laugh all at once. It was overwhelming…

everything he felt for her, for their child. It was more than he could contain, more than he could ever express, but he did his best, worshipping her with his body as he'd promised to do when they'd spoken their vows. *I'll make you happy*, he promised her silently as she cried out his name and shattered beneath him. *I'll love you both and keep you both safe and make you happy. I swear it.*

Chapter 14

Dear Jerome,

Harriet is beside herself with joy. You are to tell Bonnie at once that she is delighted with her new sister and the prospect of a niece or nephew. For my part, I only ever wanted to see you happy. If Bonnie is the one for you, then we shall welcome her with open arms. Anyone who loves you as we do can expect our unstinting support and loyalty.

I'm a little irritated that you felt the need to provide mother with a grandson with quite such alacrity, however. I had hoped to be the first to do so. Just how much of a head start did you take, you cad?

You will be pleased to know that Mother is visiting Aunt Agatha. Aunt has been unwell and demanded immediate attention, as is her way. This means if you keep your head down at Holbrooke you've at least a couple of weeks' peace before the storm breaks. Enjoy it while you may.

— Excerpt of a letter from Jasper Cadogan, The Earl of St Clair to Mr Jerome Cadogan.

18th November 1814. St Clair's London Residence, St James.

They stayed at Holbrooke House for as long as they dared but couldn't dally any longer. Jasper had written to tell his brother that Lady St Clair would be back in London at the end of the week. The staff at Holbrooke were both loyal and discreet, but Jerome said he could not risk Lady St Clair discovering the news from anyone else. Bonnie could hardly blame him. She'd likely be furious enough as it was without that indignity.

The weeks they'd shared had been idyllic, and if Bonnie had not known the truth it would have been so terribly easy to believe that Jerome really did love her and was glad to have married her. Jasper and Harriet's words of support had gladdened her heart, but she knew they were just being kind for Jerome's sake. Harriet was a dear friend, but even she must know what a dreadful *mésalliance* this was. She was just too kind to say so.

Anyway, as with all good things, their blissful little idyll was at an end and now Bonnie must face reality.

She could see the change in him the moment they left Holbrooke, the tension and worry that filled his blue eyes. He kept darting glances at her when he thought she wasn't looking, and she could only imagine what he was thinking. Like her, perhaps he had allowed himself to enjoy the time they'd shared without considering the future. He'd enjoyed the freedom to bed her as and when he wished, but now reality had struck, and he'd remembered that he was stuck with her. He'd remembered how unsuitable she was and how furious his mother would be, how sick with disappointment.

At least her own sickness had abated. Though her appetite had not yet returned, she was no longer forced to spend the early part of the morning hunched over a bowl.

As if he'd heard her thoughts, Jerome nudged her, and she turned to see him holding out a slice of apple. It was neatly peeled and cut, and she saw he'd opened the picnic they'd brought with them for the journey, although he'd only closed it an hour ago.

"I'm not hungry," she protested.

"I know, love, but you hardly ate a bite earlier and only that tiny bit of toast at breakfast. It's not good for the baby."

Bonnie gave a resigned little huff of impatience but couldn't help smiling at him. He was such a dear man and was trying so hard. Yet it only made her even more miserable to know that it was just that, he was *trying,* trying to make the most of a bad situation. Well, she'd not make it worse. She'd promised herself and him. So she poked her tongue out at him and snatched the apple from his hand, eating it and three more slices besides, though it sat in her throat like a rock and made her feel ill.

She certainly felt no better when they arrived at the St Clair's London home. It was horribly grand and the staff were a deal starchier than at Holbrooke. At least there she'd been made to feel welcome after their initial shock. Perhaps because the staff had eyes in their heads and had seen the path she and Jerome were on firsthand. In London she was a heavy blow to them, a vulgar little nobody with no family to speak of and a reputation for being no better than she ought to be. No doubt they'd heard, as everyone had heard, that her guardian had given her a generous dowry—considering she was a nobody—just in the hope someone would be desperate enough to take her off his hands.

Oh, they were polite enough when Jerome gave them the news, and they made all the right noises. Not so when he was not around. There were whispers, spoken just loudly enough for her to catch, not to mention the way they looked down their noses at her, as if she was the servant here. Even her poor maid, Agnes, was treated like a pariah and given the cold shoulder. She could almost feel the air of anticipation filling the place as they got word Lady St Clair would arrive that morning. No doubt they expected her to throw Bonnie out and have the marriage annulled. She wouldn't be surprised. Truthfully, she wouldn't entirely blame the woman, she thought as she smoothed her hand over her belly. There was a small but definite swell now and she smiled despite herself. How would she feel if her own son was taken in by the wrong sort of woman, one who threw herself at him and got herself with child to force his hand? Bonnie sighed, knowing only too well the answer to that question.

She looked up from her place beside the fire to watch her husband pace. He looked tense and unhappy and her heart bled for the misery she'd caused him. She knew how much he wanted his mother to be proud of him, and she knew their marriage and the reason for it would only bring him shame. Yet it had to be faced, and at least she could stand beside him and defend him. She'd not let Lady St Clair think ill of him. She would tell the woman it had been all her, and that she'd planned to trap him from the start. It wasn't as if it would make any difference; Lady St Clair would think that in any case, so Bonnie might as well shield Jerome from some part of the blame. At least she was used to such censure.

"She's here."

Bonnie got to her feet, the book she'd been pretending to read sliding from her nerveless fingers, disregarded. Her heart was hammering, and her skin felt clammy, hot and cold all at once. *Stop it,* she scolded herself. *You've faced Morven in a fury, you've faced Gordon Anderson. Lady St Clair is no more frightening or overbearing than they are.* Except that Bonnie rather thought she might be. Perhaps she wouldn't rant and rage and rattle the walls with her shouting and bellowing, but Bonnie suspected she wouldn't need to.

"Right." Jerome tugged at his waistcoat and ran a hand over his hair before facing her. "How do I look?"

"As handsome as always," Bonnie said, meaning it with all her heart. He was so beautiful, and she loved him so much. If only she could spare him this mess altogether, she would.

He grinned at her, though this time it didn't quite reach his eyes. "Wish me luck," he said, leaning in for a kiss.

She ducked away. "What? No, I'm coming with you," she said at once, but Jerome only shook his head and planted a kiss on her cheek instead.

"Oh, no. Not on your life. I'll introduce you a little later, once she's gotten over the initial shock. It'll be the baby and the fact we married behind her back she'll be most furious about, and I'd just as soon you not be there to watch me get raked over the coals."

"No!" Bonnie exclaimed, clutching at his arm. "We did this together. I won't let you face her alone. It isn't fair."

Jerome's face softened, and he pulled her close. "Love, I won't have you or the baby distressed, not for a moment," he said, before giving her a kiss on the nose. "Now sit down and don't worry, or go out and get some fresh air if you prefer, only don't fret, I beg of you. Mother will be cross, I know, but she's not an ogre. Once the shock has worn off, it will all be well."

There was nothing else to be said. He'd made up his mind and nothing she could do to change it. The last thing she wanted was for Lady St Clair to walk in and discover them in the middle of a row. So she watched him go like a good little wife and tried to sit and not worry, but it was impossible. After ten minutes she was beside herself and decided a walk was a good idea.

Once she had fetched Agnes, and they'd wrapped up in warm coats and bonnets, for it was a bitterly cold day, they made their way to the front door. Bonnie paused as the sound of angry voices drifted from the library and her heart clenched.

"Come along," Agnes said, her voice kind but firm as she moved Bonnie towards the door. "We both need some air."

"Best start packing, I reckon," came an amused voice from one of the footmen in an undertone.

The butler said nothing, and did not reprimand his staff, just turned his disdainful expression away from them, though he must have heard.

Agnes glared at them as Bonnie stiffened, but she knew better than to react, to give anyone the satisfaction of knowing they'd hit their mark. So the two of them walked arm in arm, out of the front door and into the street. They carried on in silence for a while until Bonnie turned to her maid.

"Thank you," she said simply.

Agnes smiled. She was a widow, her grief etched into a face that had seen life. A woman in her early forties, with greying hair swept back in a tidy bun, and kind eyes, Bonnie had been grateful for her steadfast support in the past weeks.

Employing Agnes Lacey had certainly been one of her better decisions, Bonnie reflected. During the brief interview when they'd met, Bonnie had told her, point blank, that she was unmarried and pregnant and, if that was too much for her to deal with, she'd find someone else. Agnes had just frowned for a moment and then shrugged. "I raised six brothers and sisters, helped Mama birth two of them. Reckon I can look after you, miss."

And that had been that.

"She won't cast you out," Agnes said. "She's a strong woman from what I can tell, for all everyone thinks her a featherbrain. Perhaps she'll not like it, but she'll make the best of it."

Bonnie nodded and walked on. Not that she knew where they were going. Agnes didn't ask her, just walked at her side, silent but reassuring, and Bonnie was thankful. Oh, how Jerome must be cursing himself. He must wish he'd never met her.

Her mind drifted back to that night, the night she'd cut off her hair and dressed as a young man. Goodness, what would his mother make of that? She felt the blush sear her cheeks as if she'd just confessed all. She pushed the thought aside and remembered the night instead, remembered demanding that Jerome undo the bindings she'd wrapped her breasts under, even though she'd known where it would lead. He'd tried to stop her, tried to tell her no, but she'd insisted, and then she'd led him on, practically demanding that he take her virginity. Her skin burned hotter with the shame of it and tears pricked at her eyes. She blinked hard, trying to clear them. They'd turned onto a busy street now, lined with shops, though she had no idea where they were.

All at once she was weary, weary and heartsick. She wanted to lie down in the dark and cry for every foolish thing she'd ever done, for the loss of everything she'd hoped for, yet surely she wasn't so weak? She put up her chin, breathing in deeply, trying to calm herself but her mind was a muddle and she felt dizzy. Perhaps she ought to have eaten more, as Jerome had insisted.

She stopped, putting a hand to her head as it began to pound.

"Mrs Cadogan?" Agnes said, but then there was a shout and they both turned at a commotion further along the street.

"Stop, thief!" someone screamed, and suddenly everyone was jostling and pushing, and a boy shot out from the crowds, directly at them. He stumbled as he went, tripping over someone's foot and barrelling straight into Bonnie. She gasped, her heel catching on the edge of the pavement. There was no time to right herself and suddenly she was falling backwards, and there were screams and shouts and the terrified shriek of horses, and then… nothing.

Chapter 15

Dear Sir,

*I most sincerely beg your pardon for the
lateness of this month's rent, but I must ask if
you could be so very kind as to give me a few
more days…*

**— *Excerpt of a letter from Miss Jemima
Fernside to her landlord.***

19th November 1814. St Clair's London Residence, St James.

"Am I forgiven?"

Jerome stood staring at the tense figure standing by the
window. His mother was still a beautiful woman, though her
golden hair had faded a little. He felt, as he always felt, too
inadequate to be her son. He held his breath as she turned her blue
eyes upon him, considering.

"I have despaired of you these past years, Jerome," she said,
and Jerome swallowed, wishing he didn't have to look into her
eyes as she told him what a disappointment he was. "I believed
you would never grow up, never find whatever it was you were
looking for. When you began this association with Miss Campbell,
I assumed it would be like all the others; that you would make a
fool of yourself, and us, and Jasper would be obliged to pay vast
sums of money to keep it all quiet and make the girl go away."

"You'll not make her go away, mother," he said, unable to keep silent though he tried his best to moderate the fury in his voice. "I'm not a child, whatever you may think of my behaviour. She's my wife and I love her. She's more important to me than anything else. I'm going to be a father, and I would far rather that you welcome her and our child into this family, for it will hurt her as much as me if you do not. But I cannot force you. I can make my own choices, though, and in that case I will be obliged to leave and make my own way. I'll not give her up, not for anything. No matter what you say or do."

Jerome squared his shoulders, waiting for the onslaught, trying to prepare his heart for what must surely come, but his mother just sighed with annoyance.

"I don't believe I'd finished," she said tartly.

Jerome blushed. Few people saw this side of his mother. Most people saw the elegant, fashionable lady with a frivolous passion for frocks and gossip, a tinkling laugh that could still make men turn their heads, and an attention span that made her appear something of a hen-wit. Though Jerome had always felt he stood in Jasper's shadow, everyone knew she adored her sons who—as far as they knew—could do no wrong. The truth was a little different. Although they had been allowed a great deal of freedom, likely a deal too much, their mother had always had a sixth sense when they were in any real trouble, and neither of them regarded one of her set downs as something to be shrugged off. Her opinion mattered to them, and knowing she was cross or disappointed always stung.

"I beg your pardon," Jerome said, wishing he didn't feel as if he was eight years old and had been caught stealing from the kitchens again.

"If you had been paying attention, instead of disregarding every word that I uttered, you might have realised I said, *I believed* you would never grow up, *I assumed*. Perhaps my command of the English language is not what it ought to be, for I was certain those were all past tense." She glowered at him a little and then her expression softened. "Foolish boy," she said, shaking her head. "You have changed, and why or how that happened is not entirely clear to me, but I think this young woman has had a hand in it. I could see how miserable you were once you parted, and I suspected then that this time was different, that *you* were different."

Jerome blinked hard, relief making his emotions tumble about in his chest as he nodded.

"I am different, and she has changed me. I know you'd hoped that I might make a match with Lady Helena, but...."

His mother waved this away with a laugh. "Oh, perhaps, but only because I despaired of seeing you make another mistake. But, if you love Bonnie and she's not just another infatuation, *and she loves you*, then there is no mistake. I am not such a snob as to put our illustrious family's bloodline before my son's happiness. Besides which, Jasper is the earl, and he's married well, so you ought to have the freedom to do as you please. You have my blessing," she said, smiling as Jerome felt all the tension leave his body in a rush.

He felt giddy with relief and quite desperate to see Bonnie and tell her the good news.

"Come here," his mother said, holding out her arms.

Jerome went to embrace her, still feeling a little startled that he was so much bigger than she was. She smelled familiar, of lavender and fresh cut greenery and it was so comforting he had to blink hard to clear his vision. She hugged him tighter, and he was eight years old in his heart when he considered how much that meant to him.

"I'm still angry with you, mind," she said, moving away and wagging her finger. "Getting a child on the poor girl and then marrying her behind my back. Oh, Jerome, I'm so furious I could throttle you."

"You've made that very clear, Mother," he said ruefully. "But may we put it behind us now? Bonnie will be so worried and it's not good for the baby."

She reached up and cupped his cheek, her eyes filling with tears. "There's my boy, a devil and an angel all wrapped up in one." She shook her head. "Yes, yes, of course, go and get your lovely bride and let me welcome her properly. We have a great deal to talk about."

Jerome beamed at her and hurried from the room, heading back to the library, only to find it empty. He went out again, hailing the butler: a grim-faced, miserable sod who'd always frightened him as a child. The tetchy old fogram must be of an age with Methuselah by now.

"Where's my wife, Potts?" he demanded.

"I believe she has gone out, sir," the butler replied. "She took her maid and left on foot perhaps half an hour ago."

"Damnation," Jerome muttered and began to walk back to tell his mother when there was a commotion at the front door, which flew open as the butler exclaimed in annoyance.

Miss Lacey, Bonnie's maid almost fell through it. Her face was tear-stained and her bonnet all askew, and Jerome's heart lurched in his chest.

"Oh, Mr Cadogan!" she cried, running to him. "You must fetch a doctor, at once!"

Before Jerome could ask, a dark shadow fell over the doorway and a man appeared, carrying Bonnie in his arms.

"Oh, God...." Jerome rushed forward, only dimly aware of his mother's voice behind him, shouting instructions as the entrance hall erupted into motion. "What have you done!" he bellowed, terror seizing his heart as he saw the wretched brute with his hands on Bonnie, and she was still, so very still.

"Oh, Mr Cadogan, it wasn't his fault, sir," the maid said, stepping between them. "She was pushed into the road. This gentlemen did everything he could to stop the horses, I swear he did."

Jerome looked at the fellow, to see he was white-faced with shock.

"I'm so sorry," the man said, his voice rough. "She came from nowhere. I tried...."

Jerome couldn't hear him, could hear nothing but the buzzing in his ears as he took her from the stranger's arms. She stirred as her head fell against his shoulder.

"Jerome," she said, her voice faint. "Oh, Jerome, the baby...."

***

Jasper jumped down from his horse, flinging the reins at the waiting servant and rushing up the steps to his house.

"Mother!" he exclaimed as she hurried towards him. "Where is he? What's happened?"

He'd dropped everything and rushed out of the door, though his mother's note had held little information beyond *your brother needs you, please come at once.*

He hadn't stopped to pack, leaving Harriet in charge of everything as he'd yelled for a horse and ridden back to town at breakneck speed. Now he was dusty and hot, despite the freezing weather, but cared for nothing but seeing Jerome.

"Oh, Jasper," she said, her lovely face crumpling as she ran to him. He embraced her, his heart hammering as he wondered what on earth had put her in such a state. He guided her into the library where they could speak privately.

His mother wiped her eyes and sat down as Jasper crouched before her and grasped one of her hands.

"Tell me," he pleaded, sick with anxiety.

"It's Miss Campbell, I mean… Bonnie. She left the house and took herself off for a walk whilst I was speaking to Jerome and… and I'm terribly afraid she heard me shouting at him and thought… but I wasn't shouting because of her, I wasn't. Only he's so irresponsible sometimes, but the way he spoke of her and he's been so tender with her, and he was trying to think of the baby and now… and now…."

She broke down again and Jasper took a deep breath, striving for patience.

"Mama, *please*! What has happened?"

His mother wiped her eyes again and nodded, gathering herself. "There was an accident," she said, her voice thick. "A pickpocket, I believe, he was rushing through the crowd to get away and he pushed Bonnie off the pavement and she f-fell in front of a carriage."

"Oh, God, no." Jasper felt his heart clench, imagining getting such news about his own wife.

"Yes," she said, choking the words out. "Thank God, she seems to be unharmed, just a concussion and some nasty bruises, thanks to the quick reactions of the driver, but… but she's lost the baby."

Jasper tried to swallow down the knot that had formed in his throat.

"Oh, Jasper," his mother said, her lovely eyes filled with tears. "He's devastated. He's blaming himself, b-but I cannot help but think it's my f-fault. If the child had not believed I disapproved of her so and feared my reaction…."

She couldn't continue and put her face in her hands.

"Nonsense," Jasper said, trying to keep his voice even though the world seemed terribly blurry. "Of course you would be cross, he behaved dreadfully and we both know it. He knows it too, but this is no one's fault. It's just a horrid accident. We must give thanks that Bonnie is not badly hurt."

She nodded. "I know, b-but I feel so guilty, and poor Jerome, he's been out of his mind. He loves her very much."

Jasper smiled. "I know," he said, patting her hand. "Where is he?"

"He spends every moment beside her, but the doctor came back to check on her just before you arrived, so I suppose he'll be pacing outside her door."

"I'd best go up, then." Jasper leaned in and kissed his mother's cheek. "No more tears," he scolded gently. "All will be well, I promise."

"You're a good man, Jasper," she said with a sigh. "And a good brother."

"So is he," Jasper replied, and went in search of Jerome.

***

Jerome sat beside his wife's bed as she slept. She was horribly pale, dark shadows visible beneath her eyes. Dear God, how fragile she was, and how close he'd come to losing her. Though the loss of their child was a sorrow that filled his heart to the brim, and hurt far more than he might have imagined, he knew losing her would have destroyed him.

Be thankful, he counselled himself, but it was hard to be thankful when their baby had been taken from them and Bonnie wouldn't look at him. She slept mostly, only waking for a brief time whilst the doctor came. Though Jerome had wanted him to wait, the doctor had disagreed and told him she must be given the news at once. So the doctor had explained that she had lost the baby, but that she was fit and healthy despite a few bruises, and there would be plenty of opportunities to have more.

Jerome had braced himself for tears that had never come, had waited for the doctor to leave so that he could go to her and comfort her, but she had turned away from him. She had closed her eyes and not said a word since.

She stirred now, and he sat up, reaching for her hand. "Bonnie," he said, forcing a smile to his face though he wanted to weep. "There you are, sleeping beauty. I thought you'd never wake up."

She blinked, staring at him, and then gently pulled her hand from his grasp.

"What time is it?" she asked.

Jerome frowned, his brain taking a moment to understand the mundane question. He fumbled for his pocket watch, staring at it for some time before he could answer her. "It's four thirty in the afternoon. Are you hungry? I think Cook mentioned something about chicken broth. She's made it specially."

Bonnie shook her head.

"Well, some tea, then," he suggested, feeling panic rise in his chest though he wasn't entirely sure why. "I could do with some. I'll send for tea and toast, and you liked that apricot jam, didn't you...? I'll ask—"

"I don't want tea, and I don't want toast," she said, and though the words were calm, there was an edge to them. "I want an annulment."

For a moment he just stared at her as the words made no sense to him. Try as he might, he couldn't make his brain understand what it was she meant, what she was saying, and then it sank in and his breath caught as the panic he'd been fighting down surged through him.

"An annulment," he repeated stupidly, sounding dazed and uncomprehending, which was entirely correct. It was as though someone had tilted the world on its axis, and everything had turned upside down, making no sense.

"Morven never gave his permission to our marriage," she said, so icily calm that he wanted to shake her. "He's my guardian. He ought to have been consulted."

"But you're of age," he said, fighting for breath, his heart thudding so hard he felt as if he'd run for miles and miles.

"No. In fact Morven controls my finances until I'm twenty-five unless I marry as he wishes."

"I know that!" he exclaimed, angry now. "As if I give a damn for a paltry five thousand pounds. I'd have married you no matter if it were five pounds or fifty thousand. It makes no odds to me."

"Nonetheless, we didn't get permission. That's grounds for an annulment."

"I don't give a damn if it's grounds for a stay in the Marshalsea, it's not bloody happening!" he shouted, utterly bewildered and hurt, so dreadfully hurt.

He wanted to hold her and comfort her and cry with her for the loss of their child, and she wanted... she wanted to get rid of him?

"Don't be a fool," she said, and she sounded so utterly weary he didn't know what to do, what to say.

"I'm not being a bloody fool!" he shouted, knowing he ought not to raise his voice but not having the least idea of what *to* do. "Why are you saying this? Are you trying to hurt me?"

She flinched, but at that moment the door opened and the doctor came to him, his expression stern.

"Mr Cadogan, I believe I told you that your wife needed peace and quiet and yet I can hear raised voices from the other end of the corridor."

"Well," Jerome said bitterly. "She wants so much peace and quiet she wants me gone. For good! Should I allow her that too?" he demanded, and then stormed from the room, barely stopping himself from slamming the door behind him.

He stood outside it for a long moment, too numb to speak, or to move, and then he sat in the chair that had been placed by the door for him as he'd refused to leave when the doctor was with Bonnie. How long he sat there with his head in his hands, he didn't know, but then he heard footsteps, and looked up to see Jasper coming towards him.

He paused in front of Jerome, his eyes filled with sorrow. "I'm so sorry," he said.

Jerome lurched awkwardly to his feet. Jasper drew him into a hug, and his composure cracked. Though it hurt his pride, his heart hurt far more, and he sobbed on his big brother's shoulder. Jasper said nothing, for which he was grateful.

"I'm sorry," he said, pulling away and rubbing his face with his handkerchief after such a humiliating display and loss of control. "Please forgive me."

"Don't be an ass, Jerry," Jasper said, smiling a little. "After what you've been through, you're entitled, and as if I give a damn. If it were Harriet, I'd be the same and you know it."

Jerome nodded, knowing that was true, and then met his brother's eyes. "But would Harriet demand an annulment?" he asked bitterly.

Jasper's mouth dropped open. "What?"

It took Jerome a moment to reply and, when he did, his voice wasn't entirely steady. "She doesn't want me," he said, giving a twisted smile. "After... After all of it. She doesn't want me. Realised what a bad bargain she made, I suppose," he quipped, though he wanted to break down again, not make jokes at his own expense.

Jasper stared at him and then shook his head. "No."

"Oh, I assure you, yes," Jerome replied tersely. "She was very clear about it." He sat down again, as he wasn't certain his legs were steady enough to do the job of keeping him upright.

"No," Jasper said again, harsher this time, as if that made everything all right.

"Damn it, Jasper, did you not hear what I said?"

"I heard," Jasper replied, and then crouched down in front of him. "I have a wealth of experience with bad-tempered women, Jerry," he said wryly. "And I saw for myself how besotted Bonnie was with you. She loves you, and that doesn't stop overnight. This isn't a change of heart, I'm sure of it. She's hurt. She's badly hurt, and she's lashing out or trying to protect herself, or perhaps you. Don't ask me which, because I'm certainly not clever enough to figure out what goes on in a woman's mind, but I'm telling you, she doesn't want an annulment."

"She doesn't?" Jerome asked, wanting with all his heart to believe his brother.

Jasper shook his head. "If there's one thing I've learned over the past months, it's that you must talk. You can't let her out of your sight until you know everything, every single reason, every single thought behind her demand for an annulment. You must force her to explain it to you, to reason it out. Good God, Jerry, I nearly lost Harriet because of what she heard me say to that arse Peter Winslow, and I never meant a word of it. If only I'd known we could have been married long before now, perhaps we'd already have children, but a ridiculous misunderstanding festered between us and kept us apart for years. Don't let the same stupid error ruin everything for you."

Jerome took a deep breath and considered Jasper's words, hope flickering to life.

"Thank you, Jaz," he said, meaning it with all his heart.

"That's what big brothers are for, Little Breeches," he said, grinning at the nickname he'd tormented Jerome with for years.

Huffing out a laugh, Jerome regarded him with narrowed eyes. "I'll let you get away with that this once," he warned. "But next time I'm going to pound you."

"You can try," Jasper retorted, getting to his feet. He paused, and then ruffled Jasper's hair. "It'll be all right. Just keep calm and don't give up. Don't let her hide her feelings from you."

Jerome nodded. "I won't. I can promise you that."

Chapter 16

Dear Mr de Beauvoir,

It is three weeks since my last letter, and I admit I have been sunk into gloom waiting for a reply which never came. How cruel you are to me. I waited and waited for your letter and the devastating set down I felt certain you would give me and… nothing.

I can only think I must be a deal more provoking to regain your attention.

— Excerpt of a letter from Miss Minerva Butler to Mr Inigo de Beauvoir.

20ᵗʰ November 1814. St Clair's London Residence, St James.

"I'm afraid she won't see you."

Lady Helena nodded her understanding and handed Jerome the prettily wrapped box of comfits she'd brought. "Well, perhaps you could give those to her for me, and… and tell her I'm so sorry. Hug her for me, won't you, please?"

Jerome gave a smile that made her heart clench. "Of course."

"Are you all right?" she asked, knowing she ought not to. Her maid had retreated to sit in the corner of the room but, even if they were alone, she suspected he'd not tell her the truth. Men were so touchy about feelings and she doubted he'd thank her for the question, but it had been his child too. In fact, he seemed perfectly wretched, the poor fellow, and she rather felt he needed a hug as much as Bonnie did.

They both looked up as the parlour door opened and the obsequious butler who had fawned over her on arrival showed in another caller. A man.

As the newcomer stepped through the door, Helena turned to look at him with interest. He was tall and athletic looking, with broad shoulders, and he carried an extravagant bouquet of exotic blooms. He brought with him the clean, fresh scent of a cold winter's day and his dark hair gleamed with lighter gold highlights, as though the sun shone upon it, despite the grey November weather. Rather to her surprise, he ignored Helena completely and went straight to Jerome.

"Mr Cadogan," he said, and his voice was deep and pleasant, but not at all what she was used to. "I hope you will forgive the imposition, but I wanted to check on Mrs Cadogan. I confess I have not slept since that dreadful accident. I keep seeing it and trying to think of all the ways I might have prevented—"

"Please, don't distress yourself, Mr Knight," Jerome said, and that same weary smile appeared again. "I have heard several accounts of the accident now and the one thing everyone agrees on is that it would have been a great deal worse if not for your skill with the horses. You have nothing to reproach yourself for."

"And yet I feel sick with it," he said, and Helena thought the words sounded heavy with something that sounded like loathing. "Please, tell me, is she well? The babe...?"

"We lost the child," Jerome said, his voice very quiet. "But Mrs Cadogan is unharmed and making a good recovery. For that I am grateful indeed."

Mr Knight blanched and then ran a hand through his hair, his expression stark. Helena watched him, noticing the hand was scarred and work worn and realising then why the voice was not quite correct. He *almost* spoke like a gentleman, he *nearly* looked like a gentleman, but he was not one. She studied him closer, intrigued.

"I cannot tell you how sorry I am," he said, and Helena believed him, for the man looked utterly wretched. He seemed then to remember the lavish bouquet he carried. "I brought these for Mrs Cadogan, with my very best wishes. If there is ever anything I can do for you, either of you…."

"That is most kind, Mr Knight. I'll make certain my wife gets them. She'll be touched, I'm sure. Oh, but do forgive my ill manners." Jerome turned towards Helena. "Lady Helena, might I introduce you to our guest?"

Helena nodded, impatient for him to get on with it.

"Lady Helena, Mr Gabriel Knight. Mr Knight, this is Lady Helena Adolphus."

Mr Knight gave a stiff bow, barely acknowledging Helena before returning his attention to Jerome.

"I won't keep you any longer, Mr Cadogan. I hope you will remember my offer. If ever there is anything I can do for you, you need only ask it. I beg you will, sir, for my conscience will not sit easy if you do not. Good day, Mr Cadogan, Lady Helena."

He left, once more barely acknowledging Helena's presence.

"The poor man is beside himself," she said, once the door had closed behind him.

Jerome nodded, ringing the bell for a servant. "I know. He feels responsible, though everyone said there wasn't a thing he could do. It was a miracle it wasn't a great deal worse, from what I've been told, and I've him to thank for that."

"What did he mean, if there was ever anything he could do for you? Who is he that he can make such an offer?"

Jerome looked at her in surprise. "You've not heard of him?"

Helena shook her head.

"He's vastly wealthy. Owns half of London from what I can tell, property all over the place. Hotels and shops and the like. It appears he's trying to get a foothold in the *ton,* but of course no one will give him the time of day."

"No wonder, if he's so brusque with all the ladies he meets," she said lightly. "But no doubt I was not seeing him at his best. He's obviously overset by the accident, and who can blame him? I shan't hold it against him. A generous fellow, too… such beautiful hot house blooms in November. They must have cost a pretty penny." She patted Jerome's arm, smiling at him. "Please try to persuade Bonnie to let me visit, or Matilda if she prefers, but I feel she ought to talk to one of us."

Jerome nodded. "So do I," he said, and she heard the bleak note to the words.

"Courage," she said, wishing she knew what to say, or do, to make it better, but she rather doubted there was anything that could do that. What words could ease such a loss? "I can come at any time, only tell me when. Now, I'd best be off, the Peculiar Ladies are meeting at Matilda's, and I shall be late as usual."

"You're too good, Lady Helena, thank you."

She gave a little laugh and shook her head as she moved towards the door. "Don't be silly," she said over her shoulder. "I'm not at all good, and you know it. That's why Bonnie and I get on so well."

***

Matilda looked around at the Peculiar Ladies and smiled, relieved at how many had come.

Prue, Minerva and Alice sat on one sofa, Aashini, Harriet and Helena on another. To her immense relief, Jemima had come today too and was perched on the chair closest to the fire. She seemed pale and far too thin, and the way she huddled closer to the flames made Matilda's maternal instincts all flare to attention.

Kitty was absent, as she was back in Ireland with Luke, though Matilda had written to her to keep her up to date with everything that had happened. She waited until the tea had been served and everyone had taken their pick of the delectable selection of cream cakes and sweet treats laid out for them.

"It seems so odd not to be meeting at Ruth's house," she said, casting a critical gaze over the laden table. "She always gives such delicious tea parties. I hope I've done you all justice?"

"More than justice," Alice said, reaching for another cake.

Matilda smiled, pleased that she'd taken to the idea of eating for two. She was such a tiny slip of a thing, but she had a very tidy little bump now and looked to be glowing with good health.

"But tell us everything," Alice added, her expression growing serious. "How is Bonnie, have you seen her? Oh, the poor dear, every time I think about it…." Her voice quavered and she put her plate aside and snatched up her reticule, searching until she found a handkerchief. "She m-must be so unh-happy," she sobbed.

Minerva put her arm around her and hugged her as Alice composed herself.

"Jerome is distraught," Harriet said, setting her teacup down. "I think he needs our support just as much as Bonnie. He doesn't know what to do for her, though he's trying so hard, and Jasper's wretched because he can't protect his brother from the hurt. Oh, it breaks my heart." She snatched off her spectacles and wiped her eyes.

"I agree. I called in on my way here," Helena said, pressing a handkerchief into Harriet's hand as she spoke. "She wouldn't see me, which I quite understand, only I hope she'll want to see one of us soon. Surely she needs her friends about her at such a time?"

Matilda shrugged. "I suppose everyone is different. We must give her time and make sure she knows we'll drop everything the moment she needs us. There's not much else we can do for the moment, other than write to her."

Everyone murmured their agreement and Matilda knew that they had all sent cards and flowers, rallying around Bonnie as best they could.

"But what of Ruth?" Minerva asked, the other reason for today's little gathering as everyone was worried out of their minds. "I've not had a word from her, have you?"

She watched as each of them shook their heads, apprehensive murmurs filling the room.

"I've written twice, with no reply," Prue said, her anxiety plain.

"I have a letter," Matilda said, taking it from the table beside her and holding it up. "She begs all of your forgiveness for not having written but... well, let me read it to you.

My dear Matilda,

Forgive me for not having written sooner, or for replying to all the letters that have arrived over the past few days. It is so comforting to know I am not forgotten and that all of my friends' thoughts and good wishes have travelled with me. Perhaps you would be so very kind as to read this letter to them at the next meeting of the Peculiar Ladies. Indeed I wish I could be there to tell you all everything, but I promise to write more soon and catch up with my correspondence.

I am now Mrs Ruth Anderson! How strange it sounds, and how very far away I am. It has all been rather a whirlwind and continues to be so. Wildsyde Castle is without a doubt the most beautiful place I have ever seen, if rather daunting. I adore the Highlands. I think perhaps I must have Scottish ancestry for it feels like coming home and I have only to look upon the breathtaking scenery outside my window to be utterly spellbound. The castle, as

Bonnie warned me, is in shockingly bad repair, however, and the staff are the most ramshackle, belligerent lot it has ever been my misfortune to lay eyes on. They call me 'Sassenach' and I do not feel it is a compliment. However, I do love a challenge and I intend to bring them kicking and screaming into the nineteenth century if it kills me. It feels a little medieval here, but nothing that time, money and good management cannot overcome.

Wish me luck ladies and do please forgive me for being such a dreadful correspondent but I hardly know whether I'm coming or going at present. I will endeavour to do better. In the meantime please be assured that I am reliant on your letters to keep me up to date with all your news. I love and miss you all and send hugs. Have a cream cake for me, dears.

Your devoted friend and Peculiar Lady,

Ruth."

Matilda closed the letter and looked around, wondering if they would notice what had been glaringly obvious to her.

"She doesn't mention him," Prue said, meeting Matilda's eyes.

"Not once," Harriet added as they all darted glances back and forth.

"Not even in passing."

"No mention of the wedding."

"Or the wedding night."

An uneasy silence filled the room.

"She sounded well enough," Alice ventured, a hopeful note to her voice. "Not overwhelmed or... or despondent."

"Yes," Matilda said, smiling, and wishing she could just accept that was true and put her worries for Ruth out of her mind. "Yes, she did. I'm sure she's quite all right."

"She's a very capable woman," Harriet added, though Matilda knew as well as they all did that Ruth might just be putting a brave face on it rather than admit her mistake. "She's strong and independent and intelligent. She's been running her father's household for years as her mother is such a featherbrain. If anyone can bring a chaotic household into order, it's Ruth. She's indefatigable."

"She's all of that," Matilda said, nodding and getting to her feet; "And I think we ought to raise a glass and toast her good health and happiness, and not with tea." She waved a bottle of French brandy at them and they all murmured their approval. It was utterly forbidden to unmarried young ladies and disapproved of for married ones, but they were hardly going to tell anyone. She poured them each a generous measure—to keep out the cold—and they raised their glasses.

"To Ruth," they said in unison

"To Ruth," Matilda agreed. *May you be happy and well, my friend.*

Once the brandy had been disposed of and the table rather depleted of cream cakes, they got onto any other business.

"I have a letter from Kitty," Harriet said, grinning, "who has given me custody of the hat and the dares."

There was a murmur of excitement around the room and the Peculiar Ladies who had not yet taken their dares flushed and fidgeted.

Everyone watched as Harriet fetched the hat and gave it a shake, the little slips of paper inside rustling as she did so.

"Well, who's first?" Harriet demanded. "You made me do it, you dreadful creatures, so don't think I won't get my own back."

"I feel rather odd," Helena said, putting a hand to her heart.

"Me!" Minerva squeaked, raising her hand, her lovely face flushed. "I think it's about time."

Jemima bit her lip and shook her head. "Oh, no," she said, looking like she might faint dead away. "Oh, no, I... I couldn't."

"Oh, to the devil with it, I'll do it too," Helena said, taking a deep breath. "Give me the hat," she demanded, as imperious as ever.

"She's *never* a duke's daughter," Prue laughed, to which Helena stuck her tongue out, thrusting her hand into the hat and swishing the paper back and forth before taking one.

She sat staring at the folded slip for a long moment before handing it to Aashini.

"You read it," she said, pressing the backs of her hands to her cheeks which were flushed now. "I feel sick."

Aashini took a deep breath and undid the paper. "Oh my." She gasped, darting a panicked look at Helena.

Helena wailed and bounced up and down on the seat, waving her hands at her cheeks which were now scarlet. "Oh, good heavens! What is it? What is it?" she shrieked.

"Drive your carriage past White's and wave to the gentlemen."

Helena's mouth dropped open.

"Oh, good Lord, Robert will kill you," Prue said, staring at her sister-in-law with wide eyes.

Whilst it was all well and good for a lady to drive herself about town, driving past the gentlemen's clubs of St James would be considered *fast*.

"B-But Prue, I must do it now," Helena said, thoroughly rattled. "What am I to do?"

Prue considered. "I am going to visit Robert's estate in Hampshire with him in the new year," she said, frowning. "If you must do it, and I suppose you must, then that would be your best opportunity. By the time he finds out we'll be miles away and that will give me a while to calm him down before he sees you again.

Also," she said, brightening a little. "It doesn't say *when* you must do it. If you went, say, very early in the morning, when most of the gentlemen have long since collapsed in a heap or gone home and everyone sensible is abed, it's likely no one will see you."

"Oh, but doesn't that go against the spirit of the thing?" Helena asked, biting her lip. "If I must do it, I think it ought to be done with flair."

Prue shrugged. "It's up to you, dear. Only do have a care; a dare ought to be thrilling and a little shocking, but not so much as to plunge one into hot water deep enough to drown in."

Helena nodded, but it was clear she was no longer attending the conversation, too lost in pondering what she would do.

"My turn," Minerva said, as Harriet moved closer and offered her the hat.

Matilda kept her mouth shut and just continued to watch the proceedings. With luck, two dares would be enough for the time being. She glanced at Jemima who returned a weak smile and knew she was hoping the same thing.

Harriet shook the hat, tossing the little slips of paper about as Minerva gathered her courage. "Here I go," she said, and plunged her hand into the hat.

Everyone stilled, waiting for Minerva to reveal her dare. The young woman closed her eyes for a moment, as if in prayer, and then unfolded the paper. A smile curved over her lovely mouth and it was clear that the dare suited her very well indeed.

"Well?" Matilda demanded.

Minerva sat up straighter, cleared her throat and read aloud. "Go somewhere you are not supposed to go."

"Why do I get the feeling you already know where you are going?" Matilda said, wondering if she ought to keep a closer eye on Minerva.

"Because I do," Minerva replied, an innocent expression in her eyes that fooled no one.

"Oh?" Prue asked, her tone eloquently saying exactly what Matilda had just been thinking. "Where?"

Minerva smirked and laid her hands neatly in her lap. "Why, to a lecture at the Royal Society, of course."

Chapter 17

Dear Ruth,

I read your letter to the ladies at the last meeting as you requested. Of course we are all dying of curiosity to know more and I expect you will receive a barrage of questions in the letters that are even now coming your way.

Just tell me one thing, dear, and I'll not plague you further with endless queries.

Are you happy?

— Excerpt of a letter from Miss Matilda Hunt to Mrs Ruth Anderson.

20ᵗʰ November 1814. St Clair's London Residence, St James.

Jerome jolted as his wife's bedroom door closed in his face. Miss Lacey had become as fierce as a bulldog ever since the accident, guarding her mistress from anything that might cause her distress. Apparently, that included him.

He'd gone to deliver Mr Knight's flowers and hadn't made it over the threshold. The flowers had been gently but firmly taken from his grasp by the maid as she informed him that his wife was sleeping and ought not to be disturbed. Perhaps later.

The twisting in his gut told him that *later* was likely to be about the same time hell froze over. Utterly despondent, he walked back along the corridor, at a loss for what to do next.

"Jerome?"

He turned to see his mother behind him and walked back to her.

"Why aren't you with Bonnie?" she asked, her eyes full of concern.

Jerome shrugged, trying to repress the childish urge to demand his mother make it all better. He was a grown man, for heaven's sake; he ought to be able to sort out his own problems. Except he was miserable, and he didn't know what to do or say to Bonnie to make it all right, because there weren't any words and it wouldn't be all right. He wasn't all right himself, so how could Bonnie be? And how the devil was he to even try when she wouldn't let him anywhere near her?

"She won't see me," he said, avoiding looking at his mother as the sorrow and sympathy in her eyes was enough to make his throat tighten. He stared at the carpet instead, and so didn't immediately realise his mother had walked off until he heard a firm knock on Bonnie's door.

He watched as the door opened and his mother bestowed a dazzling smile upon Miss Lacey.

"I'd like to see my daughter-in-law," she said, standing to one side and gesturing for Miss Lacey to leave the room. "In private," she added, in the *obey or suffer the consequences* tone Jerome recognised from his childhood.

There was a moment's hesitation, and then Miss Lacey stepped aside, and his mother entered, and closed the door behind her.

***

Bonnie stared unseeing at the grey winter's day beyond the window. Agnes' voice was a low murmur, and she assumed Jerome had come back to try again. Her heart clenched.

"Make him go away," she whispered. She couldn't see him, not yet. If she saw him now, she'd break down and cling to him and he'd see how weak she was. When she was stronger, she'd be brave enough to insist on the annulment that would set him free. She'd brought him nothing but trouble and heartache, and it was the only thing she could do for him. Perhaps he'd not understand at first but, in time, he'd realise she'd done him a favour. She turned around to see what was taking so long, and then froze.

His mother entered the room. Lady St Clair closed the door behind her, turning to face Bonnie, whose heart leapt to her throat. One hand went automatically to the high neck of her wrap and she clutched at it, her breathing coming too fast. Oh, not now. Please, not now. Bonnie knew everything she'd done: she'd seduced Jerome and got herself pregnant and trapped him into marriage, and now she'd made him miserable by being so hopelessly clumsy as to get herself all but run down and lose the baby. Lady St Clair could not possibly punish her any more than she was punishing herself, and yet she couldn't bear it, couldn't bear the accusation and disgust she knew would be in her eyes.

Bonnie went to turn away from her, but the woman's words were not what she expected, and she paused.

"You poor child," Lady St Clair said. "I know just how you feel. I had a similar experience with my first pregnancy, the year before I conceived Jasper. I fell down the stairs, clumsy fool that I am, and... and I felt so *responsible*." Her voice quavered a little, and she held out her arms to Bonnie, her smile warm and full of understanding.

Bonnie made a small, choked sound, and the next thing she knew she'd been enveloped in a hug. The gentle touch of her mother-in-law's soft hands stroked her hair as comforting murmurs assured her all would be well again, and the faint scent of lavender that rose around her seemed to ease the misery in her heart just a little.

Lady St Clair led her back to the bed and tucked her in as if she was a little girl. Then she got a clean handkerchief and sprinkled it with lavender water and put it across Bonnie's forehead before sitting beside her and taking her hand.

"There, now," she said, and as she smiled Bonnie saw the echo of both her sons' handsome faces. She was still remarkably lovely, and looked far younger than her years, but she must have been a truly breathtaking young woman. "I think perhaps you have taken it into your head that I disapprove of you."

Bonnie swallowed, hardly knowing what to say after being treated with such kindness. "No more than you ought to, my lady," she said, fighting back the urge to cry. "I t-trapped him into marrying me, but I-I didn't mean to, I swear it. At least, I didn't think he'd be so st-stubborn. I kept t-telling him I wouldn't m-marry him. It was all my fault, after all. I s-seduced him, b-but then he found out about the b-baby."

She could keep the tears back no longer and dissolved into an ugly bout of inconsolable sobbing.

Lady St Clair said nothing at all, but held Bonnie's hand and waited for the storm to abate.

"And now there is no baby, so he'll be better off without you."

Bonnie blinked. She'd been expecting his mother to say such a thing, of course she had, but after her unexpected kindness she'd thought perhaps…. Well, there was no point in avoiding the obvious. Just because something would make you miserable you couldn't pretend it wasn't there. It wouldn't change the facts.

She forced herself to meet Lady St Clair's eyes and found no malice, no judgement, nothing at all in fact. The woman simply appeared to be waiting for her to respond.

"Yes," she said.

His mother didn't react for a moment, then she took a very deep breath and Bonnie had the distinct impression she was praying for patience, though she wasn't certain why.

"I like you, Bonnie, despite what you may think. It is true I would not have chosen you for a daughter-in-law," she added, making Bonnie wince. She smiled and shrugged in response. "I see no reason to pretend otherwise. You are not easy in society, you bring a pitiful dowry to the marriage which is not ideal for a younger son, and you have a penchant for scandal. However, if you can make my son happy, that is neither here nor there. Jerome's happiness is all I care about. Currently, you are making him very unhappy, and that I do not enjoy seeing. You will do something about it, young lady."

Lady St Clair's lovely blue eyes settled on Bonnie, her gaze so fierce that Bonnie had to fight the urge to squirm.

"B-But that is what—"

"Have you asked Jerome what he wants, Bonnie?" she demanded, her voice rather harder now. "Have you thought to ask him how he feels about the loss of your child? It was his child too, you recollect?"

Bonnie drew in a shocked breath, taken aback not only by the sudden sharpness of her mother-in-law's voice, but by the words. She'd just assumed Jerome would be relieved, but... but what if he wasn't? She felt her chest tighten but couldn't find an answer.

"No, I didn't think so." Lady St Clair sighed. "Youth really is wasted on the young," she said, shaking her head. "Now, you listen to me, you foolish girl. I am very happy to welcome you to this family. Harriet is a wonderful daughter-in-law and I love her dearly, but she's rather too sensible and I think it will do us all the world of good to have a livelier influence, and there is no doubt whatsoever that you need the benefit of my advice and Harriet's good sense in return."

The words seemed almost foreign to Bonnie, their meaning was so hard to grasp. Lady St Clair *didn't* want to throw her out? She thought Bonnie would do *them* good? It was madness, surely, and she didn't know whether to laugh or cry. Of course, it mattered little what Lady St Clair thought. It was lovely for the family to be generous enough to accept her, but Jerome had never wanted her to begin with.

"I can almost hear the whirl of thoughts in your head," Lady St Clair remarked. "And I have the sinking feeling you still haven't understood what I've told you."

"Oh, no, my lady, you've… you've been so very kind. Far more than I deserve and—"

"Hush!"

Bonnie clamped her mouth shut, blushing at the stern command.

"This is what you will do, Bonnie. You will ask Jerome to come and see you. You will talk to him about what has happened, about the loss of your baby, and you will ask him how he feels, what he wants, and then… if that fails… well, I shall bang your heads together and see if that can't get me better results."

Despite everything, Bonnie smiled. She rather liked Lady St Clair.

"Promise me."

Bonnie nodded. "I promise."

Her mother-in-law's face softened, and she patted Bonnie's hand. "There, there, child. It may seem a trite thing to say but all *will* be well, I assure you, if you only do as I have asked of you. You need the truth between you and your husband, not what you *think* is true. A marriage only works if both parties are honest and open, and you can rest assured I shall have a conversation with Jerome before he comes in here, so you can depend on his being honest with you too."

She got to her feet and smoothed down her gown before giving Bonnie a warm smile.

"I shall send Jerome to you later, when you've had time to recover your senses, but for now I suggest you get some sleep. There's nothing that won't wait a few hours."

With that, Lady St Clair swept from the room with a brisk rustle of silk and petticoats, and left a stunned Bonnie behind her.

**

Jerome dithered outside Bonnie's bedroom door. Even though his mother had assured him Bonnie wanted to see him, he felt foolish and ridiculously nervous. It seemed his mama had sorted things out for him after all, which made him feel like an idiot, as if he was being managed, which was how—caught between his mother and Jasper—he often felt, and rebelled against. No matter the fact he was a grown man, Jasper still watched him like a hawk, as did his mother. The more they sighed and shook their heads at his behaviour, the more the devil in him wanted to make things worse. Not now. Now he wanted to make things right, to make Bonnie happy, and proud of him, and not to regret marrying him so deeply she wanted to leave. He wanted to see her, and so badly he felt the tug of longing as an ache in the pit of his belly. Yet he was afraid, afraid that his mother had only precipitated the end of everything. She had urged Bonnie to see him, to talk to him, but his mother had no way of knowing what she would say.

For all she knew, Bonnie would tell him it was over, and that she still wanted the annulment she'd been so adamant about before.

"For heaven's sake, you bloody fool, get a hold of yourself," he muttered, before pacing up and down a bit more and then grasping hold of the door handle.

It took such a surge of courage to propel him through the door that he flung it open rather more violently than he'd intended, and Bonnie gave a little shriek of alarm.

"Sorry," he said, holding out both hands in a peaceable gesture. "Uh… it slipped," he added, wishing he could go out again and pretend it never happened.

"You startled me," Bonnie said, pressing her hand to her heart.

Jerome's own heart clenched as his gaze settled on her lovely face. She made a charming picture, sitting up in bed and wearing a delightfully frivolous dressing gown that was all ruffles, lace, and pretty ribbons. The urge to go and ruffle the ruffles was hard to resist.

He looked around, wary in case her guard dog of a maid was about to leap out at him from a dark corner.

"Agnes isn't here," she said, guessing what he was thinking. "We won't be disturbed."

Jerome nodded and then tried a tentative smile. "How are you?"

"Fine," she replied at once and then shook her head. "No, I'm sorry, that… that's not entirely true and… I promised your mother I would tell you the truth."

"So did I.".

"I think she wants to tear her hair out," Bonnie added, returning his smile which made his heart leap.

"I think she wants to murder us both," Jerome retorted, which made her laugh, and his heart gave an odd sort of kick against his ribs this time.

"Won't you come and sit down?"

Jerome nodded, uneasy with this terribly polite exchange. He drew up a chair beside the bed, not feeling confident enough to sit on the mattress yet, but angled it as close to her as he could get.

"So," he asked. "How *do* you feel?"

Bonnie shook her head. "No," she said, and something sad and vulnerable shone in her eyes. "You first. How do you feel?"

Jerome looked down, wishing she hadn't asked him. He'd been ready to cry with her when they'd first learned the news. He'd wanted to hold her and weep with her, but she had turned away from him and now he was unsure of himself. Yet, he *had* promised to be honest.

"Jerome?"

Her soft voice brought him back, and he realised he was plucking nervously at the edge of the bedclothes. He forced his hands to still, placing them flat on his knees and took a deep breath.

"I feel wretched," he said, his voice a little uneven. "I came to get you that day, you know. I'd spoken to Mother and, though she was furious with me for what I'd done, she forgave me for it, and she wanted to meet you. She seemed pleased for me, for us, and I was so excited for you to meet her and then... and then you were gone and the next thing I knew Mr Knight was carrying you through the door."

He paused and looked up to find she was staring at her hands, winding the ribbons of the pretty dressing gown back and forth around her fingers.

"In the space of a few seconds I went from being so happy and relieved, to utter despair. I thought... I thought you were dead for a moment," he said, his voice cracking. It took several seconds to steady himself and try again. "And I hardly had time to feel the joy of discovering you were alive before I heard that we'd lost the baby."

He saw her flinch at his words, saw her eyes fill, but he carried on, needing to get the words out now, needing her to hear them.

"I came to you, Bonnie, and I wanted to weep. I wanted to hold you and have you hold me and grieve together for what we'd lost but... but you turned me away, and then you said you didn't want me anymore." It took him a long moment before he could speak again, and when he saw the tear roll down her cheek, he almost didn't say it, but he had to, needed to. "That was the worst moment of my life. I never knew anything could hurt so much as you hurt me then."

There was a taut silence, and then Bonnie flung herself at him and burst into tears.

"I'm s-sorry," she sobbed, inconsolable now. "I'm s-so s-sorry."

Jerome gathered her up before she tumbled from the bed and settled himself beside her on the mattress, her head on his chest as they cried together. He let it go on for a while until he caught her eye and then he laughed.

"What a watering pot you've turned me into, you wretch. All my manly pride out the window."

Her tears came to a shuddering halt, and she looked up at him. Her nose was red and her eyes watery, and he'd never loved her more. He felt his heart might burst with it.

"I know you never wanted to m-marry me," she said, and when he opened his mouth to object, she glared at him. "The truth! You promised."

Jerome frowned, finding it hard to remember the time when he'd been foolish enough to believe he was doing his duty because he had no choice.

"To begin with," he admitted. "To begin with, I was only doing what I thought I must, and when I discovered you were pregnant, well, there was no getting out of it."

"There's no getting out of it," she repeated, as though she was reciting something. "I've been such a bloody fool."

Jerome's head jerked up as he stared at her.

"You wrote that to your brother," she said.

He closed his eyes, trying to remember exactly what he'd written. "You read my private letters?" he asked, his voice even.

Bonnie stiffened in his arms. "Not on purpose. You left it out on the desk. I only saw the first few lines where it wasn't quite folded. I didn't snoop and read the rest of it."

Jerome cursed and let out a breath. "The next time you feel the need to go prying in my private correspondence, could you have the decency to do the thing properly, please?"

She stared at him and it took him a moment to speak as he needed to count to ten, or possibly a thousand. "If you had troubled to look at the rest of the letter, you'd have come away with a rather different opinion, Bonnie," he said, struggling not to lose his temper.

There was anxiety in her eyes, and he let out a breath, tightening his arms about her as she laid her head on his chest once more.

"Bonnie," he said, softly now, and he wondered if she could hear the frantic thudding of his heart, because to him it sounded like an enthusiastic marching band was living in his chest. "Bonnie, do… do you still love me?"

He looked down, waiting for her to raise her head and meet his eyes again. It seemed to take forever, so long that he felt breathless and giddy, what with the ridiculous pounding of his heart and the fact he'd forgotten how to breathe. When she finally did, her eyes were bright and her cheeks flushed.

"I never stopped," she said.

"Oh," he said, all the breath that had been locked in his lungs leaving him in a rush. "Oh, thank God." It took several seconds to gather his wits and when it finally happened it was accompanied by a furious rush of anger. "Then why the bloody hell did you ask me for an annulment?" he demanded, sitting up so quickly that she was flung down upon the mattress. He glared at her, and the flurry of ruffles that covered the generous swell of her breasts fluttered as she breathed.

"Because I love you, and I want you to be h-happy," she stammered, blinking up at him. "Because I thought I ought to set you free."

Jerome stared at her in outrage, so stunned by the stupidity of what had happened between them he didn't know how to react. He drew in a long breath and then let it out again slowly. "No wonder Mother wants to murder us," he muttered, rubbing a hand over his face.

Bonnie watched him, her eyes filled with anxiety and unshed tears.

"Oh, Bonnie," he said, uncertain of whether he ought to laugh or cry, and suspecting he would soon be reduced to some mortifying combination of the two. "You ridiculous, dreadful girl. Can't you see that I love you, that I've been falling harder and harder ever since the day we met?" Her eyes widened, but she said nothing, just stared up at him. "I adore you," he whispered, smiling now as her face grew blurry. "I never want to be without you, and losing our baby broke my heart. I'm relying on you to help me put it back together again. Can you do that for me, Bonnie? Please. Because I've been so utterly wretched, and I can't go on like this."

"Oh, Jerome," she sobbed, and tugged him down to her.

Jerome wrapped her in his arms and pulled her close and kissed her, softly, tenderly, with all the need he had been holding in since the moment Mr Knight had carried her through the door. They didn't speak for a very long time, just held each other as their hearts settled into the peace between them, with no more doubts or misunderstandings.

"Your mother was very kind to me," Bonnie said, when finally they were calm enough to speak again.

Jerome stroked her hair. "I'm glad," he said. "She was furious with me for the way I've behaved, but she said she thought I'd changed, and that it was your doing."

"Me?" Bonnie exclaimed, astonished.

He chuckled and tightened his hold on her. "I know. I can't think where she got such a harebrained notion from. Though perhaps it is true, after all. You're such a madcap creature it forces me to be the sensible one. *Me*! Can you imagine?"

Bonnie stared at him, unblinking. "No," she said, deadpan.

"Well, you have to admit, I'm not as bad as you."

"Are too."

"Am not."

"You are far more badly behaved than me!"

"Don't be ridiculous!"

Jerome decided there was only one way to settle this argument, and tickled her.

Bonnie squealed and shrieked at the top of her lungs. Jerome suspected the entire household would be scandalised, and they'd jolly well better get used to it.

Chapter 18

Dear Mr de Beauvoir,

I have recently discovered that the first lady to ever attend a lecture at the Royal Society was the Duchess of Newcastle in 1667. Pepys recorded the shocking scandal of this dangerous experiment and I can discover no evidence that it has since been repeated. I find this strange as you obviously have no problem in believing the female mind capable of scientific discovery, else you would not have recommended the book by Jane Marcet. Why have you not encouraged female natural philosophers to take their place? Why is it so forbidden for a woman to even take an interest in such subjects as science and biology?

I wonder what would happen if I attended one of your lectures at Somerset House?

— Excerpt of a letter from Miss Minerva Butler to Mr Inigo de Beauvoir.

25th November 1814. Church Street, Isleworth, London.

"Oh my God." Inigo stared down at the letter in his hand, a flicker of something that he refused to acknowledge warming his heart whilst a far stronger rush of panic burst to life in his chest. She wouldn't.

Yes, she would.

No matter how many times he assured himself she'd never get through the door, there remained the unshakable belief that Miss Butler would manage it, somehow. She'd be there at one of his lectures, and either she'd cause the most almighty scene or creep in somehow and he'd likely not know it… which meant he'd be a bag of nerves at every lecture he gave for the foreseeable future. Oh, this was intolerable.

Stop being such an idiot, he scolded himself. *You are a grown man, a man of science and thirty years of age, by heaven. You will not become hysterical because a chit of a girl has decided to plague you with her… her…*

A memory of soft, pink lips pressed to his arose in his mind no matter how he tried to keep it at bay. Along with it came the memory of her scent—something sweet like vanilla, and purely feminine—and the dark, dark blue of her eyes. Prussian blue. Oxidation of ferrous ferrocyanide salts produced Prussian blue. It was not a natural colour for eyes but then she was an unnatural creature, too bold, too daring, too… *beautiful* for a man's sanity, for *his* sanity.

He shook his head, aggravated by his fanciful notions. It had been the light in the room, that was all, that and the fact she'd disturbed his equilibrium so badly he was remembering it all wrong. Her lips had not been as sweet and intoxicating as brandy laced syllabub, the feminine scent of her had not clung to him for hours, days afterwards, and her eyes had not been that impossible shade of blue. He was imagining it all. Lust had disordered his mind and, if he had any sense, he'd pay a visit to a certain house he knew of and make use of the ladies within so he might rid himself of such base, if natural, urges.

Nonetheless, he must put a stop to this nonsense at once.

Moving to his desk he snatched up a fresh piece of paper.

Miss Butler,

Please put any ideas of attending one of my lectures at Somerset House firmly out of your mind. Not only will you not get through the door, but you will cause a scene that will no doubt be painful to both of us.

Inigo hesitated, his pen poised over the paper. Surely, rather than torment himself with wondering if or when she might appear and cause him embarrassment, it would be as well to take control of the situation? For if he knew when she was to appear, he would be prepared for it, no nasty surprises, and that was the *only* reason for arranging such a thing for her. No doubt she would be bored out of her mind and her silly infatuation for him would shrivel up and die.

Yes, that would be best.

He swallowed, refusing to acknowledge the slightest twinge of regret.

As, however, you feel compelled to make a nuisance of yourself, I shall arrange for you to attend the next conversazione at Soho Square. Joseph Banks is the president of the Royal Society but his sister, Miss Sarah Banks, often hosts such events and I have been invited to speak on the occasion she next holds one. I will ask that you are included in the invitations when the event is arranged.

Please understand, Miss Butler, that I do this only to save us both embarrassment and beg that you are not so foolish as to consider there is anything resembling a romantic note to the invitation. There is not.

M. De Beauvoir.

Inigo stared at the sheet, satisfied, lifted the pounce pot and shook the fine dust over the ink. Careful to return the excess back to the pot, he duly folded the letter, addressed it, and put it to one side to be posted.

With a sigh of relief, Inigo turned back to his work and endeavoured to put both the letter and the infernal Miss Butler out of his mind.

***

"What are you looking so pleased about?" Matilda asked, narrowing her eyes at Minerva as the carriage carried them to St James and Lord St Clair's house.

Bonnie had invited the Peculiar Ladies for tea, and they were all dying to see her. Prue had cried off, pleading illness and so Matilda, and Minerva—who was staying with her cousin, Prue— were attending together.

"Do I seem pleased?" Minerva replied, doing her best to look the picture of innocence. "Well, perhaps a little," she admitted. "Though I'm irritated too, truth be told, for I shall have to think of another location for my dare."

"Oh? How so?"

Minerva studied her friend and knew that Matilda was a canny one. She already knew Minerva was up to something, she just didn't know what. It would probably be best to keep it that way, but she couldn't resist sharing her news all the same.

"Well, I had decided to find a way in to one of the lectures at the Royal Society. You know what a bunch of stuffy old men they are," she added with a sigh. "Anyway, I have been outmanoeuvred and invited to a talk to be given by Inigo de Beauvoir at Soho Square. As I only really wanted to attend the lecture, not cause a furore, it seems I shall have to think of something else." Her lips curved into a smile as she considered what the *something else* might be.

"Minerva Butler," Matilda said, her voice stern. "What are you up to?"

Hmmm, she really was canny. "Up to?" Minerva replied, raising her chin a notch. "I can't think what you mean."

"Oh, can't you?" There was a snort which suggested Matilda didn't believe a word of it. "To what do we owe this sudden interest in the sciences, I wonder?"

Minerva bristled. Yes, she had to admit that her infatuation with Mr de Beauvoir had inspired her, but she had become fascinated by everything she read, and more so by the discovery that she understood a fair proportion of it. Her whole life she'd believed herself to be nothing more than a pretty face, to have nothing to contribute to a conversation past discussing the weather, the latest fashion or whatever *on dits* were doing the rounds. Not that she had anything against those things. She still loved fashion and gossip and dancing, and all the frivolous things she'd always loved, but now… now a whole new world had opened up to her and she wanted… she wanted *more.*

"Why should I not be interested?" she demanded, stung. "Do you think me too stupid? Harriet doesn't. She has encouraged my interest."

"As do I," Matilda replied, her expression placid as she adjusted her gloves, wriggling her fingers into the fine kid leather. "I applaud it wholeheartedly. I just wonder if the attraction is purely the subject being discussed, or the fellow giving the lecture."

One elegant blonde eyebrow quirked and Minerva looked away, out of the window, and prayed she wasn't as pink as the heat in her cheeks would suggest.

"Mr de Beauvoir is a fascinating man," she said, aware she sounded a little stiff.

"I understand you met him. In a book shop."

Minerva glanced back at Matilda to see an amused glint in her eyes. She gave a huff and folded her arms.

"Oh, very well. Yes! Yes, I met him and yes, I… I admire him greatly. I would like to know him better."

"How much better?"

Minerva felt the heat in her cheeks grow a little warmer but could not help the way her lips curved up as she heard the teasing note in Matilda's question.

Matilda sighed and shook her head. "Just when I think one of you is safely married off and out of danger, the next one shows signs of madness. I shall go grey before the year is out, mark my words."

"Now there's the pot calling the kettle black," Minerva shot back. "Exactly what did happen when the Marquess of Montagu fell from his horse during that storm?"

She smirked as two spots of scarlet blazed high on Matilda's cheeks.

"N-Nothing," Matilda stammered indignantly, only confirming to Minerva that *something* had happened. "It was just bad luck that I was there when the provoking man fell. I thought he was dead, for heaven's sake. He gave me such a start. But then he insists on escorting me back to the house, and we were alone... *again*, and you know as well as I do how little I need a story like that to get about."

"Well, I shan't say a word," Minerva said at once. "You know that, but... but is that all that happened? Didn't he flirt with you?"

Matilda made a disparaging noise. "Of course he flirted with me. The wretch has made no secret of his desire to make me his mistress no matter how many times I tell him to go to the devil." She fell silent for a moment before adding, "The trouble is he *is* the devil, so it makes no difference."

"You desire him."

Matilda looked around at Minerva, wide-eyed with shock.

"Oh, come now, you can admit as much to me, surely?" Minerva said with a crooked smile. "I understand, you know. Mama will murder me with her best fur tippet if she discovers I'm infatuated with an intellectual, of all things. Yet, from the first moment I saw Mr de Beauvoir I knew… I just *knew*. There was the strangest sensation, in the pit of my belly," she added in an undertone. "It comes back whenever I think of him and… and when I imagine his arms about me, his lips upon mine…." Minerva sighed and closed her eyes as a shiver ran down her spine. "Well, it only gets ten times worse. I desire him, though he can't stand the sight of me. I think it is similar for you and Montagu, except the other way about. He is pursuing you, and you are telling him no, even though…." Minerva fell silent, considering that in the light of Mr de Beauvoir's last letter. "Even though, at heart, you want him."

"Don't be foolish," Matilda snapped. "I would need to be out of my mind to want a man like Montagu. He wants only to dishonour and shame me."

"What has that got to do with desire?" Minerva asked, laughing a little. "It's not like it's something we have any say in."

Matilda was quiet for a long time and then gave a despairing sigh. "Oh, Minerva, why are we so ridiculously foolish?"

Minerva shrugged, a crooked smile at her lips. "I have no idea," she said softly. "But it does make life interesting."

***

Matilda embraced Bonnie and was hugged so fiercely in return that she felt quite winded. The large room of the grand house was full of chatter and laughter as the Peculiar Ladies, and this time some of their husbands too, caught up on all the news and gossip.

"I'm so glad you're feeling better," Matilda said, stepping back to look Bonnie over. "And looking very fine indeed," she added, noting with approval her friend's dashing new ensemble.

Bonnie laughed. "I've been horribly spoilt," she admitted, doing a little twirl. "Lady St Clair… Charlotte," she amended, at receiving a reproving glance from her mother-in-law, "took me shopping yesterday. She said it was to cheer me up, but I think it was a nefarious plan to exhaust me in the hopes I'd behave myself today. I never met a woman with such stamina for shopping!"

"It's true," Lady St Clair said with a sigh. "And I went and bought the ghastliest orange gown, too. I can't think what possessed me. Orange? With *my* complexion? Oh, dear me no, a fatal combination. Why didn't you stop me, Bonnie? It was very unkind of you."

She sauntered off then, leaving Bonnie open mouthed. "Stop her?" she exclaimed. "A herd of elephants couldn't stop her! Of all the nerve. I told her three times to get the green one instead, but she wouldn't listen."

Matilda laughed, delighted at the easy manner between the two women.

"There you are," Jerome said, taking hold of Bonnie's hand and putting it firmly on his sleeve. The look that passed between them was so intimate that Matilda had to look away for a moment. How lovely it was to see them both so happy. She had to admit she'd not believed Jerome would see everything that Bonnie could give him, not believed there was any option but to see Bonnie hurt, but she was more than relieved to have been proven wrong.

"Miss Hunt," Jerome said, smiling at her. "It's a pleasure to see you again. I do hope you'll accept the invitation to our engagement ball when it arrives."

Bonnie rolled her eyes at him. "How can it be an engagement ball? We're married. It's just a belated celebration, that's all."

Jerome shrugged. "Well, whatever it is, whenever it is, I hope Miss Hunt can attend. How's that?"

Matilda laughed. "I'd be delighted to. When and where will it be?"

"Here," Bonnie said, shaking her head. "And in ten days. You'll get the invitation tomorrow all being well and, oh!" she exclaimed, jigging up and down. "I can't wait for you to see the invitations before I tell you, though they're very pretty, but I must explain now or I'll burst. It's a masquerade ball!"

"Oh, yes, of course," Matilda said, laughing. "For you never did complete your dare, did you?"

Matilda watched as Bonnie and Jerome exchanged a glance and the two of them dissolved into laughter.

"Oh, no!" Matilda said, holding up a hand in alarm. "Don't tell me, I beg of you. I've already decided it's likely I'll have gone grey before the year is out, pray don't make it happen any quicker than it must."

Bonnie grinned at her and leaned in to kiss her cheek. "Poor, Matilda, our darling mother hen," she said with a sigh. "Just know that I completed my dare, but I'm certainly not going to miss another opportunity to dress up."

"What are you going as this time?" Matilda asked.

"I haven't decided yet," Bonnie said, turning her attention to her husband. "And Jerome won't tell me what he's wearing so I can't try to make a matching pair." She scowled at him, but Jerome just returned a sweetly innocent expression.

"Where's the fun in that?" he retorted.

"Won't it be a lark though, Matilda?" Bonnie said, leaning in conspiratorially. "Lady St Clair has invited everyone who's anyone, to a party in *my* honour," she said with a crow of laughter. "All the *ton* will be there, and oh my, the old tabbies will be beside themselves with fury when they were so looking forward to seeing me go to the devil."

"But you have gone to the devil, love," Jerome whispered, waggling his eyebrows at her. "You just haven't realised it yet."

The two of them laughed and wandered off to talk to some of their other guests and Matilda watched them go, smiling, for their happiness was so very infectious.

"They'll do very nicely, I think."

Matilda looked around to see Lady St Clair had returned and was also watching them with approval.

"Yes, I agree," Matilda said, allowing Lady St Clair to guide her to a seat by the window. "You must be very proud, not to mention relieved, to see both your sons so happily settled."

"I am," Lady St Clair replied, looking rather smug. "I'll admit, Bonnie would not have been my first choice, but I think now that perhaps that was rather short-sighted of me. Jerome would have been wretched if he had no one to laugh with, and there's not been enough laughter since their darling papa died." She gave a wistful sigh and Matilda reached out and took her hand. "Such a man he was," the dowager countess said, her eyes growing misty. "Everyone told me not to marry him. Such a shocking reputation he had. But I never regretted it, not for a moment."

There was a heavy silence before Lady St Clair shook off the past and turned back to Matilda with a laugh.

"And, did you know, Morven doubled Bonnie's dowry? When he discovered she'd married the Earl of St Clair's brother, he was heard to remark he'd not be disparaged for being a blasted nip cheese by an English earl, and that was that. Isn't that precious?"

Matilda gave a snort of laughter. "Oh, how like Bonnie to land on her feet, and how richly she deserves it. I am glad for her."

"And what of you, Tilda, dear?"

"Me?" Matilda echoed, alarmed by the sudden gleam in the woman's eyes. It occurred to her then that, now her sons were happily married off, the dowager countess might decide to turn her attention to other interests... like finding Matilda a husband. "What of me?"

"Well, I know you have Mr Burton dancing attendance on you, not to mention Montagu trailing in your wake. I heard he was very attentive at Mrs Manning's rout party."

To her horror, Matilda blushed scarlet and quickly changed the subject.

"Sadly, I've not seen Mr Burton since I came back to town. He was supposed to have returned at the beginning of the month but was delayed. He's called twice more but we've missed each other on both occasions." Thank heavens, Matilda silently added, thanking providence for keeping them apart for she was no nearer reaching a decision on what she ought to do about the man.

"Hmmm," Lady St Clair replied, her blue eyes a deal too keen for Matilda's comfort. "Well, just so you are not caught unawares, I shall have to invite Montagu to the ball. Perhaps I shall invite Mr Burton too," she added, studying Matilda, who endeavoured to keep the dismay from her expression at that idea.

"You must invite who you wish," Matilda said, aware she sounded somewhat brittle.

"Oh, come, come," the dowager countess said, chuckling. "Don't be like that. I shall invite all the eligible young men I can think of who might make a good husband for you."

Matilda snorted. "The ones with pockets to let, you mean," she said, not without bitterness. "For I cannot think who else you would invite who would fit the bill."

Lady St Clair shrugged. "Whether or not you marry one of them, it will amuse me to see Montagu watch you dance with a dozen potential suitors while he simmers in a corner."

"Oh, please." Matilda made an incredulous sound and wondered if happiness had addled the woman's wits. "Montagu does *not* simmer. There's ice in his veins and in his heart and, if his temperature ever rises above tepid, I've yet to notice it."

"Then," the dowager countess said with a small smile, "you've not been paying close enough attention."

Chapter 19

Dear Papa,

Dear Matilda

Dear

Whatever am I to say to them? What manner of madness has possessed me? I feel I am two entirely different people contained in the same body.

I think I may run mad…

— Excerpt of a letter from Mrs Ruth Anderson, never completed.

5ᵗʰ December 1814. Mr and Mrs Cadogan's celebration ball, The Earl of St Clair's London Residence, St James.

"How splendid it is."

Matilda looked to Jemima Fernside, who was staring about the lavish ballroom with wide eyes, and smiled. She was so pleased she'd talked the young woman into coming with her. Even better, she'd persuaded Jemima to stay with her for the week, so Matilda had the chance to fatten her up and try to find out about the problem she was hiding.

Jemima had always been a quiet girl, but still funny and vivacious when in company with whom she felt comfortable.

They'd barely seen her this year and each time she'd seemed frailer and shabbier, a little more vulnerable.

"I do love your costume," Matilda said, admiring her outfit. Jemima had come as the sea nymph, Calypso. It was rather a daring gown at first glance, but very cleverly done. It covered everything securely, but the way fabric shells and sea creatures had been arranged over her body made it appear somewhat more scandalous than it was. It spoke of a woman who had been full of confidence when she'd made it, and Matilda hoped she could help bring that woman back from whatever dark corner she'd been hiding in.

"It's an old bedsheet," Jemima confided in a whisper, and for a moment the haunted look that seemed ever in her eyes vanished, replaced by one of pride and something a little mischievous. "And I made all the sea creatures and shells out of bits and pieces of cast off material. I actually made it for a party the year before last but…." The mischievous glint evaporated and she shrugged. "Well, I never got to go, but I'm so glad to finally give it an airing. I feared all that hard work would never see the light of day. Though, I confess, it's rather more daring than I remembered."

"Well, I should think you would be glad, proud too, and never mind daring. You'll no doubt catch some handsome fellow's eye tonight. Such skill with a needle you have. I am in awe, as I haven't the least talent in that direction. I would have thought some exclusive modiste had made it."

Jemima blushed a little, but appeared pleased with the compliment.

"Now, where on earth has Bonnie got to? I can't wait to see what she's wearing." Matilda glanced around and then smiled as she saw Harriet approaching, dressed as a shepherdess. St Clair still looked ridiculously elegant and every inch the nobleman despite being decked out as a common sailor. They made quite a picture.

"Why, Harry, how well you look," Matilda said, making her do a little twirl.

Harriet gaped at her. "I look well!" she said, shaking her head. "Matilda, that dress is... simply stunning."

"Thank you," Matilda replied. She was feeling rather pleased with her outfit, it was true. It had been horribly expensive, especially as it had been made in such a short space of time, but the effect was rather lovely, a gown of shimmering gold and a mask to match, with a headdress about her golden hair like the rays of the sun, which she was supposed to represent. The dress glinted and gleamed under the candlelight and perhaps there were many here who would not speak to her for not being good *ton,* but they'd not be able to ignore her. That was some consolation.

"It's not fair," Harriet said, huffing with frustration. "Everyone else is in disguise but I can't wear the mask *and* my spectacles. So I have to forgo the mask or risk walking into everyone or dancing with someone I ought not."

"Well, we can't have that," St Clair drawled, sliding an arm about her waist. "You might end up in the arms of some shocking reprobate."

"Imagine," Harriet replied, pressing a hand to her breast and adopting a scandalised expression whilst her husband leered at her.

"Come along wench, and dance with me," the earl commanded, dragging his not unwilling shepherdess along behind him to the dance floor.

A moment later and a Harlequin had swept Jemima off to dance too and Matilda watched, not a little enviously, as the colourful costumes swirled about her.

A strange prickling sensation at the back of her neck made her turn, an awareness that she was being observed skittering down her spine. She almost shrieked and took an involuntary step backwards as she found the Marquess of Montagu standing behind her.

"Oh!" she said crossly. "Why must you creep up on me like that, you wretched man?"

One blonde eyebrow arched beneath a stark white mask. "How did you know it was me?" he drawled whilst Matilda willed her heart to stop jumping about like a crazed rabbit. "As I assume you'd address no one else in such an insolent manner."

She almost laughed as she looked him over. He was dressed in pristine white from head to toe, and the buttons on his coat glinted with diamonds, as did the pin in his snowy cravat. The harsh colour made his eyes glint ever more silver and his hair gleamed white blonde in the candlelight. No one else could have worn it and seemed so utterly masculine, no one else had the kind of magnetic presence that made people get out of his way and turn their heads to watch, either.

"Lucky guess," Matilda retorted, repressing the urge to roll her eyes. As if he didn't know the effect he had on the assembled company. "What are you, anyway?" she asked, trying not to look him up and down but finding the effort of dragging her gaze away from his magnificence too herculean a task. Instead she tried to infuse the question with a mocking tone, which was not altogether successful.

"Why, Miss Hunt, surely that's obvious? I'm an angel."

Matilda made a very unladylike snorting sound and covered her mouth with her hand, a little mortified.

"Oh," she said, her voice not entirely steady. "I do b-beg your pardon but…."

It was no good. She went off into whoops of laughter, quite unable to control herself, and so violently it made everyone in earshot turn and look at them.

Montagu sighed.

"Must you make a spectacle of us?" he asked. "I suppose I had better dance with you until you have gained some semblance of control."

"What?" Matilda's laughter came to an abrupt halt. "Oh... *No... I....*"

Too late. By the time Matilda had gathered her wits she was halfway to the dance floor and could hardly refuse now without causing a scene. "I never said I'd dance with you," she muttered, exasperated by his high handed manner.

"You never said you wouldn't, either. You were too busy cackling."

"I do not cackle!" she shot back and then gasped as his hand settled at her waist, pulling her just a little too close for decency.

"Of course not," he said, his voice soothing now. "I was only teasing you. I do enjoy teasing you, Miss Hunt. You are so wonderfully... responsive."

Matilda glared at him until she realised he was teasing her still. She felt colour rise to her cheeks.

Amusement glinted in his wicked eyes. "Ah, there you are. Now, you shine like the sun you are supposed to represent, and I beg you to believe that I am not teasing any longer." He lowered his voice, dipping his head to whisper in her ear. "You cast everyone else here into the shade, Mademoiselle Soleil. There is no one to outshine you."

"An angel, of all things! It's a wonder you didn't get struck by lightning," she muttered, striving to keep her voice even when the warmth of his breath fluttering against her neck had her temperature climbing. "*Again*," she added, daring to shoot a furious glance his way.

"It wasn't lighting that struck me, as you well know."

He made a sudden turn and the combination of his words and the speed of the dance set Matilda's head whirling. She stumbled and a strong arm lashed about her, hauling her against the hard, masculine body she'd been trying so desperately to ignore. It was impossible now, and the breath rushed from her lungs. Heat, everywhere was heat and desire, burning through their clothes, searing her from the inside out as though she really was the sun, hot and fierce and dangerous.

There was a satisfied glint in his eyes as he looked down at her, and she knew he saw the shock in her eyes. Though she'd righted herself and they were once more the correct distance apart, the damage was done.

"You did that on purpose," she said, wishing she didn't sound so breathless.

"And if I did? It isn't as if you don't want me closer."

She stared up at him, incensed. More so because it was true, damn him to hell. "I'll tell you how close I want you. Let me see," she said, adopting a thoughtful expression. "How about Peru?"

"I see you are still intent on lying to yourself," he said, his voice softer now. "Why must you continue to deny what is obvious to us both? It doesn't affect your ability to keep saying no, after all, or... does it?" he asked, his gaze far too knowing. A glimmer of a smile touched his mouth. "You can't escape this any more than I can."

"Oh, please," Matilda said, irritation fighting through her confusion strongly enough to make her voice sound almost steady. "You expect me to believe you are a slave to your *feelings*?"

"You could make me your slave."

The words were spoken so fast she almost didn't catch them, as though he'd spoken without thinking, something she suspected he never, ever did. There had been an edge to the words too, something that might have been anger. Montagu never got angry, either. Never. She stared up at him, wanting to search his expression, to seek out any tiny chink in that icy armour he wore, but his arrogant face was turned away from hers.

"Yes, whores are often the masters of noblemen, aren't they?" she said in disgust, frustrated that he was as impervious to her scrutiny as always. "Perhaps I'd rule you for a week or two, a few months perhaps, if I was very clever. What an achievement. Should I die happy knowing I had your undivided attention for such a time?"

"Not a whore," he countered, his voice smooth now, disarming, all traces of anger vanquished in an instant. "Why must you always speak so? The mistress of the Marquess of Montagu is no whore."

Matilda laughed at that, at the way he could view the world from his lofty vantage point.

"Yes, your mistress would be an entirely respectable position," she said, so annoyed by his mollifying tone her fingers itched with the desire to slap him, or possibly wring his neck with that snowy white cravat. "I'd have vouchers to Almacks and any number of proposals of marriage from eligible gentlemen once you were done with me and cast me aside."

"You'd not need to marry," he countered, perfectly unruffled by her sarcasm. "I'd give you everything you could ever need. Financial security. More than any marriage could give you. You'd be independently wealthy, in charge of your own future. Surely that's worth a little thought, at least?"

"And what of children?" she asked, furious with herself as she heard the wistful tenor to her question.

Too much sentiment on show. *Weak*, she scolded herself. It made her sound weak and emotional and she didn't want that, not in front of him. Yet she couldn't stop herself from asking.

"You need not worry on that score. I am very careful not to sire bastards."

She froze in his arms, almost coming to a complete stop but he bore her on, forcing her through the steps when she would have halted the dance.

"Don't make a scene," he warned her. "It will only damage you, not me."

His words washed over her, his previous response making her so enraged she could hear nothing but the ringing in her ears.

It took a long moment before she was calm enough to answer but, when she did, the words were every bit as icy as she'd hoped they would be. "I want children, my lord. A family. Even if I was so far out of my wits as to consider the possibility of being your mistress, which I assure you I am *not,* that would put an end to it. No one will marry me once you've grown bored and cast me aside, and no child of mine will bear the disgrace of illegitimacy. I will marry or die an old maid. There is no middle ground. I'll not shame myself with an affair that will ruin everything I dream of."

He said nothing, the silence a weight between them. The dance seemed to go on and on, his powerful body guiding hers with such surety she felt she was being swept along by a tide, pulling her under, into dark water. She dared to look up at him and their eyes met. Her breath caught. She'd been wrong, he hadn't been struck by lightning, he *was* lightning, his touch shocking, lighting her up and burning away her will. The force of the connection between them seared her, and fear gripped her heart as she recognised the pulsing of desire coursing through her veins. He knew it, damn him. He knew what she felt. She could see it in the intensity of his gaze and could not look away. To her surprise, he did not look smug. There was no triumph in the winter grey sky of his eyes. Did he fear it too, she wondered, and then laughed at the very idea. Of course not. What on earth did the Marquess of Montagu have to lose?

The music drew to a close but still he gazed down at her, until it was too much, too terrifying to endure. She pulled away from his grasp and almost ran from the dance floor.

***

Helena watched Matilda hurry away from Montagu and glanced at Minerva, who stood at her side.

"I wonder what he said to her," Minerva said, biting her lip.

"I don't," Helena replied, taking a sip of her lemonade and wishing she could drink champagne like the married ladies. "It's obvious enough."

Minerva sighed. "I know. I worry for her."

"Not as much as she worries for herself, I'll wager. The air fairly crackles when the two of them are in the same room."

"Is Mr Burton here?" Minerva asked, looking around.

"I've not seen him." Helena watched a waiter go by, a silver tray filled with glasses of champagne held aloft. "Curse it, I hate being a lady. I wish I'd been born a man."

Minerva looked at her with amusement. "I think it's too late to change your mind," she said, her lips quirking as she took in Helena's costume.

Helena had come as Eve. Her gown was perfectly respectable, though so well fitted it highlighted her assets in a manner that had pleased her and brought her many compliments this evening. It was a heavy white satin dress, trimmed all over with silken fig leaves, most especially in the appropriate areas. A faux red apple, studded with glittering red jewels hung from a ribbon at her wrist and a silken snake coiled about her waist and up over her shoulder, its red forked tongue arrowing out in the direction of her décolletage. Her brother, Robert, had almost had an apoplexy when he'd seen her. It was always the mark of a successful outfit.

Helena huffed out a laugh. "Doesn't it make you wild, though? All the things nice young ladies do and don't do? Sometimes I feel so... so constricted I want to scream."

"Is your corset too tight?" Minerva asked, her expression the picture of innocent enquiry. "Or is that snake squeezing you to death?"

"Wretch," Helena replied, knowing she was being teased. "Don't you know what I mean?"

"Of course I do!" Minerva exclaimed, giving Helena a look of pure exasperation. "Honestly, Helena. You have a deal more freedom than the rest of us. The daughter and sister of a duke can get away with things that would cause us lesser mortals to fall off the edge of polite society into an abyss. My position is far more tenuous than yours, and look at poor Jemima. She's so close to the edge I fear she'll slip any day now."

Helena nodded, a wash of shame rolling over her. "That's true. Did you see that dress she was wearing the other day? It was clear she'd turned the cuffs, and it was so far out of style. Oh, you're right, of course you are. I'm spoiled and headstrong, and yet I'm so... so bored! Poor, poor me. Rich and popular and spoiled, how tragic."

Minerva gave her a sympathetic smile and linked their arms together. "You need an interest," she said firmly. "Something to occupy your mind, to challenge you. Take me, for example. I've discovered I'm not quite as hen-witted as I supposed. In fact, I have the most fascinating book on chemistry if you care to borrow it. I'm even going to a lecture. You can come if you want...."

Helena was aware that Minerva had stopped talking and was watching her intently but could do nothing to redirect the focus of her gaze nor to curb the smile that she felt tug at her lips.

"What?" Minerva asked, following her line of vision to look across the ballroom. "What is it that's so captured your attention?"

"That thing you said about having something to challenge me, to occupy my mind," Helena murmured, her eyes fixed on the far side of the ballroom.

"Oh dear," Minerva said, her voice faint. "That's Gabriel Knight."

"Yes," Helena replied, grinning. "I know."

"Oh, but, Helena, no. Your brother… if he had the slightest idea…."

Helena tore her gaze away and glared at Minerva.

"Oh, no!" Minerva squeaked, alarmed. "I wouldn't dare, but it'll get about if you so much as dance with him. He wants to gain a foothold in the *ton*, everyone knows it. His only option is to marry well, but he's too proud to make himself agreeable, so he puts everyone's backs up."

Helena felt her curiosity, already piqued, flare to life. "How fascinating," she murmured.

"Oh, Helena, no," Minerva pleaded. "Robert will be furious. They don't like each other. How do you not know this?"

The more Minerva spoke, the more determined Helena became to get better acquainted with Mr Knight. He was proud, ruthless, and her brother didn't like him. What an irresistible combination. She looked him over, considering all the other reasons that would make him a fascinating conquest. He was tall and lean, ruggedly handsome, with a strong jaw, a cleft in his chin, a firm set to his mouth that hinted at a stubborn streak a mile wide, and dark, dark eyes. Helena suppressed a shiver.

She had plenty of beaus fawning over her, writing her poetry morning, noon, and night and comparing her to Helen of Troy or waxing lyrical about her green eyes, likening them to emeralds or spring leaves or some such nonsense. Pretty saps, the lot of them. Oh there were one or two who were nice enough, possible husband material if she were desperate, but not one of them stirred her interest, and not one of them offered her a challenge. Now, to have a man like Gabriel Knight fall at her feet… *that* would be a conquest.

"Come along," Helena said, taking Minerva's arm and strolling in a leisurely fashion around the perimeter of the ballroom.

Minerva sighed. "I do understand the fascination, the desire for something you know you ought not want," she said to Helena, her voice low, and there was a note to it that made Helena look at her a little more closely. She *did* understand, all too well, if Helena was any judge. Well, well. "All the same, do have a care, Helena. He's not... well, they say he's not an indoor cat."

Helena paused and then burst out laughing, causing everyone around them to stop and stare at her. Minerva flushed scarlet, though Helena couldn't care less; she *was* a duke's daughter, after all.

"Whatever do you mean, not an indoor cat?" she asked in an undertone.

"Well, I didn't say it," Minerva muttered. "It's said of him. That he's not quite tame, I suppose. Not used to being in polite company. His manners are appalling."

"Minerva, darling, you could have said nothing more precisely calculated to make me want to further our acquaintance."

Minerva nodded, her expression resigned. "I rather feared you would say that," she said and then shrugged. "Oh, well, it looks like we're both bound for perdition. I suppose we may as well enjoy it."

"Certainly we shall enjoy it," Helena said as they drew closer to her target, who was deep in conversation with Silas Anson, the Viscount Cavendish.

Lord Cavendish looked up as they approached and smiled warmly at them. "Ladies," he said. "How lovely to see you both."

"And you, Lord Cavendish, Mr Knight," Helena said, giving Mr Knight a dazzling smile before turning back to the viscount.

"Is Aashini here?" Helena asked, trying not to allow her attention to wander to the dark figure glowering beside her. He seemed to radiate hostility, though she could not determine why exactly.

"She is. Dancing with a rakish looking sailor, I believe."

"Oh, that's St Clair," Minerva said, laughing. "So I think you mean a rakish looking earl. No one could ever mistake him for a sailor, surely?"

"I know what I mean," Cavendish replied, chuckling.

"Breeding will out, no matter the disguise," said Mr Knight, his voice mocking, his dark eyes returning to Helena with slow deliberation. "Though some disguises are more apt than others," he added, his cold gaze sweeping over her costume of Eve and leaving a wave of heat in its wake.

"Are you calling me a temptress, Mr Knight?" Helena asked, pleased by the flash of surprise in his dark eyes, though it was quickly gone. Lord Cavendish's eyebrows shot up, and Helena knew that remark would travel directly to her brother who would lecture her for being so brazen. It had been worth it.

Mr Knight studied her for a long, silent moment before replying. "No."

He turned away from her and walked off.

"Well!" Helena fumed, despite having been prepared for his reaction. She stared after him until he disappeared into the crowd and then burst out laughing. "What a dreadful man," she said, feeling a surge of excitement coursing through her.

Oh, Mr Knight, she thought to herself, *you have no idea what you've just done.*

Chapter 20

Mr Briggs,

Though it is with great reluctance I write, I must confess that you were correct in your assumption. I am in dire financial difficulties. I had to borrow money to pay for my last month's rent and now I cannot afford the repayment and have no way of paying the next month's rent either.

It seems I have no choice but to put my pride and honour aside and enquire about the man you spoke of, the one who was looking for a 'paid companion'. You said he was a gentleman, and very discreet. Can you assure me of this...

— Excerpt of a letter from Jemima Fernside to Mr Gerald Briggs.

5th December 1814. Mr and Mrs Cadogan's celebration ball, The Earl of St Clair's London Residence, St James.

"Well, are you ready for your big entrance?"

Bonnie looked at her mother-in-law and then back to the mirror, wondering if perhaps she'd been a bit too bold for her own good. When she'd told the dowager countess about the costume she had in mind, Lady St Clair had stared at her before saying, quite calmly, that she was a diabolical, wicked and outrageous young woman who would cause the family no end of trouble. Her mother-in-law then clapped her hands together in delight and thrown herself into Bonnie's plans with gusto. Even Harriet had joined in, though mostly to try to keep a rein on some of their more shocking ideas. She said someone had to.

A queen gazed back at Bonnie and her lips curved into a smile. She'd wanted to give the old tabbies who been so certain she was destined for ruin something to chew on and Queen Elizabeth, *the virgin queen*, had been so perfect as to be irresistible. Lady St Clair had pretty much emptied her jewellery box over her, and everywhere she glinted with diamonds, emeralds, and rubies. It was outrageous, a show-stopping shout of triumph and not a little vulgar. Bonnie couldn't have been clearer if she'd stuck her tongue out at them. The dress was gorgeous, a rich, dark blue, heavily embroidered with gold thread. It weighed a ton and Bonnie was grateful for the change in fashions as it was rather unwieldy too, but she felt like a queen and that had been her intention.

"Yes," she said, flashing Lady St Clair a cheeky smile. "I am ready."

Her mother-in-law returned her smile, and Bonnie recognised a kindred spirit at last. It had taken her a while to realise it, but after all, Lady St Clair had married a wicked rake, a wild fellow with a dreadful reputation, and she'd tamed him. Well, up to a point, at least. He'd stopped his womanising ways but had remained a rather dashing figure, which made sense, considering the two sons they'd turned out. Lady St Clair, though, was not the rigid, moralising woman Bonnie had feared. Far from it. She was warm and understanding, with a fine sense of the ridiculous and a rather dreadful sense of humour to rival Bonnie's. She also got away with saying the most shocking things by adopting the vague and frivolous mien those who didn't know her well thought was the sum of her parts. They simply thought she didn't mean whatever scandalous thing she'd said the way she'd said it, when she'd meant every word, as her intimates knew full well.

In short, Bonnie belonged at last. She'd found a family, a husband who adored her even when she was dreadful, and a mother-in-law who admired her even when she was dreadful—up to a point at least. Plus, her brother-in-law was an absolute darling, and her sister-in-law one of her closest friends. How much more perfect could life get?

Lady St Clair offered her arm, dressed rather outrageously herself as Queen Boadicea. She'd taken her inspiration from an engraving by John Opie of 'Queen Boadicea Haranguing the Britons'. If Bonnie was to be a queen, she'd said with a haughty sniff, she was certainly not about to be outdone.

They'd agreed it would be far more spectacular to make a grand entrance once everyone had arrived. There was nothing the *ton* liked better than a bit of theatre, after all. They had also decided she would enter on Lady St Clair's arm, a show of solidarity and approval from her new mother-in-law that would force many of the high sticklers to accept Bonnie into their ranks without further protest.

"Do we know what Jerome has come as yet?" Bonnie asked, her heart thudding with excitement as they made their way to the ballroom.

"No, he wouldn't tell me, the aggravating boy," Lady St Clair said with a sigh. "No matter how I plagued him. Though I wouldn't tell him what you were wearing either, so I suppose it's fair."

They paused just outside the grand double doors and Lady St Clair looked Bonnie over, a critical gaze that surveyed her daughter-in-law from head to toe.

"Very regal," she said with an approving nod. "Now then, come along, let us set tongues wagging. I'm just dying to put Lady Sumner's nose out of joint, spiteful cat that she is."

Bonnie threw her head back and laughed as the footmen opened the doors and Lady St Clair swept them both through into the ballroom. Everyone stared.

"Don't fail me now, Bonnie," Lady St Clair murmured as Bonnie's breath caught in her throat at the sight of the hundreds of people watching her. "Chin up. You're a queen, remember."

Bonnie turned to her mother-in-law, who winked at her, and her nerves melted away under that supportive gaze. She grinned.

"Now, where is Jerome?" Bonnie demanded, staring about the assembled company as they moved through the ballroom, searching for him, until her gaze settled on a man dressed all in black. There were horns visible in his thick blond hair and a wicked glint in the blue eyes that glittered behind the mask. The devil.

Bonnie gave a squeal of delight and launched herself at him.

"Ooof!" Jerome said, staggering back a pace. "Bonnie Campbell, you wretch. I always said you'd go to the devil."

"So did everyone," she laughed, kissing him, right there in front of everyone as gasps and murmurs of mingled amusement and shock rippled through the ballroom.

"Well, I think you've set the tone for the evening, Bonnie," Lady St Clair said dryly. She made a shooing motion at them both. "Run along and play, wicked children, but if you're too dreadful, I shall disown you both."

"That sounds fair," Jerome replied leaning in to kiss his mama. She gave him an adoring look and patted his cheek before turning back to Bonnie.

"What are you waiting for? Go and dance with your devil. Show the world how happy we are to make you a part of this family, and just how perfectly you fit in."

Bonnie did not need telling twice and, seconds later, she was in her husband's arms, being whirled about the dance floor. It was a moment of pure, unadulterated happiness. After everything that had happened, she had finally found what she'd been searching for. Though the loss of their child was still a tender corner of her heart, she knew they had time, that there would be other children, and that she was a part of something now. She didn't have to be alone any longer. So she danced as though it was her last day on earth, though it felt like the first, and she laughed, her heart bursting with joy and gratitude for everything she had.

"This is what I love about you," Jerome said, drawing her attention back to his handsome face. He was staring down at her with such a look in his eyes that her breath caught. "You're so alive. Everyone else just moves through the steps of a dance but dancing with you… it's like an adventure."

"That's the nicest thing anyone has ever said to me." Bonnie's voice was a little thick, emotion catching in her throat. How was a girl supposed to hear such words and keep her composure? She wondered if this evening could possibly be any more perfect.

"Really?" Jerome said in surprise. "Goodness, I shall have to do better than that, then."

"Oh, yes please," she murmured with a sigh, before adding, "But not yet, for you'll make me cry and I don't want to do that. Not now."

"I'll save it for later, then," he promised, his expression grave, and swept her into a series of turns that made her feel as if she was flying.

***

"Are you all right, Matilda?" Bonnie asked. She had been on her way out of the ballroom, her plans for the rest of the evening something she had not yet confided to her husband. A respectable married lady she may be, but she didn't see why that should put an end to her fun. Matilda looked pale and rather out of sorts, though, and Bonnie could not pass her by without speaking to her. "You look a little peaky."

Matilda turned towards her, a distant look in her eyes that suggested she'd not heard what Bonnie had said. Her expression cleared as she focused on Bonnie, and fixed a smile to her face that was not entirely convincing.

"Oh, I beg your pardon. I was wool gathering. Yes, I'm quite all right. Though... I wanted to speak with you, if you have a moment. About Ruth."

Bonnie nodded, guilt tugging at her stomach. She too had been thinking about Ruth. The thought that she might have failed her friend nagged at her. At the time she'd been so overwrought by her own situation that she feared she'd not done enough for Ruth, and not explained just what she was letting herself in for. She ought to have taken more note of the look in Ruth's eyes, the one she recognised well enough, as she'd felt the same overwhelming *need* when she'd first seen Jerome. As impulsive as Bonnie was, however, she'd still taken a bit of time to get to know him first. Though, being fair, if she'd had a dowry of fifty thousand to bribe him with, perhaps she'd have proposed to Jerome on the spot too.

It seemed strange to her that Ruth should feel that way about Gordon, but to each his own. She'd found him too big and clumsy. He was an ignorant brute in her eyes, fit only to live out in the wilds of the Highlands. How Ruth, a gently bred woman who'd been brought up to fit in with the young ladies of the *ton,* would cope with him she didn't know. Not that Ruth was a shrinking violet, far from it, but surely her new husband would frighten the life out of her. Yet it hadn't been fear she'd seen in Ruth's eyes, not even close.

Matilda drew her to one side. "What is he like?"

Bonnie didn't need a name to identify that Matilda spoke of Ruth's new husband.

"I hardly dare say," Bonnie said with a weak smile. "After everything I told you."

Whenever she'd mentioned Gordon Anderson, she'd maligned both his character and his appearance. Not to mention his personal hygiene. She wasn't entirely sure why, except that she resented being forced to marry against her will and the fact that he only wanted her for her dowry, as he couldn't stand her any more than she could him. It was a petty revenge perhaps, but it had been strangely satisfying.

"Did you exaggerate his character as much as you did his appearance?" Matilda asked, a hopeful expression in her eyes.

"Not entirely," Bonnie said carefully, not wanting to alarm Matilda and wishing she could be more comforting. "Oh, Matilda... the thing is, Gordon and I have never gotten along. We only have to be in a room together for a few minutes before we're at each other's throats, so I can't pretend I've seen the best of him. He isn't used to a woman standing up to him and speaking her mind, and you know I can't keep my tongue between my teeth. The trouble is," she added, feeling anxiety for her friend bloom in her heart, "I don't think Ruth can, either."

"But would he hurt her?" Matilda demanded, fear glinting in her blue eyes. "Come along, Bonnie. I must know. Is Ruth in any danger? Is he... violent?"

"Oh, no!" Bonnie exclaimed, shaking her head. "At least, yes, he can be, but not to a woman. He'll not hesitate to knock a man down who insults him, he's a rather brutal sort, but I've never known him lay a hand on a woman. No, it's not that, he's... he's just a bear with a sore head. He'll either not say a word for days on end or bark orders. There's nothing tender about him, no soft feelings. Ruth is in no physical danger, but I fear for her happiness."

"Well," Matilda said, her voice grim. "I suppose she's made her bed, as we all must. She wasn't forced to act as she did, and we'll never know exactly what was in her mind. How can we ever know what anyone else truly thinks?"

Bonnie stared, taken aback by the bleak tone of her friend's voice. Somehow, she didn't think it was only Ruth that she was speaking about. Matilda noticed the concern in Bonnie's eyes and gave a short, humourless laugh.

"There's little any of us can do for her now," she said with a sigh. "Though I shall go and fetch her and bring her back with me if I have the slightest sign she needs to escape."

"You're a good friend," Bonnie said, laying a hand on her arm. "And I will happily go with you. If Anderson makes Ruth unhappy, he'll have me to deal with, too."

Matilda smiled and patted her hand. "That, if nothing else, ought to give the man pause," she said, making Bonnie grin. "But how wretched of me to waylay you, and on such a glorious night. What a triumph for you, you truly do look like a queen, and you ought not be thinking of anything but your own happiness at such a time, you deserve it, love."

Impulsively, Bonnie hugged Matilda tightly and kissed her cheek. "Thank you, Mama Hen. At least you have one less chick to fret over. In the morning, I shall check my correspondence. I haven't had a moment to read my letters so I don't know if there is anything from Ruth, but if there is not, I shall write to her again, and beg her to confide in me."

Matilda nodded. "Yes. We ought not fret before we know there is a need to. You ought not, at least. Enjoy your success, Bonnie, and kiss your husband. I've no doubt he's pining for you."

That, Bonnie was more than happy to do, and ran off with a smile on her lips.

Chapter 21

Dearest Bonnie,

I am so sorry that I did not write sooner. I'm not sure why I didn't, only ~~things have been dif...~~ It's taken me a while to adjust.

How delighted I was to hear of your marriage to Mr Cadogan. I wish you both every happiness, though I suspect you do not need my wishes. It was clear the last morning I saw you that he adored you. Lucky girl!

I by contrast, have not married for love and went into this arrangement with my eyes wide open and yet... oh, Bonnie, dearest. I urgently need your advice regarding my husband...

— Excerpt of a letter from Mrs Ruth Anderson to Mrs Bonnie Cadogan.

5th December 1814. Mr and Mrs Cadogan's celebration ball, The Earl of St Clair's London Residence, St James.

Jerome looked around the ballroom. The evening had been a wild success and his mother was in raptures. The people she'd wanted to make green with envy had turned suitably chartreuse in tint. Those she wanted to eat their words of condolence at having had such a terrible daughter-in-law foisted upon her had been made to see the error of their ways. Their friends and family had rallied about them and been caught up in the triumphant happiness of the evening. Everyone was having a marvellous time, Bonnie and his mother most of all. They were thick as thieves, and no doubt cooking up plans for future devastation.

It had rather taken him aback how well and how quickly Bonnie and his mama had taken to each other; in truth it was a little daunting. He'd always known of his parents' well-honed sense of the ridiculous. It was only now, however, that he realised it hadn't only been his father who'd caused mischief and mayhem. His darling mama had a touch of the devil in her too. Well, at least she could no longer take him to task for his bad behaviour, as he could take pleasure in reminding her that the pot was every bit as black as the kettle.

Nonetheless, it was irritating if the wretched woman had taken Bonnie off somewhere, as he wanted to be alone with his wife. He'd been very patient all night, but now he'd had enough of dancing and chatter and he wanted Bonnie, preferably somewhere dark and secluded.

He gave a huff of irritation and snatched up a glass of champagne from a passing waiter. Where on earth had she gotten to, the provoking creature? Jerome jolted as someone gave him a jovial, and none too gentle, slap on the back.

"There you are old man," crowed an amused voice. "I've been looking everywhere for you."

With an ominous feeling of déjà vu, Jerome swung around and looked into a glittering pair of pale green eyes.

"Oh, good Lord," he murmured, torn between a groan and hysteria. She'd gone and done it again. "Plague take you, Bo— Bart," he stammered, correcting himself at the last minute. "What are you doing here, and dressed like that?"

Jerome looked her over and felt his body tighten as he noticed the way the well-fitting breeches clung to her shapely legs. No doubt her delectable bottom was equally well highlighted and, if he remembered rightly, not nearly well enough covered by the tails of her coat. How anyone could mistake her for a young man was beyond him.

"Why, looking for you, Coz," she said, adopting the swaggering pose of a young buck. "Thought you might like to go elsewhere for a bit of sport? What say you?"

"I say, I ought to tan your hide, you dreadful creature," he muttered, trying hard to glower at her but his lips kept turning upwards and spoiling the effect. "Come along, then," he said, setting down his empty glass. "If it's sport you're looking for, I have just the thing."

Jerome let his young *cousin* out of the ballroom and along the darkened corridors as if they were heading for the front door, and then diverted, opening a door and shoving her inside. It was a small room, done up as a parlour though his mother thought it too dark and seldom used it. Tonight it was quiet and vacant, only illuminated by the moonlight flooding through the windows as the curtains had not been closed.

"Oh, Jerome, I thought we were going to—"

Jerome didn't give his madcap wife a moment more to remonstrate but simply backed her up against the nearest wall and kissed her until she was breathless.

"You've caused quite enough of a stir for one evening," he told her, when he finally came up for air, trying his best to sound like a stern husband who ought to be obeyed. Bonnie simply snickered.

"We'll cause a deal more of a stir if anyone catches us like this," she said, raising one eyebrow as she gestured to her breeches and tailcoat.

Jerome snorted despite himself. "You are, without a doubt, the most provoking creature I have ever come across. It's a good job I married you. No one else could have possibly kept you in line."

Bonnie blinked up at him, her eyes wide and innocent. "What makes you think you can do it?"

Hiding his smile, Jerome ducked his head and nuzzled her neck whilst his nimble fingers made short work of the buttons on her breeches. He slid his hand beneath the fall, seeking out the feathery triangle of soft curls between her thighs as Bonnie's breath hitched.

"This," he murmured, kissing the tender place beneath her ear and trailing his lips along her jaw to her mouth as his fingers slid lower. The faint sounds of the orchestra were still audible, but the party seemed a long, long way away now as he caressed her.

"Oh," Bonnie said, her head falling back as her eyes closed.

"Bonnie," Jerome whispered, giddy with desire, with the nearness of her, the warmth and the scent of her. He slid his fingers into her wet heat and felt his own breath catch as she gasped. "I'm mad for you, you wicked girl. I've thought of nothing but you since that night at Green Park. You were lit up brighter than any of the fireworks, did you know that? The sky was full of colours and light and I couldn't see anything but you. You dazzled me, and I've still not recovered."

She opened heavy-lidded eyes and focused on him. "Please, don't recover," she murmured. "I don't want you to come to your senses."

"I shan't," he promised, unbuttoning her waistcoat with his free hand. "I couldn't if I wanted to, and I don't want to. There's no cure for you, Bonnie, and I thank God for that."

As he tugged her shirt free, he also thanked God that she hadn't bound her breasts as tightly as the last time. With one deft tug, he loosened the edge of the binding and freed the end. It took a few moments pulling and cursing but then her splendid breasts were mercifully freed, and he pushed the shirt up and out of the way.

"Lovely," he murmured, before pressing his lips to the generous mounds, kissing along the full curves before dragging his tongue over her nipple until she sighed and made an incoherent sound of need. He took pity and suckled first one breast, then the other, as she squirmed, and his fingers caressed her intimate flesh until she was moaning and helpless beneath his touch.

"And here I was thinking I'd have a queen to command me," he murmured, smiling against her skin as she panted. "Though I admit, these breeches are easier to access than acres of skirts and petticoats."

"I c-can still command you," she said, the challenge audible in her voice, faint as it was.

"Oh? And what would you have of me?" he asked, excitement shivering over him.

"I think," she murmured, her dark, desire-hazed eyes glinting in the dim light of the room. "You should kneel for me."

Jerome gave a wicked chuckle and wasted no time in obeying. He dragged the breeches from her legs, freeing her as she held the shirt out of his way. The sound she made, desperate and wanton as he touched her with his tongue made desire burst inside him like the firework he'd compared her too. It glittered through his blood, making him ache with need, making his heart pound with elation and joy, a heady combination that Bonnie alone had the recipe for. Good Lord but she was audacious and fearless: his beautiful wife, his madcap, naughty girl.

She was bold, too, too bold perhaps as the sounds she made became louder and ever less restrained. She glared at him as he sat back on his heels and tugged her to the floor.

"You are so noisy," he said, barely containing his own laughter as she huffed and muttered at him. "You'll be heard above the noise of the orchestra if you keep on."

"Well, what did you expect," she grumbled, "when you do *that*?"

Jerome showed her exactly what he expected of her, tumbling her onto her back and fumbling with his own buttons with unsteady fingers. Exhilaration coursed through him and he muffled his own cry of triumph against her skin as he slid inside her. As he loved her with his mouth and hands and body it became clear that Bonnie was incapable of discretion, so he softened the decadent sounds she made with kisses until the final cry which he prayed no one else had heard over the din of the ballroom. He laughed then, rolling off her and onto his back, tugging her with him as the laughter bubbled up inside him and the ridiculous joy of it, of life with her, made him helpless with mirth.

"You're mad," Bonnie said, propping herself up on one arm and staring down at him with amusement.

"Mad for you," he said, breathless still as he reached a hand up and tangled his fingers in her short, dark curls.

"It's not blonde," she said with a sigh of regret, tugging at one of the curls and squinting sideways at it. She gave a rueful smile as she looked over the generous curves and valleys of her body. "And I'm no sylphlike lady. I *was* in need of rescuing, though," she added, brightening. "So there's that at least."

"What are you wittering on about?" he asked, bemused.

"The woman of your dreams," she said, a flicker of something uncertain visible in her eyes. "Everyone told me I wasn't your type. That you always fell for fragile looking blondes in need of rescuing."

Jerome stared up at her. He supposed the words were true enough. He'd thought the same not so long ago, yet it felt like a lifetime.

"You are everything I dream of, Bonnie," he said, his voice low. "But so much better, because you're real, and you're so much more than I realised I wanted or needed." He reached out and filled his hand with her breast, squeezing a little. "So much more," he added, with a sly grin as she squealed and laughed. He rolled her over onto her back again and stared down at her, dazed with his own good fortune. "Thank God for you, Bonnie. For being brave enough and strong enough to show me what I needed. If you hadn't…." His voice quavered a little, and he gave a soft huff of laughter. "I love you, you dreadful girl, don't ever change. I love you just as you are, even though you'll turn my hair grey. Let's have lots of children, and lots of laughter, and as much chaos as any couple can possibly handle."

"I like the sound of that very much," she whispered, her eyes full of everything he wanted to see there. "And I love you too, Jerome. I have from the start, as you well know. But…."

Jerome waited, wondering anxiously what came after that *but.*

"Can we concentrate on the *lots of children,* please?"

He grinned down at her, relieved. "Now, you mean?"

"Of course now," she said, sliding her hand under his trousers.

"Bonnie," he groaned as she caressed him. "You're wicked, and insatiable, and I will be a husk of a man if you keep this up."

"Oh, you'll survive," she said with confidence as he grew hard once more beneath her touch. "And you love me for my wickedness, you just said so. You can't take it back."

"I do, and I wouldn't," he admitted, sighing and closing his eyes in bliss before opening them again with a start. "Oh, God," he said alarmed.

Bonnie's hand stilled. "What?" she asked, staring down at him. "What is it?"

"Oh, good Lord," he groaned. "I've just realised. We… we might have daughters… like *you!*"

Bonnie snorted with mirth at his obvious consternation.

"It's not funny," Jerome objected. "They might get caught up with... with—"

"A wicked fellow like you?" Bonnie suggested. "Perhaps," she said, her tone soothing as she pushed him back down again. "But I'll make sure any daughter of mine knows how to deal with such a troublesome creature."

"That is *not* reassuring," he grumbled, as Bonnie moved over him and kissed his neck and his jaw, working along to his mouth.

"They'll be fine," she soothed him. "Because they'll know they are loved, that they belong, and that their papa will murder any man who dares to treat them unkindly."

"I would," he said, meaning it, and feeling a swell of emotion at the thought of a daughter, with laughing green eyes and dark, lustrous curls like her mama. "And I will. I love you, Bonnie."

"I know," she said. "I love you too, with all my heart."

And she made a point of showing him just how much that was.

Girls who dare– *Inside every wallflower is the beating heart of a lioness, a passionate individual willing to risk all for their dream, if only they can find the courage to begin. When these overlooked girls make a pact to change their lives, anything can happen.*

Ten girls – Ten dares in a hat. Who will dare to risk it all?

Next in the series

To Winter at Wildsyde.
Girls Who Dare, Book 7

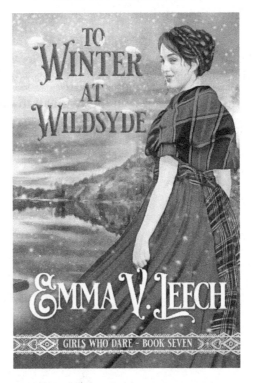

A dare to change a lifetime …

Miss Ruth Stone, a wealthy heiress, is struggling to fulfil her father's dream to marry into nobility, despite her hefty dowry. Dared by the

Peculiar Ladies to "Say something outrageous to a handsome man," Ruth outdoes herself and proposes marriage to the heir to an earldom.

A decision she may live to regret...

Before she can think better of having opened her big mouth, her gorgeous, hulking husband-to-be has hustled her into a carriage and borne her off to his remote, tumbledown castle where he intends to put her dowry to good use.

A marriage or a business affair...

Ruth has no illusions. She's a strong, sensible woman, not a fragile beauty and she knows her husband will never fall madly in love. Their marriage is one of convenience, her children will inherit title and legitimacy among the *ton* and she will have the home of her own she's dreamed of. Yet her pig-headed, obstinate husband rouses her temper and her passions like no one before.

Her first winter at Wildsyde is about to set the old castle alight.

Turn the page for a sneak peek of To Winter at Wildsyde, out February 7, 2020

Chapter 1

My dear Kitty,

I hardly know where to begin. I only went out for an hour, yet in that brief interval everyone seems to have run quite mad.

Do you remember Ruth's dare, 'To say something utterly outrageous to a handsome man'? Well, I'd say she's outdone herself.

— Excerpt of a letter from Miss Matilda Hunt to Mrs Kitty Baxter.

29th October 1814. London.

Ruth tried not to stare. She really did, but it was impossible. After a valiant battle she gave up and gazed across the carriage at a man she'd met barely twenty minutes earlier. A man to whom she'd just proposed marriage.

Her luxurious carriage ought to accommodate four people with comfort. Gordon Anderson made it look like something a child would play with. His massive frame shrank everything around him, and he appeared somewhat ill at ease against the plush velvet and gold trim of the comfortable seats. No doubt he was wondering if he'd been a little rash himself, but then he was getting fifty thousand pounds as part of the deal. He'd been desperate enough for Bonnie Campbell's meagre five thousand to come to London after her, so his change of fortune ought to be something to celebrate. Of course, he'd also had Bonnie as part of that original arrangement. A voluptuous Scottish girl, she might be a hoyden, but she'd still have been a beautiful wife he'd have enjoyed bedding if nothing else. Ruth blushed as she considered how she would appear by contrast.

Ruth had no illusions. Her friends were all beautiful women to a greater or lesser degree, and it was impossible not to be aware of one's attributes when there were so many fine examples to compare oneself to. Not that she was jealous or resented them… well, maybe she was just a touch envious, but they were her friends and she loved them all dearly. Besides which, she knew her own worth. Perhaps she was no beauty, but she was a capable woman more than able to make her husband's life comfortable and well organised. She had run her father's vast household since the age of twelve, as her mother was a featherbrain, to put it politely, and a tumbledown castle in the wilds of Scotland should hold no terrors for her.

Why then was she trembling?

Well, perhaps that was because she'd just agreed to marry *a complete stranger!*

Still, Mr Anderson had given her leave to redecorate the castle as she saw fit and had given no restrictions. Though he might regret that when he saw her father's house. Happily she did not share her parent's taste for opulence and ostentation. The running of the household and the staff was also to be her domain and he would not interfere. That was a good start. If they could be reasonable there was every chance they might make a go of their rather unconventional marriage.

"Tell me about Wildsyde, Mr Anderson. What is it like?"

Ruth was relieved to discover her voice was steady, which was a wonder, given that every other part of her was shaking now, as the reality of what she'd done sank in.

A pair of rather unsettling whisky coloured eyes turned upon her and she caught her breath. Good heavens but he was beautiful. That seemed an odd choice of words, perhaps, but he *was* beautiful, in the same way a harsh and rugged landscape was beautiful. Uncompromising, dangerous, and breathtaking.

"Wildsyde is old and draughty and at this time of year, cold enough to freeze yer ballocks," he said, his gaze on her placid, showing nothing resembling curiosity or interest. "Have ye changed yer mind then, lass?"

"No," Ruth replied, a little too quickly lest she give herself time to think about it.

She'd spent far too long thinking and fretting over the kind of husband she might end up with. There had been offers. They came on an almost weekly basis when such a hefty dowry was up for grabs, and not one of them had been remotely tempting. Her father dismissed most of them because they were not illustrious enough. Her optimistic papa seemed to think she still had every possibility to snare a duke, if she only put her mind to it, but he'd settle for anything above a baron if push came to shove. That being the case, now and then she had to suffer through proposals from desperate noblemen who were either on the brink of ruin and a protracted stay in the Marshalsea, or with one foot in the grave. Some of them had made her shudder to consider, others had simply made her want to cry.

She was not some fragile miss to be pushed around, though. Her father had long since realised his daughter had a will as iron-clad as his own and no amount of bullying or wheedling would make her change her mind or accept a match she didn't favour. This man had at least been her choice, for good or ill. The problem was, she had no idea which was the most likely. *It's not worth it for a title,* Bonnie had pleaded with her. *He's not got a brass farthing, the castle is practically in ruins and miles from any society and, what's more, he's a dumb brute with as much sensitivity as a rock, and not a civilised bone in his body.*

Despite her best intentions, Ruth could not help but survey that body now. It certainly didn't look civilised. It looked virile and powerful and so shockingly masculine it made her breath catch.

His knees were bare and the ungainly sprawl he'd adopted in the carriage had hiked his kilt higher to expose a few inches of muscular thighs. Ruth stared and stared, never having seen anything resembling male skin beyond face or hands in her life before. The sudden awareness that she was being observed filtered through her stunned brain and she blushed scarlet as she realised she was right. A smirk played at his lips.

"Think ye can wait until we get to Scotland?"

Ruth sucked in a breath at his audacity but refused to look away from him. That it was true enough ought to make her ashamed perhaps, but she'd not let him intimidate her. This man needed to know she'd not be bested, no matter if his physical presence made her quiver inside. She could hardly deny that it had been desire that had motivated her. Oh, yes, he had the title she needed to satisfy her father's longing for a foothold in society and, more to the point, he was desperate enough for money to agree to wed her. Those things had been high on her agenda, but not the sole motivating factor. She'd taken one look at him and *wanted.*

Mine, had screamed a voice in her head and perhaps it was the aura he carried of something not quite tame that had awakened this savage part of her she'd not known existed. Either way, it was awake and clamouring now, and no amount of second thoughts and anxieties were enough to make it give way.

The carriage drew to a halt outside her father's lavish home on Upper Walpole Street and Ruth let out a sigh of relief. She needed to get out of this confined space and fast, before she lost her senses entirely.

Mr Anderson got down and then reached his hand back to her. Unlike most men of the *ton*, he did not wear gloves, and though she did, his touch seemed to sear through them as if they were not there at all. His hand engulfed hers, suntanned and work roughened, not the hand of a gentleman, for all he was heir to an earldom.

The butler, Garrick, smiled at her warmly as they entered, though his smile faltered as he took in the man with her.

"Garrick, is my father at home?" she asked, blushing a little as she evaded his eye.

Not that he would comment. Garrick was a prince among butlers and Ruth was extremely fond of him. To say that she would miss him more than her own parents was not an understatement. A tall sparse man with neat black hair, twinkling blue eyes, and an air of absolute certainty about him, he'd been her ally for many years. He had quickly learned she was the force that ran the household and only took instruction from her and not her foolish mama—not unless Ruth had sanctioned whatever it was the idiotic creature had demanded. Leaving him behind would be a wrench and not only for her, she suspected. Where her father was a doting but absent parent, Garrick had been there since she was twelve years old.

"Yes, Miss Stone. I believe he is in his office."

"Thank you." Ruth smiled at him as she handed him her gloves and hat.

She was well aware that among the *ton* servants were never thanked, but she considered such ill manners to be improper, no matter if it showed up her lack of breeding. If staff looked down upon her for appreciating their efforts, they were at liberty to go elsewhere to be treated with less respect.

Once Garrick had left them alone, she turned back to Mr Anderson and tried not to gawk at the picture he made: a wild looking, unshaven Highlander standing in her father's opulent entrance hall. Ruth knew the house was vulgar, with far too much gold and ostentation on show. She'd done her best to keep a lid on her father's appalling taste, but there was only so much she could do. It was his house. Seeing Mr Anderson in such a setting was jarring, though, only highlighting the fripperies and ridiculous expense, and akin to seeing a lion prowl the ballroom at Almacks.

It was not his natural habitat.

"Holy God," he murmured, staring about in awe.

"Yes, well," Ruth said, a little impatient now as she felt awkward... more awkward. "Perhaps it would be best if you waited here while I... I...."

"Go and break the news?" he suggested drily.

"Yes," Ruth agreed, not seeing any point in pretending that wasn't the case. Whilst her father would be delighted at the prospective earldom, his new son-in-law might give him pause. She needed to prepare the way.

"Will yer da nae like the match?"

"Oh, he'll like the earldom just fine, Mr Anderson," Ruth said, trying to focus on keeping things business-like. She was used to dealing with her father's associates and if she kept things impersonal, for now at least, she might get through this without swooning or becoming hysterical. One could only hope.

"Until he finds his son-in-law is about as welcome among the English elite as a dose of the clap?" he suggested mildly.

Ruth ignored his turn of phrase, certain that he was trying to rile her, though she didn't understand why. That he needed her money was obvious. Did he find her so unattractive the thought of keeping his end of the bargain was enough for him to hope she'd cry off? The idea could not be disregarded, as lowering as it was.

"You might be unwelcome, but I will do well enough I've no doubt," she said coolly. "A countess is due a measure of respect, no matter who her husband is." Though Ruth hadn't the slightest intention of allowing her father to use her for his own ends. She'd done quite enough to elevate the family and its fortunes and wasn't about to become a martyr to the cause.

That seemed to shut him up, for the moment anyway, and so Ruth ordered him some food—for no doubt a man of his size was always hungry—and set off to find her father.

***

233

"Bleedin' 'ell," murmured Mr George Stone as he looked up at his prospective son-in-law, despite having been well primed in advance so that he wouldn't gawp.

Ruth elbowed her father, who shook off his rather daunted expression and held out his hand, giving Mr Anderson the benefit of a broad grin. A practical man, her papa. It hadn't taken him long to realise that the heir to an earldom in the hand, was a better option than a so far mythical marquess or duke who had yet to show themselves. Yes, the man was a Scot, which was regrettable, but the earldom was an old and venerable one, if not terribly wealthy. Not that it mattered. Mr Stone had wealth in spades, and he wanted his grandson to be born to a title. The Earl of Morven would do very nicely. Except that Ruth could see the calculation in her father's eyes and the realisation that Ruth had not been exaggerating. Entry into the *ton* would not happen in this generation, not easily at any rate. Not unless Ruth took her husband well in hand, something of which her father seemed to believe her more than capable.

Not being a fool, Ruth did not rush to agree.

Looking at the man now, she doubted her ability to survive the wedding night. She'd either die of shock or anticipation. Best not think of that. Still, once she'd got his measure, she didn't doubt she could manage him to a degree. In her experience—which was admittedly limited mostly to her father—men were content enough in their home lives if they were comfortable and well fed, and that at least she could achieve.

Much to her chagrin, Ruth's witless mama took one look at her prospective son-in-law and swooned. Ruth regarded her mother as she fell with an elegant rustle of silk with an impassive expression. Neither Ruth nor her father rushed to catch her, being far too familiar with the routine, though she suspected Mr Anderson would have done so if the horror on her mother's face hadn't been quite so blatant before her eyes had rolled up.

"Ring for Mrs Grisham, Papa," she said with a sigh, before finding a small bottle of sal volatile and waving it beneath her hopeless parent's nose. She didn't dare look at Mr Anderson. She didn't doubt it was the kind of display which would not find favour with him.

Once her mother had been taken off for a lie down in a dark room, Ruth returned her attention to the men.

"Well, Ruthie, run along then, and leave us to discuss the details, there's a good girl," her father said, rubbing his hands together and looking pleased with himself at the prospect of the coming negotiation.

Ruth levelled her papa with a stern look he was familiar with by now, and which chased the smile from his face. "No, Papa, this is my future we are discussing. I shall stay."

Mr Stone's expression darkened.

"Would you leave your secretary to arrange the details of an important deal?" she demanded, folding her arms.

"I'm not your bloody secretary, you cheeky mare," Mr Stone retorted.

"No, of course not, dear," Ruth agreed with a placid smile. "But you are not me, either."

She sat herself down before the desk and then craned her neck up at Mr Anderson.

"Do sit down, Mr Anderson," she said. "Papa, why don't you offer some brandy? You know a little snifter always clears your mind."

Mr Anderson gave her a long, hard look which she couldn't read, but sat as she bid him, and her father poured out two generous measures of brandy.

"Right then," she said, smiling as the two men settled themselves down. "Shall we begin?"

Chapter 2

Today, I leave my friends behind and begin a new life in the Highlands of Scotland. When we reach Wildsyde Castle, I will become Mrs Anderson.

Oh, my word. What have I done?

*— **Excerpt of an entry by Miss Ruth Stone to her diary.***

30th October 1814. London.

"It was good of you to agree to delay our journey to visit my aunt in Tunbridge Wells, Mr Anderson," Ruth said, drawing those unsettling amber eyes in her direction.

Mr Anderson snorted and raised one eyebrow. "It was nae *good*, lass as ye ken well enough. It was clear ye would nae give me a moment's peace if I dinnae agree to it. I'm nae so foolish as to endure a journey to Scotland with a woman holding a grudge."

Ruth frowned for a moment, a little irritated that he had to point the fact out, but it was true enough. "I suppose that is a fair comment, but my Aunt Ethel has been vocal in her disapproval of my unmarried state."

"And ye want to go and rub her nose in it, aye?" he said, a flicker of amusement behind the words.

"Aye, I mean yes, yes I do, if you must know."

He shrugged and Ruth watched his massive shoulders lift and settle with avid interest. "It'll delay our journey by a day, but ye can consider it a wedding gift. I've nought else to give ye."

"It is a very fine wedding gift," Ruth said, meaning it.

She was beside herself with delight at the prospect of presenting this magnificent specimen of manhood to her widowed aunt. The woman had given a deal too much advice and become far too exasperated by Ruth's inability to snare a husband. She'd made Ruth feel every bit the oversized, ungainly and unfeminine lump she'd always feared she was. Finally, Ruth could hold her head up.

"Though…" she began, before losing her nerve and closing her mouth again.

"Well, out with it," he said, his voice a pleasant rumble over the noise of carriage wheels.

"Well," she said, gathering her courage and leaning towards him, her expression hopeful. "Do you think you… you might…?"

"If ye are asking me to act the part of besotted fool, Miss Stone, ye are barking up the wrong tree."

Ruth flushed. "Not a besotted fool, Mr Anderson," she said, her voice tight. "My aunt is neither blind nor a halfwit, she'd never believe it, but if… if you could try to… to…."

"Be less of a brute?" he suggested.

"Do you think you might allow me to finish my own sentences?" she demanded, irritated, although he was right on both counts, even if she'd perhaps not have phrased it in quite such terms.

"If ye stop hemming and hawing, aye."

Ruth sighed. "Well, then, *can* you manage to be less of a brute?"

Mr Anderson regarded her with a resigned expression. "How long are we going to be there?"

***

They made Aunt Ethel's by midday and, as far as Ruth was concerned, it could have added a whole month to the journey and still have been worth it.

Her aunt was a bracket-faced woman with a thin mouth, set eternally into a narrow line, and protruding eyes that were currently in danger of falling from her head, so profound was her astonishment.

"Betrothed?" the woman repeated, her voice faint as she stared at Mr Anderson like he'd dropped from the skies. Ruth couldn't really blame her. It was the kind of figure that ought to have dropped from the skies, bringing with it as it did thoughts of warrior gods and ancient deities.

Mr Anderson bore her aunt's scrutiny for about five minutes, which was four more than Ruth had bargained on, before he made his excuses, albeit politely, muttering something about seeing to the horses. Ruth didn't care. Her aunt had seen him, knew he was not a figment of her imagination—who in the world could have imagined such a man? — and was suitably speechless.

"Well, I never," said Aunt Ethel, snatching up a fan and waving it vigorously even though she was swathed in shawls and blankets. "Goodness me."

"We'll marry in Scotland. Mr Anderson has a castle there," Ruth added, rather enjoying herself now. She looked around, startled as Aunt Ethel reached out and grasped hold of her wrist.

"Well done, Ruth!" she said, a look of such approval in her eyes that Ruth was quite taken aback. She'd never pleased her aunt before. Indeed, she wasn't sure anyone ever had. "Well done, my girl."

"Oh." Ruth blinked in astonishment. "Well, thank you," she said, uncertain if thanks were due in the circumstances. It was her money he was marrying after all, not *her*. She'd made no secret of the fact. What was the point?

"Oh, such a man," Ethel sighed, waving the fan faster still. "My own dear Alfred was a big fellow, you know," she added, her eyes growing misty. "A pig-headed, stubborn ox of man, he was." She blinked, a wistful sigh at her lips. "Oh, he took a deal of managing, I can tell you. My word, the rows we had."

A beatific glow lit up her aunt's face, changing it dramatically. It occurred to Ruth that she'd never thought of Ethel having been anything other than a widow. Her husband had died young, long before Ruth was born, and they were not a close family. Now Ruth wondered how much of her aunt's bad temper resulted from grief, for it was clear in this moment that she'd adored her husband.

Aunt Ethel looked up, aware perhaps of Ruth's scrutiny.

"That one will lead you a merry dance," she said, looking positively gleeful. "You'll want to murder him a time or two, mark my words. Oh, but it will be worth it."

"Do you think so?" Ruth asked, daring to voice her doubts to this woman whom she'd never have dreamed of confiding in before now. "Because he's awfully.... Well, he's very...."

"Yes," Ethel said with a wry smile. "I reckon he is. He'll not be used to having a wife, or to heeding anyone's advice but his own, and I doubt he'll be intending to give you an inch, so you must take it Ruth. Don't put up with any nonsense. You're a Stone through and through, and we're aptly named, I tell you. Your pa may have made the money, but he'd never have gotten so far without me and your grandmother pushing him on, though he'll never admit as much," she added with a snort. "You take his measure, my girl, but if you ask me, you're more than a match for him."

Ruth smiled and let out a breath, feeling a sudden rush of affection for her usually belligerent aunt. She leaned in and kissed Ethel's cheek. "Thank you."

Ethel laughed and shook her head. "Oh, don't thank me. I'm looking forward to watching the sparks fly, albeit from a distance. You'll write and tell me how you're getting on?"

Ruth smiled and nodded. "You may count on it, but only to receive tactical advice in return."

"Done," said her aunt, and gave her a very uncharacteristic grin.

***

They returned to London that night and, to placate Mr Anderson for the day he'd lost in accommodating the visit to her aunt, they left at daybreak. The stops were brief and infrequent and clearly more for the horses' benefit than for Ruth's.

Mr Anderson was not a conversationalist.

Most enquiries met with grunts that seemed to either be positive or negative, but if he had spoken more than ten words during the entire day Ruth would have been astonished. That he appeared to have no interest or curiosity about her at all was galling, but Ruth had no illusions. She was no sultry beauty, nor a fragile blonde that needed mollycoddling. Mr Anderson did not desire her and, beyond keeping to the terms of their agreement, didn't give a hoot about her. Well, fine. That was fine.

She would have a house—a castle in fact—and she would have staff to manage and plenty to keep her busy. No doubt soon enough she'd have children too, and... and that thought led her imagination down quite a different avenue. She forced herself to stare out of the window and not at Mr Anderson's bare knees.

He had sprawled out across the carriage once more, his arms folded and his eyes closed and, despite her best intentions, her gaze drifted away from the landscape and back to him. He was a landscape all of his own, as strange and impenetrable as any foreign terrain, fraught with unknown dangers. What she suspected was a deceptive calm had settled over his powerful frame. Even the language of this new world was foreign to her. *He* was foreign to her, yet as with any undiscovered place, exotic and beguiling despite the dangers. Everything feminine in her felt the pull towards him, the longing to explore, to make the foreign familiar. Hers.

His hair was a rich, dark brown and too long for fashion. It fell almost to his shoulders, with a distinct wave running through it. His lashes were darker still and so long and thick any woman would have wept with envy. The contrast against such a starkly masculine and forbidding visage was profound. Though he'd been cleanly shaven when they'd left, now the dark stubble at his jaw made it appear he had not done so at all, as though his body defied any attempt to civilise it. The longing to reach across the carriage intensified. She wanted the right to touch him, to stroke her hand across his cheek and feel the rasp of his whiskers. The desire was so sudden and intense that Ruth curled her hands into fists, as if she could restrain the wanting by holding it closed in her palm. Her eyes drifted down, over the muscular arms folded across his chest, down the plaid of his kilt, to the exposed skin of his knees. One leg stretched out, the other bent and fallen against the door of the carriage. Once again, his kilt had rucked up an inch or so, giving her a fine view of his lower thighs.

She wondered if he'd done it on purpose to unsettle her and felt a sudden prickle of unease, as though she was being watched. Ruth darted a glance back at his face to assure herself his eyes were still closed, but couldn't shake the feeling he'd been well aware of her scrutiny. The air in the carriage was cold and Ruth drew it in, filling her lungs and forcing her gaze back to what lay beyond the window. She would not stare at him, not torment herself with thoughts of what kind of man he was, what manner of wife she would be to him. What would be, would be, and she would make the best of whatever befell her.

***

The inn at Dunstable was neat and clean, not that Ruth noticed. She was too exhausted by the events of the past few days to do anything beyond swallow a little soup in the privacy of her own room and fall into bed. A wide-eyed maid servant had helped her undress and prepare for bed. Ruth disliked her on sight and failed to hide it, making the girl nervous and clumsy. Her animosity was not rooted in frustration at her incompetence. Much to Ruth's dismay and shame it had been instantaneous when they'd entered the inn. She was pretty and slender and made Ruth feel like a fool for even hoping the gorgeous man she was with would ever look twice at her. When the girl had stared at Mr Anderson with an expression Ruth very much feared mirrored her own whenever she looked upon him, it had made all her insecurities rush to the surface. By the time the girl's wide eyes had fallen to Mr Anderson's knees, she'd had enough. Ruth had coughed, loudly, and demanded she prepare her room at once.

Her own maid, Rachel, had deserted Ruth immediately upon hearing the news of her engagement. She'd taken one glance at Ruth's husband to be and turned as white as a milk pudding. This shock followed by the mention of *Wildsyde Castle* in *Scotland* was too much. Their destination might have well as been The Tower of London, such was her obvious revulsion. Either way, it was more than the woman could bear. She made her views on living in such a remote part of the country, and amongst such crude people, abundantly clear. So, with no time to make alternative arrangements, Ruth told Mr Anderson she could well look after herself and made no fuss. If she'd been hoping for a word of appreciation at not forcing him to delay their journey whilst she sought another maid, for propriety's sake at least, she was to be disappointed.

Now, alone in her bed and staring up into the dark, Ruth felt far from home, though they'd only been on the road one day. *Chin up,* she counselled herself sternly. *This was your idea, your chance for independence, for the life you wanted for yourself. No one said it would be easy.*

You could change your mind, urged another, louder voice in her head, which she silenced. Impossible. She'd travelled for a day in an enclosed carriage with no maid for propriety. They must marry now, or she'd be ruined. Just as well, she thought with a sigh, pounding her lumpy pillow and hoping to get comfortable. There was no going back, so she'd just have to make the best of it. She turned onto her side, forced her eyes closed, and willed herself to sleep.

***

The journey continued in much the same fashion over the following days. Mr Anderson was a huge if silent presence that consumed the majority of the available space in both Ruth's carriage and her mind. When they crossed the border into Scotland she had come to a breaking point, out of patience with his monosyllabic responses to her efforts to talk with him and decided it was time they had a conversation, whether he liked it or not. A furious determination swept over her and she reached into her reticule, retrieving a small notebook and pencil.

"Tell me about your staff," she said, watching the dark sweep of those luxuriant lashes lift and the whisky coloured eyes turn upon her. "Are there many working at the castle at present?"

There was a heavy sigh.

"Five," he said and then yawned, scrubbing a hand over his bristly jaw.

The rasp of his whiskers set her all on edge and her temper ratcheted up another notch as she waited for him to elaborate. He did not.

"Only five?" She frowned at him. "Surely, a property of the size you've indicated...."

He favoured her with a look of scornful impatience.

"Did ye forget already, lass? I've nae a brass farthing, as the wee hellion told ye plain enough. 'Twas nae a falsehood."

Ruth nodded her understanding.

"Tell me about them, please," she asked, and got only an irritated sigh in response. "What are their names and their duties?" she demanded, the words bitten off as she fought to keep her frustration at bay.

"I'll introduce ye," he said. "Ye'll meet them soon enough."

He stretched, yawning again and lifting his arms to the ceiling, extending his limbs as best he could in the confined space. Ruth stared, captivated momentarily by the shift of muscle beneath his clothing before she caught the amused glint in his eyes. Gritting her teeth, she glared at him.

"I would like to learn their names and duties before I arrive."

She held his gaze, realising how imperious she sounded as one dark eyebrow lifted just a fraction. He'd better get used to it if he was going to ignore her. If he thought to test her, to see how far she would bend to his will or how she'd respond to such treatment he'd not discover a biddable little mouse for a wife. He'd gained fifty thousand in taking her, but she would make him earn it.

He gave her a long, considering look before he replied. "Hilda MacLeod is housekeeper and cook. Dougal Clugston is the estate manager. There are three maids: Sheenagh Baillie, Flora Moffat, and Jessie Irwin."

Ruth nodded. "I shall need to hire more staff."

"That's yer own affair," he said, and crossed his arms once more, closing his eyes.

Damn him, he was going back to sleep.

"Will you invite anyone to the wedding. Your family, perhaps?"

"Na."

"Why not?"

No answer.

"Why not, Mr Anderson?"

Silence.

"Why, Miss Stone," Ruth said, adopting a conversational tone. "Because my kin are loud and talkative, and I fear you'll not get a word in edgeways. Why, Mr Anderson," she continued, deciding she may as well carry on both sides of the conversation. "How thoughtful you are. Shall we take a honeymoon, do you think?" She paused and cleared her throat, attempting to imitate his thick Scottish brogue. "Nae, lass. I'll be too busy spending yer blunt, but ye may sleep with the beasts while I make the castle fit for ye."

Ruth thought perhaps his lips twitched but otherwise he made no sign of having heard her.

"Why, Mr Anderson," she said with a breathy sigh, holding a hand to her heart in the manner of a swooning maiden. "How lucky I am to have married such a man. "Aye, lass," she said, lowering her voice and giving a sharp nod. "Ye are indeed. I am a paragon among Scotsmen." Ruth fluttered her eyelashes at the motionless male opposite her. "I'm so relieved," she said, adopting a simpering tone. "For I was sore afraid I had agreed to wed a mannerless brute without a civilised bone in his body."

She stilled as one tawny eye cracked open, glinting in the dim light of the late afternoon. Heat flared in her cheeks under his scrutiny as she waited, for what she wasn't sure. Fury? Amusement? For one excruciating moment, she wondered if he'd put her over his knee. Then he grunted, closed his eyes, and went back to sleep.

Chapter 3

Dear Papa,

We expect to arrive at Wildsyde Castle tomorrow afternoon. The journey has been long and fatiguing and I confess I shall be glad to sit still. Many of the roads have been in poor repair and I feel my bones still jolting and swaying as I try to sleep at night. The weather has not been entirely kind either but tomorrow looks to be better. Perhaps I will see the castle for the first time in sunshine. I shall write more and describe it in detail as you asked me to once I have settled in.

— Excerpt of a letter from Miss Ruth Stone, to her father, Mr George Stone.

6th November 1814. Wildsyde Castle, Scotland.

Gordy watched the English woman covertly from under his lashes. She had been silent today, the endless questions she'd insisted on peppering him with since they left having dried up. Her one-sided conversation had also ground to a halt. A pity, that. It had been amusing to hear her cool English accent try to round and soften the words to approximate his Scottish brogue. He'd been hard pressed not to laugh, but he was determined things remained formal between them. With luck she'd have scurried back to England and her idea of the civilised world by Christmas. The way her mother had fallen into a swoon at the mere sight of him only confirmed his suspicions that Ruth Stone was far too fine to survive at Wildsyde, even if he wanted her to, which he did not.

He'd not wanted to marry her. Well, no more than he'd wanted to marry Bonnie, or any woman, sly, deceitful creatures that they were. He'd no doubt at all that this one would cause him trouble, but he was ready for her, for whatever lies and tricks and wiles she would use to wind him around her finger. No woman had managed it yet, and she'd not be the first to have tried. Fifty thousand pounds, though? His heart still leapt at thoughts of the enormous fortune. He was rich! It seemed impossible, improbable at best. Yet, he'd seen the marriage settlements himself.

Anticipation thrummed beneath his skin as he considered everything he could do with the money, all that he could build and mend and create. For the first time in his life he'd be able to look his tenants in the eye without feeling weighed down with guilt and shame. The Highland clearances had sent displaced families pouring towards the coast, searching for work in the fishing villages around Wildsyde. He'd been impotent to do anything before, only the fertile land about the castle keeping them afloat as he poured every penny into repairing what fell apart before his eyes. It was never enough though. No matter how hard he worked to patch things up there was never enough money to do the job as it ought to be done. Not so now. He wondered if this woman had the slightest idea what she'd done in marrying him. The gaudy opulence of her home, the sheer scale of the fortune her father must have amassed for such a display had staggered him and left him bereft of words. He'd stood in the gilded, fussy hallway feeling every bit the heathen she no doubt believed him to be.

And she'd asked *him* to marry *her*.

He still couldn't believe it. If he'd seen her in the street, he would have expected her to turn her nose up at him, to blush and scurry away as many of her ilk would do. It was his good fortune that she'd been the other sort, the kind who looked at him from under their lashes and wondered what it would be like to bide in the dirt a while. He had no illusions about how such a fine English lady would view him, about what she wanted from him, and it wasn't refined conversation or an arm to lean on to escort her to the opera.

No. He'd read the look in her eyes with no difficulty. Well then, it was a fair deal. He'd have her money, and he'd pay her in kind, do his husbandly duty until she was with child. That should be long enough for her to have had her fill of him and all he could offer her. There was nothing else she could want from him. He knew that well by now.

Though he'd given her free rein with the staff and the castle, he had no expectation of her staying, and had no desire for her to stay. The sooner she grew weary of him and of living in such a remote part of the world and returned to her own kind, the better. Then he could get on with his life. He'd have done his duty by his name and the title that would one day be his and they could both live as they wished. He smiled inwardly, beyond satisfied at how everything had worked out. Well then, if she wanted to try to manage him in the meantime, let her. She'd soon learn her mistake. Besides, he had his own managing to do, and by the curiosity burning in her eyes when she looked at him, he'd fare a great deal better than she would.

He studied the rapt look on her face as she stared at the rugged landscape beyond the window. At least she was a fine, healthy looking lass, not some milk-and-water miss. He liked her height, liked that he'd not have to fold himself in half to kiss her, and he liked too the generosity of her breasts and hips. Soft, plentiful, comfortable. Yes. Her body was well made, sturdy and generous. Christ, she'd need to be to bear his bairns. A swell of heat rose as he considered bedding her, considered showing her what that look in her eyes would lead to.

Keeping his distance had not come easy during the journey. He never dallied with those that worked for him, nor anyone who might feel beholden to him, but that meant an hour and a half—in good weather—travelling into Wick to find a willing bedmate, and he had little enough time for such self-indulgence. Now, though, he had a wife to keep such frustrations at bay. On hand, willing, warm and soft. He let out a long, slow breath, imagining it. *Careful,* he warned himself. Bed only. It would not do to grow too familiar, too accustomed. She would leave. They always left.

For his own sake, he had best make sure it was sooner rather than later.

The English woman made an exclamation, a soft gasp of wonder, and Gordy lifted his head, watching the smile that curved her mouth. She leaned closer to the glass, her breath clouding her view, and she wiped it away at once, impatient. He frowned, wondering why she looked so delighted and then the carriage turned a little, showing him what she saw. Wildsyde. He'd been so lost in thought he'd paid no mind to the familiarity of the landscape, had not realised how close they were.

There it stood though, shabby but proud, like a warrior, scarred and exhausted but willing to fight still, to the death. A sudden rush of something akin to pride rose in him, warmth and pleasure that she approved of it. He shook it off at once. He did not need nor want her approval. She was not staying.

To Winter at Wildsyde

Want more Emma?

If you enjoyed this book, please support this indie author and take a moment to leave a few words in a review. *Thank you!*

To be kept informed of special offers and free deals (which I do regularly) follow me on *https://www.bookbub.com/authors/emma-v-leech*

To find out more and to get news and sneak peeks of the first chapter of upcoming works, go to my website and sign up for the newsletter.

http://www.emmavleech.com/

Come and join the fans in my Facebook group for news, info and exciting discussion...

Emmas Book Club

Or Follow me here......

http://viewauthor.at/EmmaVLeechAmazon

Emma's Twitter page

About Me!

I started this incredible journey way back in 2010 with The Key to Erebus but didn't summon the courage to hit publish until October 2012. For anyone who's done it, you'll know publishing your first title is a terribly scary thing! I still get butterflies on the morning a new title releases but the terror has subsided at least. Now I just live in dread of the day my daughters are old enough to read them.

The horror! (On both sides I suspect.)

2017 marked the year that I made my first foray into Historical Romance and the world of the Regency Romance, and my word what a year! I was delighted by the response to this series and can't wait to add more titles. Paranormal Romance readers need not despair however as there is much more to come there too. Writing has become an addiction and as soon as one book is over I'm hugely excited to start the next so you can expect plenty more in the future.

As many of my works reflect I am greatly influenced by the beautiful French countryside in which I live. I've been here in the South West for the past twenty years though I was born and raised in England. My three gorgeous girls are all bilingual and the youngest who is only six, is showing signs of following in my footsteps after producing *The Lonely Princess* all by herself.

I'm told book two is coming soon ...

She's keeping me on my toes, so I'd better get cracking!

KEEP READING TO DISCOVER MY OTHER BOOKS!

Other Works by Emma V. Leech

(For those of you who have read The French Fae Legend series, please remember that chronologically The Heart of Arima precedes The Dark Prince)

Girls Who Dare

To Dare a Duke

To Steal A Kiss

To Break the Rules

To Follow her Heart

To Wager with Love (November 15, 2019)

To Dance with a Devil

To Winter at Wildsyde

Rogues & Gentlemen

The Rogue

The Earl's Temptation

Scandal's Daughter

The Devil May Care

Nearly Ruining Mr. Russell

One Wicked Winter

To Tame a Savage Heart

Persuading Patience

The Last Man in London

Flaming June

Charity and the Devil

A Slight Indiscretion

The Corinthian Duke

The Blackest of Hearts

Duke and Duplicity

The Scent of Scandal

The Rogue and The Earl's Temptation Box set

Melting Miss Wynter

The Regency Romance Mysteries

Dying for a Duke

A Dog in a Doublet

The Rum and the Fox

The French Vampire Legend

The Key to Erebus

The Heart of Arima

The Fires of Tartarus

The Boxset (The Key to Erebus, The Heart of Arima)

The Son of Darkness (October 31, 2020)

The French Fae Legend

Audio Books!

Don't have time to read but still need your romance fix? The wait is over…

By popular demand, get your favourite Emma V Leech Regency Romance books on audio at Audible as performed by the incomparable Philip Battley and Gerard Marzilli. Several titles available and more added each month!

Click the links to choose your favourite and start listening now.

Rogues & Gentlemen

The Rogue

The Earl's Tempation

Scandal's Daughter

The Devil May Care

Nearly Ruining Mr Russell

One Wicked Winter

To Tame a Savage Heart

Persuading Patience

The Last Man in London

Flaming June

The Winter Bride, a novella (coming soon)

Girls Who Dare

To Dare a Duke

To Steal A Kiss

To Break the Rules

The Regency Romance Mysteries

Dying for a Duke

A Dog in a Doublet (coming soon)

Also check out Emma's regency romance series, Rogues & Gentlemen. Available now!

The Rogue

Rogues & Gentlemen Book 1

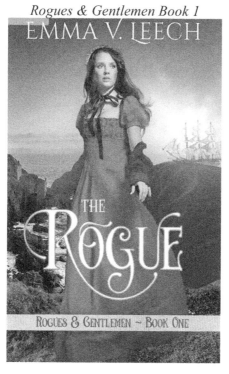

1815

Along the wild and untamed coast of Cornwall, smuggling is not only a way of life, but a means of survival.

Henrietta Morton knows well to look the other way when the free trading 'gentlemen' are at work. Yet when a notorious pirate, known as The Rogue, bursts in on her in the village shop, she takes things one step further.

Bewitched by a pair of wicked blue eyes, in a moment of insanity she hides the handsome fugitive from the local Militia. Her reward is a kiss that she just cannot forget. But in his haste to escape with his life, her pirate drops a letter, inadvertently giving

Henri incriminating information about the man she just helped free.

When her father gives her hand in marriage to a wealthy and villainous nobleman in return for the payment of his debts, Henri becomes desperate.

Blackmailing a pirate may be her only hope for freedom.

Read for free on Kindle Unlimited

The   Rogue

Interested in a Regency Romance with a twist?

Dying for a Duke
The Regency Romance Mysteries Book 1

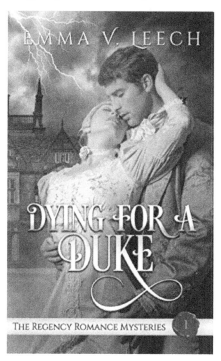

Straight-laced, imperious and morally rigid, Benedict Rutland - the darkly handsome Earl of Rothay - gained his title too young. Responsible for a large family of younger siblings that his frivolous parents have brought to bankruptcy, his youth was spent clawing back the family fortunes.

Now a man in his prime and financially secure he is betrothed to a strict, sensible and cool-headed woman who will never upset the balance of his life or disturb his emotions ...

But then Miss Skeffington-Fox arrives.

Brought up solely by her rake of a step-father, Benedict is scandalised by everything about the dashing Miss.

But as family members in line for the dukedom begin to die at an alarming rate, all fingers point at Benedict, and Miss Skeffington-Fox may be the only one who can save him.

FREE to read on Amazon Kindle Unlimited.. Dying for a Duke

Lose yourself in Emma's paranormal world with The French Vampire Legend series…..

The Key to Erebus
The French Vampire Legend Book 1

The truth can kill you.

Taken away as a small child, from a life where vampires, the Fae, and other mythical creatures are real and treacherous, the beautiful young witch, Jéhenne Corbeaux is totally unprepared when she returns to rural France to live with her eccentric Grandmother.

Thrown headlong into a world she knows nothing about she seeks to learn the truth about herself, uncovering secrets more shocking than anything she could ever have imagined and finding that she is by no means powerless to protect the ones she loves.

Despite her Gran's dire warnings, she is inexorably drawn to the dark and terrifying figure of Corvus, an ancient vampire and master of the vast Albinus family.

Jéhenne is about to find her answers and discover that, not only is Corvus far more dangerous than she could ever imagine, but that he holds much more than the key to her heart …

FREE to read on Kindle Unlimited The Key to Erebus

Check out Emma's exciting fantasy series with hailed by Kirkus Reviews as "An enchanting fantasy with a likable heroine, romantic intrigue, and clever narrative flourishes."

The Dark Prince
The French Fae Legend Book 1

Two Fae Princes

One Human Woman

And a world ready to tear them all apart

Laen Braed is Prince of the Dark fae, with a temper and reputation to match his black eyes, and a heart that despises the human race. When he is sent back through the forbidden gates between realms to retrieve an ancient fae artefact, he returns home with far more than he bargained for.

Corin Albrecht, the most powerful Elven Prince ever born. His golden eyes are rumoured to be a gift from the gods, and destiny is calling him. With a love for the human world that runs deep, his friendship with Laen is being torn apart by his prejudices.

Océane DeBeauvoir is an artist and bookbinder who has always relied on her lively imagination to get her through an unhappy and uneventful life. A jewelled dagger put on display at a nearby museum hits the headlines with speculation of another race, the Fae. But the discovery also inspires Océane to create an extraordinary piece of art that cannot be confined to the pages of a book.

With two powerful men vying for her attention and their friendship stretched to the breaking point, the only question that remains...who is truly The Dark Prince.

The man of your dreams is coming...or is it your nightmares he visits? Find out in Book One of The French Fae Legend.

Available now to read for FREE on Kindle Unlimited.

The Dark Prince

Acknowledgements

Thanks, of course, to my wonderful editor Kezia Cole.

To Victoria Cooper for all your hard work, amazing artwork and above all your unending patience!!! Thank you so much. You are amazing!

To my BFF, PA, personal cheerleader and bringer of chocolate, Varsi Appel, for moral support, confidence boosting and for reading my work more times than I have. I love you loads!

A huge thank you to all of Emma's Book Club members! You guys are the best!

I'm always so happy to hear from you so do email or message me :)

emmavleech@orange.fr

To my husband Pat and my family ... For always being proud of me.